dear
mr.
capOte

dear mr. capote

a novel by
gordon lish

a william abrahams book
holt, rinehart and winston   new york

Published by Holt, Rinehart and Winston,
383 Madison Avenue, New York, New York 10017.
Published simultaneously in Canada by Holt, Rinehart and
Winston of Canada, Limited.

Library of Congress Cataloging in Publication Data
Lish, Gordon.
Dear Mr. Capote.
I. Title.
PS3562.I74D4   1983   813'.54   82-15543
ISBN 0-03-061477-5

First Edition

Designer: Lucy Albanese
Printed in the United States of America
10 9 8 7 6 5 4 3 2 1

ISBN 0-03-061477-5

for helen deutsch
and our adele

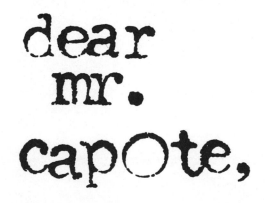

dear
mr.
capote,

this is the twelfth start of the letter I am sending. Here is the reason it's the twelfth start. The reason is to try out voices! I want the right one. Granted, they sound like the right one for a while. But is a while long enough? It is like years ago when I did a voice for fifteen minutes, time out for commercial announcements.

I am making reference to my former profession on the radio, a quarter-hour for each voice. Sometimes two in less than that.

Nothing's changed. I know how long a minute is.

Here are some of the starts I tried.

Dear Mr. Capote, Effectuate a good grip on your socks! Get ready to shake, rattle, and roll! Is this your lucky day or is this your lucky day?

Dear Mr. Capote, Please listen. All I am doing is begging you to listen. Listen, *effectuate* is one of the words so far.

Dear Mr. C., You know who this is? Answer: This is the person who can make a certain writer millions! All he

3

has to do is play his cards right, which I do not have to tell you is not what a certain Mr. Norman Mailer did!

Dear Mr. Capote, With your permission, I will go ahead and introduce myself. Hint: I am the one who is killing the people. Correction: Just the ones which when Nature calls sit down to you-know-what.

Dear Mr. Capote, Credit where credit is due. I do not have to suck up to someone in your circle. I myself am in the papers and also on all of the channels. I am a household word. I am the party which Gotham looks for, except name me the Gothamite who is (joke) using both eyes to do it, ha ha. All right, I ask you—who has Gotham scared shitless, Norman, me, or you?

Dear Mr. Capote, Call Random House! Tell them to clear the deck, stop the presses, whip out their checkbook and start practicing zeros!

Dear Mr. Capote, In all humility, I am already more famous than you are even if in the public nobody knows my name by heart. But I say do not try skipping to the sign-off to find it. Reason: It is not there yet (joke) because I'm not, ha ha.

Dear Truman, Norman muffed it. In other words, he had the ball and fumbled it. Do I have to tell you why? Okay, too many children! Believe me, I am familiar with the situation. It is the one a man with children gets in. So this in a nutshell is my personal analysis, take it or leave it. Whereas present company is clean as a whistle in the department I just made mention of. Granted, this is why I should be horsewhipped for picking Mr. M. in the first place.

Dear Mr. Capote, It is my pleasure to inform you respective to the fact that this letter is germane to the legalized disposition of the media rights pursuant to my story, it being lawfully agreed I shall deem it correct and

4

acceptable to authorize you to deliver aforesaid story to the public in accordance with the terms set forth herein.

Dear Mr. Capote, It's all right, admit it. Hint: You knew you were next in line. So where else could yours truly go, considering? There is Norman Mailer, sure, but is this individual still a legitimate factor? Let's face it, the nervy s.o.b. played himself right out of the picture!

*t*hat was ten of the starts. The other one I tore up. Correction: Eleven, not counting the one I am doing now, which is No. 12.

Listen, do me a favor and don't ask me what the missing start was. Between you, me, and the lamppost, it is not overly important. The major thing is proof. Here it is. What I say I am is one hundred percent the facts! This is a person which is reliable talking.

The other thing of it is, forget it, all the business about the different voices. Meaning, I have to talk the way I talk. But the thing is, I don't overdo it. Let's face it, everything is a question of the right word in the right place so long as the right one (joke) starts out being the wrong one, *ha ha*.

Capstone, for example, that's another one of the words. But which one is it?

I go between five-nine and five-eleven. God is my judge, you can depend on it. Granted, right-handed is also the situation.

You know as well as I do this is what the media is guessing. Or let's say the authorities the media is quoting.

But these are the only two guesses which come anywhere close. Okay, the police figure five-six to five-seven on account of "angle of entry." Whereas the right-handed part comes from the fact of which eye the knife gets in. I know I don't have to tell you, it's the left one!

But forget it. Because the rest of the guesses they are way off-base about.

Hey, take my word for it! (Ha ha.)

So all in good time, okay? Meaning, when it comes to what's what, you will be the first to know. For example, going back to radio, check it out—Ann Shepherd's real name was Scheindel Kalish.

Here is another one. Ann Shepherd (S.K.) was also Hope Evans on "Big Sister."

Look it up if you don't believe me. Go ahead and look it up all you want. You think if yours truly says it, it does not check out from top to bottom?

Okay, the media are saying I am violent and crazy. But these are the two biggest things they are wrong about. I do not have to tell you they are all wet from the word go. So what if I was put away once? This was when? We are talking about the age of sixteen! Forget it. You know how old I am right this minute? Forty-seven! I said forty-seven, and no further episode has befallen me since the one I just made mention of.

I know what you are thinking. You are thinking he is already all balled up. This is because I said you were going to be the first to know but meanwhile said I already told Norman. So any way you slice it, present company is second! Is this what you are thinking, or is this what you are thinking?

Well, I did. But let's face it, sometimes an individual has to wait his turn, even a famous celebrity. So who is the one which really regrets it? Listen, do not make me laugh. You know as well as I do, Norman had his chance. But what he did is took me for a fool. Which is what I was when it was him I wrote instead of you. So let's say I was jumpy and not thinking things through. Meanwhile, the dumbest part is how I go for a family man. Whereas let's say I wasn't thinking things through by my Number One rule. If I was, would I touch a family man with a ten-foot pole?

This is my first major rule—think a thing all the way through. I say you have not thought it through enough when you come out on the same side you started on.

Okay, this is something else I'm going to get to. Sit tight. I am going to get to everything.

Listen to this. If you live long enough, there is nothing you are not going to get to.

Here is a fact. I am a thorough type of individual. One thing I do not do is leave a thing out. So okay, I left out a thing here and a thing there when I wrote to you-know-who. But just between you, me, and the lamppost, it's not true it was because I forgot. In other words, I had to.

Here is something else. I go slow. It is the lesson I learned going all the way back to Janet R.'s bathroom. Go fast and get balled up. Go slow and stay one hundred percent. So this is the second major rule.

Not that I do not know what it is for the people who have to listen. I know how they don't want to, and how they can't wait for me to speed it up. But this is the voice I have and I have to go slow with it. Hey, look at what happened to Bobby R. Meaning, Mr. C., feel free if you have to skip. Okay, I give you permission to take a peek at the sign-off—except if you really did it, it wouldn't be there yet if you did!

all right, you can tell what I am doing—you can see that I am stalling. It is because I am nervous and can't catch my breath yet. This is the start I cannot take a chance to make a mess of. I do not have to remind you what number start this is. Not that I am superstitious. It is just that there is no reason to risk what you don't have to.

You are saying he is crazy because he is killing so many people. Whereas I say you are saying this because you have not thought it through yet. But even if I was, we could still do business. Being crazy is no impediment to doing business.

Impediment. That was another one of the words so far, *effectuate* and *impediment* and *capstone.* Like this: "Impediment."

You'll see.

Here's another one. Ann Shepherd was also Pearl Taggart on "Our Gal Sunday." In other words, Scheindel Kalish was!

Okay, I am catching my breath. My thoughts are getting collected. But before I get down to cases, I have to straighten out some things so far.

Number One) If I sometimes don't follow my rule and always don't go slow enough, it is because of Norman and of what he is doing right this minute. I know how long a minute is.

Number Two) I said all the channels, but not on 13 here in Gotham—"The Big Apple" being an expression I have nothing but disdain for. *Disdain,* by the way. This is another one of the words from the word-calendar which I bought for the boy a birthday ago.

Number Three) I have nothing but disdain for all the other channels. This is not due to my years on the radio and what the television did to me. This is because Channel 13 is the serious channel!

Number Four) I say *years* even though I know as well as the next one months is all it was. *Years* is a manner of speaking, so to speak.

Number Five) There are twenty-three so far, so if yours truly is forty-seven, you can guess how many I have to go before I finish up. Meaning, I am writing to you at the stage of not being over halfway there yet. Norman I wrote when I was up to twelve. This was because I did not want to get in touch with him until he could see I was a serious person. But by now there is no question if I am, okay?

Number Six) The wife watches 2, 4, and 7, whereas the boy and me stick to Channel 13. I don't have to tell you I do not let him watch the others because what are the others but blood and guts? Do the others ever teach? I am very fussy about this. I do not want the boy not to know the things I didn't and vice versa. T.C.'s the wife, and she says I am too conscientious, whereas I say a person can't be. This is why the boy has the calendar and also the walkie-talkie. You understand what I mean, the Word-a-Day calendar? The words come from there, whereas where yours truly comes from is from the seven-watter.

Number Seven) They are just beginning to make mention of me on 13 now that I am up to so many individuals. Hint: One more than Berkowitz! It is on "Newsline," Catherine Campion reporting. She I think is pretty. In my personal opinion, Catherine Campion looks like Janet R., especially if you look at the hair. But T.C. says Watch 2 and see Sue Cott. She says Cott leaves the other one in the dust.

Number Eight) T.C. stands for Tamara Chris, the ball and chain for the last ten big ones—also for seven more of "keeping house" before we tied the knot. Not that I wouldn't leave T.C. in two seconds flat if Janet R. showed up. I would take the boy and go.

Number Nine) You are probably wondering why I am only doing it to women. Stop wondering. Here is the answer. Better targets. Bigger eyes. Correction: I don't need *both* of them.

But I am being ridick to say a thing like that, Number Eight above. I cannot take the boy and go. This is because of the whole point of the thing, which is get to forty-seven and then get caught. On the other hand, no one is going to catch anyone until yours truly comes to terms with a certain famous author.

Three guesses who this person is.

Hint: He is *not* Mr. Norman Mailer.

I know I do not have to tell you I would be honored and thrilled if you took over. But I also do not have to tell you I negotiate on behalf of the boy. And when I do anything on behalf of the boy, it is a big mistake for somebody to get cute with me. Which I do not have to tell you is what a certain Mr. You-Know-Who did. I promise you, he is the one who is crazy if he thinks I got an idea like this just to get it all balled up at the last minute. "Last minute" is a manner of speaking.

All right, I am not in the business. Granted, I am just a beginner when it comes to making things happen in the media. But I am the father of the boy, and the father of the boy is no pushover!

No offense intended. Believe me, I don't like to shout.

10

But I guarantee you, the boy is the one subject yours truly gets touchy on. This particular subject aside, no individual is a milder individual. Name anybody, and I will meet this party halfway, Norman Mailer included. Listen, I may be killing lots of people, but not for some mean or ridick reason.

I will tell you how to think about me.

Think about me as being an inventor who is selling his invention. Don't think about me as a Bundy or a Berkowitz. I am nine million miles from individuals of that type. I am a fellow who knows what he has to work with and is working with it. In this day and age, you tell me where the choice is.

In other words, this is for the boy! This is for the big bucks! This is the boy's dad talking, who is your solid American citizen from soup to nuts!

Okay, here are the facts.

I am dependable. I work in a top-ten bank. Seventeen years I have been in the same position. Seventeen! Ask anyone. You can check it out with my immediate supervisor. My immediate supervisor will give you every assurance. Everything I tell you is one hundred percent. I am aboveboard as the day is long.

Here is an example.

Peartree's.

Peartree's surprises you?

All right, so I know about you and Peartree's, corner of First and Forty-ninth.

You'll see. I know a lot.

I even know the bartender's name, which is Gary. I don't drink, but I know the name. I always order soda. Can you beat it? Liquor salesman's son, but does he ever touch a drop?

I never eat there, either. I guess I do not have to tell you what the reason is. No offense. You can afford it. I say more power to you because you can. On the other hand, you are keeping an eye on your waistline. I know. I watch. I say an individual has a right to do this. I mean, to keep his tummy flat. This is one of the things about T.C. Hers is not the way it was when we started out. Hint: It used to be like Janet R.'s, only now it's not.

I guess this makes you sweat, me knowing things about you and where you go and so on.

I know it does.

Believe me, I am a sensitive person to what another person feels. I know what it is like to be a famous celebrity and have other people know things. Let's face it, aren't I famous now myself?

I mentioned Peartree's to make a point. I could walk over and show you what I use. But I respect your privacy. Anyway, I could. I could let you see Paki for yourself. I could put my hand down on the bar and lift it up and let you look. You would see the knife. Personally, I do not think you would try to brush me off. I make a good impression. I used to be an actor. Granted, it was on the radio and nobody saw me. But my appearance is okay. I am neatly dressed. I know how to behave with famous people. I also have a way with words. My manners are without impediment. I know how to say something. I mean a word that makes you stop and stare. *Impediment*, for instance. And what about *capstone*?

In other words, I think you would have given me my due. Given my due, I could have told you the plan right then and there. We could have worked the deal face-to-face. You would have seen what I use when I do it. You could have seen Paki with your own (joke) two eyes, *ha* ha. Sure, I can give you the mental picture, but the mental picture is just a picture!

So why didn't I do it at Peartree's?

Here is the answer.

What if you didn't look long enough?

i am going to start with how I got Paki.

I found it. I never would have had the nerve to buy one. Does this seem outlandish, considering? But it is one hundred percent, I swear. Knives make me afraid. It could be because of when I was little and I went into Simon's or it could be because of something else. I don't know. Maybe buying knives just scares people. Maybe buying them does this, whereas who can say why?

Not that knives scared her. She could be in a place with knives. She could say, "I'll only be a minute," and be hours and hours with knives. Or I could be on the television and have enough money instead.

Just think. Suppose I did not have to negotiate. Suppose the boy was taken care of. Suppose the future was all set. I could be like every other fellow who walks into Peartree's and sees the famous author. I could say, "Have a drink on me." We would be two celebrities shooting the breeze. I could show you Janet Rose's snapshot and you could show me one of yours. We could talk about me and you being on the television.

But I never even got back on the radio after I was you-know-where. So where is the money going to come from?

Meanwhile look at what is happening to the future.

Do I have to tell you what they are saying? The facts are the facts! Meaning, the future which is coming up is going to be the worst future we ever had. And I don't have to tell you that's the one the boy is going to be in!

It is enough to make you sick, everybody in the whole future worse off than the one we're having right now.

Let's face it, this was the United States Government talking—they said it was going to happen—and for your information, a certain person was listening with both ears.

So now you have the reason.

Here it is again.

The boy does not have a chance!

It is like his three-speed racing against a tenner no matter how hard he pedals. It is like what is the good of the Word-a-Day calendar and his learning all those words? Or me making the rule against him watching the wrong channels?

You see why I am using the knife?

The type is the folding type. Here is the mental picture. When the blade is back in the handle, Paki comes to four and three-quarter inches, which means almost double when the blade is out.

This is when you see PAKISTAN stamped where the steel is.

It got me wondering when I saw it. You just never stop to think if they make hard things in a place like that, a place like Pakistan and so forth and so on. I thought it was only baskets they made and other soft things, period.

The other thing is, turn the blade over. That's when you see this.

13010.

Here is the truth. I don't like looking at that number. It makes me get a little sweaty.

When I was little, everything made me sweaty. But this is just the word I use. Meaning, as a person, my skin is on the dry side.

It didn't happen until Buddy Brown. Getting sweaty, I mean.

I don't know. I can't explain it.

Up until we moved, I was the happiest boy there was. She was always saying I was out of this world. This is how happy I made myself—and everybody else because I was. Just looking at me made the people feel good.

Tell the truth. Weren't you a boy like that?

She said I was a picture-book boy. But what did she say after she saw Buddy Brown move in next door? Did she say it anymore?

I thought everything loved me. I thought the sky and trees and clouds did. I thought the sky wanted to reach its arms down and hug me. I thought everything wanted to grab me and squeeze.

Okay, I lied. Meaning, even before Buddy Brown, I sometimes got a little sweaty. Here's why. If things loved me so much, maybe they were going to get me and keep me!

This is the reason I did not go out unless she made me. It wasn't safe outdoors. Whereas inside, it was a little less sweaty.

If it was raining and I had to play in the house, saved

is how I felt. You know what I thought? I thought I was saved for one more day. I thought outside I'd go away. I thought the sky would come and get me.

So I tried to stay indoors. That's how I first made up the voices. In other words, I said I was sick. Then I got a voice to go with it, whichever sickness I said.

Strictly for the sake of argument, let's say it was sunny. That meant go out and play. But I said I hurt somewhere and I made up the voice to prove it. Also, here is the face if you are looking. But the thing of it is *afterwards*. Do you see what I am saying? I mean, the voice and face I just made up. I mean, even if nobody is listening or looking, the voice and face stay right where they are. Here's why. Because I am, and I see and I hear.

Let's face it, where Mr. M. is concerned, you keep your mouth shut about things like this. Am I right or am I right?

So this is how sunny days I stayed inside. Which is also how I saw the dust. It was the dust between us. I mean, between me and her.

Here is the mental picture.

It was when she was sewing. Listen, I don't have to tell you this is what I loved.

We had Venetian blinds. We had them in both houses, the first one and the second. She is sitting in the chair, whereas I am on the hassock. There is this window that is behind her, the slats fixed for just the right angle. In other words, when you have a needle and thread, you need plenty of light to go with it.

Now here's the thing. The light lights up the air!

Maybe the light was different in that day and age. I mean, maybe it was brighter or a different color. Because I ask you, have I seen the specks ever since?

16

I did not know they were dust, okay? No one ever told me. This is something I had to find out. But did anyone tell me when I saw?

They glittered! They jumped! They switched direction like a wave!

You see what I mean about breathing? That's how thick it is when you breathe.

But here's the point. I thought they were little animal things. I thought they flew around in the air. I didn't think she would laugh.

It was like when I used to listen to the motor. This is the motor when she is cleaning. Before she went to business, she was always sewing and using the vacuum. So here she comes with the thing running, and I hear like voices in the noise. You know what they're doing? They are saying my brother's name!

It was just like with the specks I thought were animals. Meaning, I thought everybody heard them. So why make mention if she didn't? Granted, she laughed. But wasn't this because they switched direction?

You can see the child I was. But in my personal analysis, every child is.

Hey, so *you* tell *me*. Believe me, I'm listening with both ears. For me it was the specks and the motor. So what was it for present company? I'll bet you thought of some things yourself. You just forget, that's all. Guess what. If I heard you mention your things, I would think, "Hey, wait a minute, what's that? That's ridick!"

This is just human nature. Am I right or am I right?

Actually, I know some of your things. Let's face it, you have made reference in your best-sellers. But did I laugh?

Meanwhile, now is the time to laugh if you have to. T.C. does. It's okay if you have to. But here it is.

I used to think there were little people in the radio. But I say so what? It was just my parents didn't tell me.

Here's a thought. Maybe they didn't know. But I say even if your parents know everything, there is going to be something that nobody stops you from thinking. So big deal! Let's not kid ourselves, by the time you are a certain age, you are in the know.

The boy, for example. He knows how to work the walkie-talkie. "You copy, Red Dog? This is Blue Dog, over and out."

Guess who that was on the seven-watter.

You see? Face facts. The boy is only nine! But he is almost in it already. Meaning, in the know.

Hey, you can thank the Word-a-Day calendar for it. And let's not forget him watching the right channel!

time out. I just thought of something. It is another place where I was maybe less than one hundred percent. But I'll bet you would have caught me at it anyway without me even telling you.

It's this. I said why it is strictly women only. In other words, your range of females. I said it was the bigger eyes which is the reason. But let's not forget there are these other things, which is these things like this—mascara and eye shadow and eyeliner and eye pencil and sometimes your cream and your glitter.

Another thing is the extra lashes.

You see what I mean when I say target?

Here's something. It's easier to hit it. It's like the archery concession at Coney Island, rings and rings around the black spot in the center. The difference is, this is Paki and the black spot's a million times smaller.

You know how small I mean? Ask T.C.

Hint: She calls it a part of the Devil's body. But does the Devil really have one?

Anyway, it's the size of that, the Devil's heel, more or less.

Here is something else. Where your female is concerned, one eye is bigger than the other. In my personal experience, this is the case, whatever they tell you.

So go ahead. Guess which one it is. Except don't bother.

I mean, talk about your lucky breaks!

So what if I was born left-handed? Did you ever stop to think about that? Listen, I do all the time, believe me.

Okay, here is one more thing so long as this is the subject which we are talking about. Okay, so far it is just a theory. But for what it's worth, this is my analysis.

With your female, the brain is closer!

So what do you think? I mean, you think you can use it or not?

On the other hand, don't hold me to anything. I mean, when you do the book, take it easy. I say don't put it down until you check it out. Let's face it, with material like this, we're crazy if there is something we don't get one hundred percent! But just so you don't forget to check it, make yourself a note. True or false: From the eye to the female brain the distance is shorter than the male brain is.

Enough said?

Hold it. I just thought of one more thing. What about when they wear contacts? I didn't tell you about those. In other words, if they've got on glasses, forget it. But when they've got on contacts, who knows?

You see what I am getting at?

With the pigeon-toed one which was the first one, was that the sound I thought I heard—true or false? I mean, the click. You know, Paki clicking on one of her contacts?

So when I was a little younger than the age the boy is now, I was always waiting for something to grab me. This is why I locked the car doors when you-know-who made me shop with her. I'm talking about back before she went to business. To make a long story short, she was always parking somewhere and also in a hurry. So she leaves me in the Plymouth because it's faster when I am. In other words, she says it's faster if she goes by herself.

She says, "I'll only be a minute."

But she never is. I don't think she ever was. It is more in the neighborhood of fifteen to thirty, and the time at Simon's, I don't know, maybe double that or more.

Granted, I know as well as the next one it is just a manner of speaking. "I'll only be a minute." But when it was happening, it was like the specks and like the radio. I mean, nobody told me what a minute was. You understand what I am saying? It's just dust and waves. But how do you know if they don't tell you?

What is a minute? I think I had an idea. I mean, I knew it wasn't long. This is how I figured I could wait it out. But then I couldn't. I would try and try, but then it got to be too much longer than I thought it was, and who could hold it anymore? So I lock the doors and get on the floor.

Listen, I do not think I would hold it against him if the boy did that. Let's face it, we don't have a car, but I don't think I would. The thing is, I would be all for it if he did, seeing as how Safety First is one of my major rules.

The boy is nine. But I say you cannot be too careful.

As for yours truly, seven is the age I am talking about—and you can quote me on that.

Here is how I know.

Seven was the most important age of my life!

Seven was the year we moved.

Seven was when my dad went with the liquor company, so we had the Plymouth there at home, whereas him they gave a special vehicle to drive around and sell the liquor from. That's one thing I can tell you. I was seven when we changed houses—and when we did it, everything else changed too.

Number one, we moved. Number two, guess who came to live next door.

Something happened because of Buddy Brown. The same thing goes because of Simon's. I can't say what did. But it was something.

Simon's was the hardware. Here is what happened.

One day she goes, "I'll just be a minute." It was a nice day. I think it was October after school. I don't have to tell you I felt good. That's the time of year I always do. Let's say it makes me think of Janet R. walking. But back when I was seven, I don't know. Maybe it was the leaves or light or colors.

I was sitting in the seat watching all the people. That's a thing I really like. Meaning, seeing people through the glass. So as bad as it is to be in the Plymouth, it isn't so bad at the start. And then it comes to me how it's so amazing, my head. This is because I have stopped counting for what a minute is!

Okay, you are going to have to think back to when you were the age I was. Norman couldn't, but you could. So think back and *you* tell *me*, am I right or am I right? I mean, you do something you didn't think you could, okay? And *then* what?

It's like you get so proud you tremble!

Say you're a young individual and people are always telling you how you're going to outgrow this, that, or the other. But do you believe it for a minute? For example, he was always telling her how I'll outgrow locking the doors. And then, bingo, you outgrow it! Because there I am, and I know it has to be way more than a minute is. But did I lock the doors and get down on the floor?

Hey, here's the truth, I was really trembling. It made me shake the way I was just sitting there and still looking at all the people. Even now, here in Gotham in this kitchen, you think I can't see the boy I was and how I was shaking in the Plymouth?

Listen, I was shaking. It was wonderful.

But then it's getting dark, and she's not back at all. So it keeps getting darker, and I can see how the people on the sidewalk are starting to look cold and go home. You see what I'm saying when I say they did? They are not shopping now. They are leaving places and going home and looking cold.

So I just had to do it. I tried hard not to. But it was no use. It was like having to go to the bathroom. It was like squeezing and squeezing to stop it. But then you can't. And you start knowing here it comes. So this is when I get the feeling I mean when I say I get sweaty.

But meanwhile I am looking all around. In other words, she must be coming and I want to see where she must be coming from. Granted, sometimes I was more or less in a position to make a guess. For example, she maybe says, "I'm just going into the market," or "I'm just going into the dimestore," or "I'm only going to pick up a few drug items and I'll only be a minute."

But sometimes all she does is go, "I'll just be a minute."

So I get so sweaty, I can't remember. Meaning, did she or didn't she give me a hint? This is when I get up on my knees and keep turning my head around to see. It is also when I think if I lock the doors and spot her coming, I can get them open again before she sees they aren't. In other words, who's to say I didn't outgrow it? Because didn't I really?

The next thing is, even looking around is no good. It's too dark. I can't see unless it's close. The only thing is the lights inside the stores and the shapes of the people in the ones which have some windows.

It was terrible. It was the sweatiest time I ever had up until the time of Buddy Brown.

I ask you, would an individual like a Norman Mailer see what I am saying? Would your Norman Mailer type of individual put it in when it came time to write the book?

Now I see how it was just wasting my breath to give him the background material. You know what? I think it lowered me in his eyes. Whereas in yours it doesn't do that, true or false?

So now there is this second thing, which is this. I was afraid to lock the doors! I know it's crazy, but I am more sweaty about her catching me than I am about still waiting in the car. Here is when I squeeze the hardest, and then I let go and push the door.

I ran. Across the sidewalk and into the first store.

It was Simon's.

It was the hardware.

I was never in it before. I was never in anyplace anything like it. Never anywhere had I smelled anything like what it smelled like in Simon's.

It had long aisles. Everything all over was all stacked up. You couldn't see around them. You couldn't see anyone. You couldn't see her. All you can see are things and things on shelves.

I keep looking up for her.

Then I look down.

And this is when I see it right in front of where I am.

It was a case. It was maybe the size of this table. What is in it was under glass.

I am talking about the knives!

But none of them was like this one. Paki is curved. The handle is curved so you can hold it and it fits.

The thing of it is, I do not remember the next thing after that. I can't tell you if she was there in Simon's or how she got me home. I just remember looking at them and how they looked under glass.

Here's something.

Only over my dead body will the boy ever see a thing like that.

but who knows what you are going to see? If you live long enough, there is nothing you miss. For example, what happened on Fourteenth.

Last year I was down there. It was just before Christmas. Believe me, I know better. Fourteenth Street, nobody has to tell you what's doing in a neighborhood like this. But I was checking out a thing for the boy, which was a bicycle, to make a long story short. Let's just say I was shopping all over Gotham for the best buy for the money.

Okay, you are a person in your circle, so you don't know about buys to begin with. But take it from me, in this day and age it is a scandal what they get in this particular department. Especially with gears, if this is what the doctor ordered.

The boy wanted one with gears. The truth is, he did. Even if he said he didn't. I don't have to tell you he was just saying no because of the money. You see the point I am making? In my household, everybody knows money and safety are the two categories.

Let's face it, he's only in the fourth grade, but the boys in the classroom are getting bikes with gears galore. This will interest you, make a special note. Much as you will not believe it, by fourth grade even your coloreds are pedaling around on tenners! Even your colored *girls*.

I don't have to tell you what a ten-speed goes for in

the world of today. We are talking about an item that is in a whole different department than your item with no gears at all.

So T.C. decides we meet him halfway. Which is when I go out to see what we can do on a three-speed. It is a Saturday and I am all over Gotham checking. But who am I kidding? I mean, the one place to go is the place way over west on Fourteenth, which is nothing but bicycles wall-to-wall. You never saw anything like it! So I go over, and I ascertain the prices. Okay, they are high. But let's not forget the advantage of service! Also, if something goes haywire, you can bring it back and get satisfaction. In other words, you have your year's guarantee—in *writing*. So I am making up my mind in the right direction when it comes to me in a flash. May's! Meaning, you've got to be crazy to sign on the dotted line without first checking out the situation at May's.

You would not know because of your circle. But I am here to tell you, May's is a store at Broadway and Fourteenth. In other words, this places it right in the vicinity! So you get the picture. I got to walk how many blocks to save a dollar? Believe me, you could double it and yours truly is not complaining!

Granted, May's is not in the business of catering to a person of your level. But I say whoever you are it makes sense to save a dollar! Besides, it's ridick to be in the vicinity and not see if at May's I can't do better, irregardless of the question of service and this, that, and the other.

Now here's the mental picture.

I start walking east. I'm going to May's. Okay, it's cold out. When I say cold, I mean cold as you-know-what. So why not get a crosstown? Okay, the fare is sixty cents. And this was only a year ago, right? Meaning, I don't have to tell you what the going rate is now! But in my personal opinion, the time could come when bus fare is what stands between you and God-knows-what. Does this make sense or does this make sense?

Correction: I meant to say *catastrophe*. I guess you know why. Which is it was one of the words of the twenty-three so far. Like this. "Catastrophe." But the thing of it is, I can't tell you which one it went with or whether with her I heard the same click which could have been her contacts.

Wait a minute. We were talking about money.

Here is a perfect example. The knife. Setting aside the fact I am not the type of individual to go in a store and buy one, I wouldn't have, even if I was. You see what I am saying? Paki is going to set up the whole deal for the boy's future. In other words, millions! But would yours truly fork over the few dollars?

Okay, it look like a contradiction, right? *Wrong!* Because the contradiction is just what you *want!*

Listen, when I was in the seventh grade, the teacher reads us something. She says this writer is named Whitman, this Walter Whitman from the borough of Brooklyn. I'll be honest with you, the name of the thing I don't remember. But it said something that goes right up at the top of my list. It said, *Of course I contradict myself. I am large.*

I love that. Even if it comes out of the same borough as Norman. Look, I won't kid you. No offense to present company, but this Whitman really said it. I mean, this is your real writing.

Let's face it, contradictions, that's the whole story. That's how I am and how we all are, end of discussion, period!

I say you can say anything. I say if you live long enough, you will!

Okay, I admit it. This is how Norman got into this in the first place. Put aside the fact he is a famous celebrity. Because the other thing is, he is into this thing of where you can say anything. In other words, he does not knuckle under when it comes to this, that, and the other. He knows that if you can think it, you will do it, and who can't think of everything?

Listen, I have read some of Norman's best-sellers. But you do not have to worry. What he knows you know double! Just don't make me have to spell it out for you. Some people know this, and some people don't. I am someone who does.

the point is, I am walking crosstown when it happens. This is not a neighborhood you are familiar with, okay? So let me fill you in. It is mainly your Spanish, so far as I can see. In other words, your Spanish and your coloreds. Meaning, dope addicts and so on and so forth. To make a long story short, face facts—it is an unwholesome district.

Now here is the mental picture. On both sides there are these little shops which are like hanging with all types of merchandise. Meaning, whatever they are selling, they hang it out and show it to the people walking by. So do I have to tell you what the level is of the quality? Add to this the vendors on the sidewalk, which is, for argument's sake, like pushcarts one right next to the other. In other words, this is how come the foot traffic is almost not moving. Actually, this is good. Reason: If something breaks out, it gives you your warning!

Okay. Here is the thing. People make a wave.

This is how it happens. When they do it, what you know is something is definitely coming.

You see what I am saying?

It is like a wave of water coming. The second thing is, it always goes in a direction which isn't the one it's supposed to. It's like when water goes against the natural nature of things. In other words, watch out, something is definitely coming!

I, for one, am always set up for this when I am on the streets of Gotham. This is because a decent citizen has to. Otherwise, here comes bodily harm or worse. So you have to be ready to get out of the way. You have to look with both eyes. You have to watch for the wrong type of wave.

I say make it second nature.

I don't have to tell you the number of times the boy has been told to do this.

You think I want to scare him? The answer is no. But meanwhile, which is worse, true or false? The jitters if he has to have them, or not being set for the wave when it comes?

I know some people think nine is already old. T.C., for example. She says there are fourth-graders who do things. Go down to the store on the corner or pick up an item at the market or take off for school by themselves. I, however, do not think nine years old is old enough. This is my personal analysis. Whereas, T.C., she says, "Lord, Lord."

But I say little boys are there one minute and gone the next. And when they are, I say blame the parents!

Look at the papers or listen to the channels. Let's not kid ourselves, does a day go by where there isn't a child which isn't maimed to death or dismembered? Add to this all the cases you never even hear about because there is too much blood and guts to fit it all into the papers.

Take my word for it, the papers and the channels do not have enough room for all the terrible things which always happen. One thing you can always count on, the blood and guts is going up like the cost of living. Hey, you have to have more and more just for someone to pay attention! That is why yours truly says what is all the hurry about? Sunday comes, I can see my way clear to maybe letting the boy run down to the corner for the *Times*. But do I let my guard down before he is back where he belongs? Listen, I am in Constant Touch on the seven-watter.

"Red Dog, Red Dog, all clear? This is Blue Dog, answer please."

In my household, the training is my department. I don't have to tell you, where T.C. is concerned, she does not have the patience for it. The thing is why take chances? Let's face it, the wave can come out of anywhere!

This is what I am teaching him. Which is it just comes, end of discussion, period.

Okay, this is the thing I have mainly noticed, how fast. Bodily harm is the fastest thing that can happen. I know. You better believe it, yours truly is the expert.

Like this. Suddenly something terrible is coming and no one knows from where. This is why I watch the foot traffic for the first sign of the wave. Which is how I am training the boy. I tell him to keep his eyes open for how the foot traffic is moving. You have to keep your eyes peeled for these tiny changes in direction. That's how the wave starts, first this little speeding up here and there, then the next thing you know the whole thing is going crazy and racing in the wrong direction!

Come on, the facts are the facts, this is Gotham! Meaning, you can't act like it is the middle of the Mojave!

All right. I was going to say desert. But I made it Mojave because of the story. I know you wrote it. "Mojave." I read it. I read all your wonderful writing.

I mean, you can write. In other words, you can write something and get the money. You just have to have the paper and the pencil. Whereas take me. What can I do? Sure, I used to be on the radio, but where are the soap operas of today? I don't have to tell you what happened to them! You say, okay, there is your television. But I say that's cameras and people looking.

You don't understand. I'll explain later.

No, forget it! What's wrong with right now?

Here's the thing. It's like with the eyes of all the women. So you say a word, okay? "Impediment," for example. Whereupon whoever it is stares—stops and stares, okay? Are you getting this mental picture?

So far, so good. Meaning, stopping and staring is what happens when you say the word to the women.

"Disdain." There's another, for instance.

So she stops whatever she's doing. Let's just say for argument's sake, you are all the way at the end of the subway platform and she is reading the paper.

You're in position. This is the first thing. In other words, the end of the platform and here comes the subway. This way there is the noise. Except not too much of it yet. Hey, check this. If there is going to be too much of it, can she hear it when you say it?

"Disdain." You can hear that, can't you?

Listen, who's kidding who? The thing of it is, you put your face right up close to hers. I'm talking about just this much away from her face. Hey, a matter of picas, right?

So here come the eyes. Like whatever it is she is reading, forget it. Because, wait a minute, *disdain*? Somebody said *what*? Or maybe it was *effectuate* or *catastrophe*, just for argument's sake.

So, where are we?

The eye, okay?

You've got your mascara and your eyeliner and your so on and so forth. So meanwhile there's the thing that's the size of the Devil's heel, which is to quote T.C., of course. I mean, it's there in the center of the colored part. So this is your target.

Bingo!

What I'm saying is, Paki sticks it—the mush, the brain, the whole business. So here's another one for the boy and the question of the future, right? But meanwhile you are forgetting something, which I for one don't blame you. Because from when she looks up to when you put

Paki in there, it's what? Not even a second. But that's long enough for it to be like a *camera*.

Listen, I don't have to tell you about those!

I mean, do I have to tell you who had one? Don't make me have to tell you. Also, who she took a picture of it with.

Don't kid yourself. I found it!

I don't know. Maybe I didn't. Maybe it was where I couldn't miss it.

I have to think about it. Sometimes I think she had it taped to the door of the refrigerator. On the other hand, sometimes I don't remember.

Wait a minute. Here's something. When you do it in the subway, forget about the sound. In other words, even if she has on contacts, you think you're going to hear a click even if there really is one? On the other hand, sometimes I think it always clicks and it's not a question of contacts.

But let's not kid ourselves, what with the circle you are in, this is not your type of transportation.

Am I right or am I right?

I mean, present company on even the Lexington line? Hey, do me a favor and don't make me laugh.

You are thinking, okay, so a camera, what's that? It is just an item and who has to look? But I say the thing of it is, you have to. This is because you better! Hey, what if you don't?

It's just like with the wave. It's the same thing

exactly! Meaning, does the wave see you? Hey, forget it. You just happen to be where the wave is going, and the wave starts rushing over. You see what I am saying? It's like a camera. It gets you caught in it.

Whereas I say it wouldn't if you stayed on your toes in the corners of your eyes.

I keep telling this to the boy. I say, "Stay on your toes in the corners of your eyes."

T.C. says, "Lord, Lord." She says quit it before I give him a case of the nerves. I tell her why doesn't she pitch in with the training. But she says, "Let's not and say we did."

I have disdain for the words which go with that subject. Meaning, your words which go with nerves and so on. You are saying this is because I was in a place. But it isn't. I guarantee you, this is not the reason.

Whereas the reason is, who can count on them?

Here is an example. When I was in the first one, let's take the thing with the laces. So I don't have to tell you what its name is. But then I'm in the second place. But in the second place they say its name is different. You see what I mean? It is the same thing, even the way the sleeves go and the way they have the laces. Except if you listen to what they say it is, you hear them say it's a camisole.

So you see what they do to you? They say it's a camisole. This is what they say to you even when the sleeves are the same and so are the laces.

God is my judge, this is the situation. They change the words. But they don't change the thing it was in the first place! Take it or leave it, this is what they are doing in the subject I just made mention of. Which is why you can't count on the words which go with it.

34

Camisole.

Here's another one. *Paraldehyde.*

t ake the calendar. It has a different word for every day. This is so you get a better vocabulary. Okay, it cost three dollars. But I say it was a solid investment. I say you can't cut corners in this particular connection. You see what I am saying? I want the boy to know what's doing when they say something. I do not want him to have to guess as he goes along. This is why a word a day is a step in the right direction. Take the one which comes up after *catastrophe.* Okay, you'll never guess. *Snickersnee!* Can you beat it? It means knife. Hey, live and learn, right?

On the other hand, let's not kid ourselves. I mean, it gets stuck in you, what's the diff what they call it? Am I right or am I right?

Hey, forget it! Does it hurt? Do you scream from just the waiting for it?

I mean, stop to think, the thing going in and where it's going and then it's in there. You see what I am getting at? The thing of it is, it's a thing which doesn't *belong* there. And let's not forget you see it first! You know something? Even if your back is turned, you do.

Check it out. Don't take my word for it. A knife, you don't even have to be looking to know it's on the way. This is why you scream. Meaning, it's because you have to wait. At least this is my personal analysis. In other words, you're waiting and waiting to see how much it will hurt. So here is where your scream comes in.

You take that day on Fourteenth Street when yours truly was going to May's. So here are the things—Christmas, the three-speed, and save a dollar. These are the things I am thinking about. When out it comes from where all this merchandise is hanging! Lo and behold, here it comes! It's coming sideways across the sidewalk. You see what I mean about it going in the wrong direction? In other words, it's your wave which is going against the nature of things.

You see this at the beach.
I saw this at the beach.
I grew up almost on a beach.

The town was even called it—it was called Long Beach. It's the town we moved from house to house in when I turned seven. Remember Buddy Brown? That's what he was.

Buddy Brown was a funny wave.

You know the ocean. You know how the ocean is. Something under it makes the water go in the wrong direction. This is when you get the wave. Go figure it. I mean, am I right? Meanwhile, here comes the wave.

Let's face it, I used to see this plenty. Listen, who is the expert in this department? When it comes to oceans, yours truly knows what he's talking about from the word go.

The thing of it is, on account of the ocean I got on the radio. Here's how. I was working on the boardwalk at a certain concession. So next comes Janet R. It is due to her

I get on the radio. Okay, to make it one hundred percent, let's say it's due to Janet Rose's mother's brother, who is Bill Lido.

But first there was the wave which took Davie away.

hey, listen, Janet R. is almost the most important part of everything I am telling you. You'll see—the boy, Janet Rose, my father, these are the things and that's the order. These are the people which are the reason for everything. The rest is just to fill you in. I mean like Bobby R. and Davie and my brother's mother, not to mention Buddy Brown and also Ben Bernie.

You know what? This is really something! I mean I never noticed, the two of them, they're both B.B.! You know what I am doing? I myself am stopping and staring! Hey, and look at this. I don't believe it! T.C. and guess who! Tamara Chris and Mr. Truman Capote!

You see when you stop and stare? You see what starts to happen? Hey, it's the old story. You know, step on it quick, somebody, before it starts having babies!

Okay, this reminds me. *Fascination!* It is the name of the concession I was getting ready to tell you about. This was on the Long Beach boardwalk. Which is where I worked the all-important summer. Which is the summer when yours truly is fifteen years old. In other words, it's the same summer when Davie gets his medicine. I guess I did not tell you yet, but Davie is my brother.

So here is where we are. It's the summer which Davie has the job of a dancing instructor at one of the hotels on the boardwalk. Whereas yours truly is calling color at Fascination.

I am trying to remember the name of the hotel. But I can't and it doesn't matter. The Traymore? Forget it. The thing of it is, Davie is giving lessons in the basement. Sometimes also exhibitions. Granted, he was as good as they come! But not just at dancing. Swimming also. Swimming and dancing, Davie was the expert!

Okay, here are his specialties—the mambo, the rhumba, the samba. It is the summer right around the time the cha-cha-cha is starting to come in. But don't kid yourself. That's another one Davie was already great at!

It goes without saying, I know you like dancing. This is why I make mention of the history of these dances.

You take her and my dad, they said they were great ones. They said they danced as a team. I don't know. I never saw it. Except for the one time when they said that's what they were doing. But I am willing to go along with the idea that maybe it was back before I was born. The thing of it is, they did not look like the kind of individuals who used to be dancers. Take my dad, he looked like what he was, which is a liquor salesman until he lost his license to operate a vehicle. And so far as she is concerned, she didn't look like anything. All I know is the color her shoes were.

You take the old house, she stayed home. But in the new one, she went to business. In other words, this is the word she uses. She says, "I am going to business now."

But it was like, "I'll just be a minute."

You see what I am saying? It didn't mean what she said it did.

The facts are the facts.

She worked in a store. She took in the money and

made change. I mean, if you wanted to find her, you went to the cash register, and this is what she looked like—she looked like a person you didn't look at.

Maybe it was a McCrory's or a Woolworth's or a Kresge's. I don't know. Maybe it was McClellan's. I don't want to remember.

I think about it, but I don't mind if I don't.

i t's like what happened on Fourteenth Street. I think about it. But it's better when I forget. Is this another one of my contradictions?

I don't know. Maybe it is and maybe it isn't.

I am large.

I love that. It makes everything make sense.

Did I tell you I was in this wave that goes across the sidewalk on Fourteenth? God is my judge, here it comes, whereas not even Christmas and how cold it is could stop it! But who is on his toes in the corners of his eyes, okay? Sure, I am thinking about the three-speed and the money. But the wave is what I am always thinking about even if I'm not thinking about anything. When it comes, it comes and you have to be crazy not to be ready! So say I am a block and a half from May's when it does.

Here is what I was thinking. It's Christmas. I made the walk all the way over and saved the bus fare. Also, how cold it is. So isn't there bound to be a payoff? Meaning, I will find a ten-speed for the price of a three-speed, with change left over. Look, I figure Christmas, God will make a miracle.

Okay, so this is the character of my thinking. But

don't think I'm not also thinking this is one of your worst vicinities. The other thing is the sidewalk. There's all these Spanish and coloreds all over it, not to mention the pushcarts and so on and so forth. You can't move, is the thing! But don't worry, a certain person has his eyes peeled. In times like this I am definitely on my toes in case of the wave which will come before you know it. Forget it, it does not matter that I am thinking about money and a miracle. I'll be honest with you. I am always thinking about money and a miracle. I think about those things even more than I think about Janet R., and her I think about more than I think about anything except the wave! Correction: I think about you-know-who more than anything in the world.

"Come in, Red Dog—this is Blue Dog, do you copy?"

T.C. says I go overboard in this department. In her personal opinion, the only place which worry gets you is right behind the eight ball. But I say your average person doesn't do it enough! Nobody does. Present company, for example. Are *you* worried?

Or take me. Was I worried enough when Bill Lido has me up against the building? Or what about when Janet R.'s mother says I should follow her to the bathroom? Listen, the answer is don't ask.

And doesn't this go double for going into Simon's? Not to mention writing to Mr. M. before I started writing to you.

Notice, I am not even counting leaving Buddy Brown to Davie. But do I really have to? Enough is enough, okay?

Face facts, nobody worries as much as he would if he had the brains to do it! Even *I* don't. And when is yours truly not doing it?

It was so cold. I don't suppose you were in town last Christmas. So how can you know? The television said it was a record. It was freezing even inside. We went to bed with sweaters on and socks. The boy had to wear three pairs of them! Reason: They did not send much heat up. Meaning, the super and the owners. These winters they send up less and less. But don't think yours truly can't see it from their side of the picture.

Hey, it's murder everywhere. But this is just the start. If it costs a nickel when you sit down, get ready for a dollar by the time you stand up! So meanwhile I was making reference to last Christmas, which let's say you were not here for and instead you were in Palm Beach or Palm Springs, which is where I know you always go when the weather is not fit for decent people. So in your case you wouldn't know how cold it was.

No offense, what I said about Palm Springs and Palm Beach. I mean, I realize how it sounds. But I say more power to you! I give you my personal guarantee. Let's face it, you are an artist bar none! You have given the American public great classics to get where you are. A thousand years from now they will still be singing your praises, and I will be the first one to say you earned it, every red nickel. I personally do not begrudge you one penny of the mountain of money you have. Also, what I said about Palm Springs and Palm Beach. I mean, it might scare you, me already knowing where you go when the weather in Gotham is as cold as it was last Christmas. On the other hand, August is also out of the question altogether. This is when your regular people really go ape—since did they have the smarts to get rich and plan ahead? I don't have to tell you this is what I mean when I say every individual, whoever it is, he can't worry enough! I promise you, if yours truly had done a little more worrying back when, T.C. and the boy could have been right out there with you the day you take off for your place in the Hamptons every August on the dot.

Listen, did I tell you I used to live on the Island too? Okay, I did not live there just for the summer, number one. Whereas number two, Long Beach is a long way from the Hamptons. But you can see the point I mean. On the other hand, the thing of it is, who needed Long Beach once I got to Gotham with Janet Rose and her mother? Hey, this was when I became a definite Gothamite like yourself. True or false, Gotham is our kind of town, present company and yours truly? But look at Norman, right? I mean (joke) Brooklyn, ha ha.

Time out. You think I was mentioning the distance from Long Beach to the Hamptons in miles? Because no way is miles what I was making reference to! Pay attention. It would be very perturbing if you started taking me for what Norman did. Meaning, maybe I am not educated, but I know what to measure things in!

I will tell you something I did last week. I measured Paki in picas. Do you know what a pica is? No offense. I was just kidding. Asking you a thing like this is like asking DiMaggio if he knows what a bat is.

It was my birthday. Forty-seven big ones! So the boy gives me this really thoughtful thing, which is a see-through plastic ruler for true accuracy of measurement. In other words, it has every scale you can think of—including one for measuring in picas.

I thought it was quite a thing for a person of his age to think of—something wonderful to look at but also something with its practical nature.

Here is something. Paki comes out fifty-two picas with you-know-what when it's out of the handle!

I don't know. Eight and three-quarters still sounds

longer to me. But maybe this is because a pica sounds like something smaller, not to mention it really being something which is.

This is a perfect example of why you have to think a thing through. For example, fifty-two is a bigger number than eight is. But the smaller number sounds bigger even if it isn't. But maybe this is because of how we think about knives. Let's face it, so far as yours truly is concerned, this subject is a mystery!

T.C. made her usual, which is the Duncan Hines with cherry icing. Outside of this, that's it and that's it for all the fanfare. I won't kid you, I do not go in for carrying on when it comes to your red-letter days. Too much fooling around and somebody pays the piper in so many dollars and cents. Besides, the more of a big deal you make, the more of a fake of it everybody starts making. Add to this how they are already putting on an act in the first place, and you can see how things will get out of hand even before you start going overboard.

Be this as it may, we had an outstanding time irregardless. T.C. and you-know-who sang "Happy Birthday" and then I unwrapped my surprises—the ruler, and the key ring from T.C., which was really a woman with no clothes on. So far, so good. Then we all go out to take in a PG afterwards.

Naturally, I do my best in this department. But I do not have to tell you even your PG is going to have parts which are not fit for a certain party. In this day and age, let's not kid ourselves, wherever you turn, something is disgusting! In other words, it is not what it was in our day and age, end of discussion, period.

Listen, I am here to tell you, there was nothing a nine-year-old could not listen to when yours truly was on the radio. Did someone have to worry about this, that, or the other? But that's gone. That's definitely bygones. Those days are finished and done with.

Did I tell you I was just a boy myself when I was on the programs? I'll be honest with you, I was on some of the top ones. Go ahead. Check it out. You ask Bobby R. Bobby R. could tell you. Or what about Bill Lido?

I'll give you an example. You name the voice and I could do it. I could sound like anybody, you just name the individual. Okay, you want to hear the payoff? I could sound like Bobby R. himself!

I promise you, this is no exaggeration. You ask anybody so long as they are somebody who was listening. Meaning, the time he had to take it easy, the time on "Young Doctor Malone." Hey, starring Bobby Readick! But who was really doing it when Bobby R. was vomiting?

Janet Rose, for instance. Didn't she hear just like anybody else? Ask her. She'll tell you everything I am saying is one hundred percent!

I t was Sunday. In other words, the day he rides his bike. Except the Sunday I'm talking about is the one that's my birthday. Meaning, T.C. is getting her face on for the PG, so I am using the see-through to measure things around the house. This is how you give the boy an educational experience. Whereas he could just be waiting for someone to make herself presentable. Just between you, me, and the lamppost, I never miss an opportunity. On the other hand, take my parents. When they saw me listening to the radio, they should have said, "All right, here is how it works." And that goes double for the dust and for the vacuum cleaner! Isn't this how a person learns things? In other words, it's up to those in the know to tell you! I mean, am I supposed to wait for the radio to tell me how it works?

Okay, the same thing goes for words. Am I right or am I right? This is why the calendar is staying where it is, whatever T.C. says irregardless! You want to know where I mean? Hint: When he gets up in the morning, it's the first thing he sees. This is because it is on the table and the table is next to his bed!

Listen, I guarantee you, a certain person is never going to have to worry about not knowing how long a minute is.

A minute is sixty seconds.

So the next thing is, how long is one of those?

Answer: As long as it takes to get Paki out. And here's how long the next one is.

Long (joke) enough, *ha ha.*

i do not want you to get the opinion that yours truly is the kind of individual who does not do something about it when the PG gets off-color. Meaning, I have it worked out where yours truly covers his ears and he himself covers his eyes. I don't have to tell you your average PG means it's four times the boy and me are going to have to do this. T.C. says I make mountains out of molehills. But I say T.C. needs to have her head examined, end of discussion, period.

So it's Sunday, and guess what! The word for the day is

absterge. But meanwhile here is the thing of it. Didn't I just go from forty-six to forty-seven? So this means I have to add one. In other words, to make a long story short, I have to do an extra first chance I get. Do you see this mental picture? The PG is up on the screen and yours truly is sitting there with the page in his pocket when it comes to me I have to add an extra.

Here is when I get up and whisper this. "What say you to some popcorn or some Good and Plenty?" This is when T.C. goes, "Shush," and I go, "I'll just be a minute."

Don't forget it's August. Meaning, who is still in Gotham? Just between us, it's your coloreds and even worse. Meanwhile, this is also why the lobby is more or less empty. But so far as the ladies' room goes, it couldn't be better.

All right. Are you following me so far in my thinking?

Are you seeing this mental picture? I get out the page in the lobby and I check out the word to be definite. Then I go into the facility to see the situation.

Okay, there is one at the mirror and there is one on the toilet, and it goes without saying, I start with the one at the mirror. But do you hear anything in the way of a scream when she sees me? I'll be honest with you, it's all she can do to turn around so Paki's in position.

Listen to this.

"Absterge."

But don't think I don't know I am wasting it on a person of this level.

In other words, what's the diff, a word which is to these people a foreign language?

Here's something else. Purple lipstick. Also purple where she was putting on more eye shadow until Paki took care of it.

46

Anyway, bingo. But meanwhile I am thinking three things.

Number One) Hurry before more come in.

Number Two) What happens when the one in the toilet hears this one hit the floor?

Number Three) What's the word for the one in there?

Forget it! It all turns out to have no influence one way or the other. Because when I go in under the door of the stall, this particular individual is already out like a light. Who knows? But I say she heard and keeled over.

All right, I am not going to kid you. So far as yours truly was concerned, even with the eyelid down, I did not see any reason not to make the best of it. Meanwhile, you probably read the paper. I figure open it up—since for the media you are definitely crazy if you do not stick to your trademark.

Listen, I'll just say this one thing and then I will get back to the original subject. This eye is so bloodshot, who can get a good aim at anything? Another thing is, I have to hold the head up. Enough said? I mean, I am personally no more against anybody than the next one is, but don't make me have to tell you what this colored's hair felt like. Meaning, whatever she put in it, you could touch it and cut your hand off.

Here is the last thing. I say thank God I get back to the seats when I get back to them. This is because, lo and behold, here comes something where the boy needs to get his hands up over his eyes, not to mention yours truly over his ears. So while I am doing it, guess what!

T.C. says, "Where is the Good and Plenty? Didn't you get something?"

I have to laugh. You know what I said? "Shush."

Time out. I just thought of what you are thinking. You

are thinking did I take a look the way I did the night it was me that was sitting? Meaning, on the toilet and a certain someone has to shave her legs. Am I right or am I right?

Okay, this is the answer.

No!

First of all, don't forget the factor of the time. Second of all, the smell, inasmuch as she was doing you-know-what. Third of all, T.C. cannot be trusted. You and I know what to watch for when it comes to unsuitable material. But does T.C. even have a clue? And even if she did, would she do it? In other words, it could be my birthday, which it was, but would T.C. meet me halfway, even for the welfare of the boy?

Forget it!

She would go, "Lord, Lord," and roll her eyes and meanwhile act like I was the one who was acting crazy!

Last thing, I promise. But here is something really good. Which is that there is not one peep in the whole theater even by the time the PG finishes. Listen, let's face it, your average Gothamite does not want to know from nothing nohow!

Hey, live and let live. Am I right or am I right?

You won't believe it when I tell you how come I remember certain words and don't remember them all. Like *capstone*. I don't really remember that one yet. This is because (joke) so far I haven't used it, *ha ha*.

Camisole. Is this a word I will ever forget? And how about *paraldehyde*? But I don't have to tell you, you are not going to find them on any calendar, period. Listen, they would not put ones like those on it. I promise you, you don't have to check. On the other hand, you are the wordsmith—so *you* tell *me*. How come *camisole* is the sweatiest word in the world? Or *paraldehyde*, that's even sweatier. Or *pulmotor*, there's another sweaty one for you. But here's something—*pica* and *inch*. They're sweaty too if you start thinking what they mean.

Hey, I was just thinking. Of course I cover the boy's ears. It could be like Fourteenth Street! Or even worse. Meaning, the pizza maker and the man he climbed on. Except the real thing is much faster than the thing you see in the movies. But this is not the only thing which makes the real thing different. There are these other things. You have to see. You have to hear.

I did. I saw it on Fourteenth. In other words, I saw the one who was afraid the most was the one who had the knife. Four boys, but who's afraid the most? Forget it. It's dancing. They move. It's like sleepy people dancing in the goo they're dancing in. This is what it's like—fast things going slow because you look and see the parts.

It's different than anything else. It looks gooey. But it isn't. It's in a class by itself. You know what it is? It is bodies moving how they never had to. That's it! It's gooey. But that's because you see it and it's new!

I did and didn't look. It was freezing. There was ice. Add to this the wind. Oh, all the things I heard!

Personally, I do not like it when this is how cold it gets. Ice is another thing. Ice is even worse. I'll be honest with you, when people fight, ice is the worst thing they can fight on. Okay, this is only one man's analysis, but my theory is ice makes it as bad as it can get.

Here is the mental picture.

One of the boys slips.

Which one? Guess!

I call them boys, okay? But let's just say who knows exactly. Maybe the twenties, maybe the teens. Granted, when it comes to your Spanish, yours truly is no expert.

I am forty-seven. Didn't I tell you I had a birthday? Most people wouldn't say so. Most people would say thirty-five, give or take. First of all, I have not lost my looks. And I know I don't have to tell you that in my day and age I was very nice-looking. I guarantee you, when Janet R. passed a remark to the contrary, I for one could tell what she was up to. Okay, looks. So what do you think Buddy Brown looks like in this day and age? I promise you, nobody's mother is taking Buddy Brown's picture now.

All right, so looks are more or less the thing. You think I don't know that this theory will not fall on deaf ears so far as present company is concerned? Even after we moved, people made over me. I still had my looks when I turned eight. I was still a picture-book boy. Let's face it, to this very day, people still stop and stare. Not that I spend big bucks on it. Far from it. Listen, just a normal haircut nowadays, I don't have to tell you. Whereas if you want a little style to it, forget it! Am I right or am I right? I mean, you could buy a new head for what they quote you for a good haircut in the world of today. You know what? I could write a book about what they're doing to the price of everything. Let's not kid ourselves, you get haircuts. You know what the score is. It's time somebody said something, enough said? I'll be absolutely honest with you, back in our day and age you could get a ten-speed for what today's haircut is going for in a decent location!

Okay, an actor has to watch his hair. On the other

hand, I don't see laying out that kind of money if all you are is on the radio. They can't see you on the radio. It's like a writer's hair, okay? I mean, who sees it when he's sitting down with his pencil and his paper?

On the other hand, there's the picture on the cover of your books. Whereas I am just in Payroll when all is said and done.

You see what happens when I don't go slow enough and think a thing through?

bill Lido had great hair, curly and brown. Janet Rose had the same kind. T.C.'s got this almost white hair, whereas Sylvia Berman's was long and black and came straight down. Meanwhile, Buddy Brown had the best you ever saw—blond and like the light was in it all the time. Here's something. It's the kind a mother uses her own hairbrush on.

In other words, I wasn't born yesterday. Meaning, looks are definitely the thing. Listen, if I didn't have them, you think they would have had me calling color? I mean, at Fascination, you think they would? That summer or any other? Hey, do me a favor and don't make me laugh.

But who am I to tell you?

You think I don't know about the pictures you put on your best-sellers?

It's what the people notice. Hey, you are not just another wordsmith with a college education! Forget it. You are a wordsmith who looks like a million bucks!

This is how it was with me. In other words, I wasn't just a good boy—I was a good boy who also looked like that. I'm telling you, everything loved me for it. I was loved. I was watched. In a manner of speaking, everything was taking pictures. You see what I am saying? The sky was taking pictures. So big deal if she didn't! Big deal if it would have broken her arm to get out her camera for anybody but Buddy Brown!

The thing of it is, it was a feeling I had. You see what it was? The feeling was what I moved in. I mean, the same way you move in the air. Or in the water if you're in that instead.

Naturally, there is nothing I have greater disdain for than the disdain I have for being photographed. I mean, there's no camera that's fair to your face! You see the thing I'm getting at? Let's say there was a camera which could really do it. So if there was, then you'd have how many brands in the business? Does this make sense or does this make sense? Hey, it's like I told you, yours truly was definitely not born yesterday!

Radio was a different proposition altogether. There was the microphone. You talked into the microphone. It didn't look back at you and take a picture when you weren't ready. It didn't measure you in so many picas. It didn't say it took so many of you to make one Buddy Brown!

forget acting. Forget radio. That's bygones, ancient history, water under the proverbial bridge. In other words, I work in a bank. This is where I found Paki. I think I already told you—meaning, in Payroll, right?

Another thing, it is one of your top ten in Gotham, this banking establishment. According to the figures which come out, that's where it is in the figures. Up there in the top ten, end of discussion, period.

We're Midtown. Let's just say East Side in the lower Fifties. This means I can make it over to Peartree's on the lunchbreak. Whereas for you from your place, it's what? A block, right? I mean, your apartment, it's how far from Peartree's or from there to Antolotti's? Okay, for you it is a matter of let's say convenience. In other words, let's face it, what they put on a plate at your P.'s and your A.'s is not exactly what they put on a plate at your Cote Basque!

Believe me, I am not saying it is my custom to dine at this level. Listen, it's no secret. I mean, even P.'s is out of the ballpark for yours truly. I'm talking, of course, about your full-dress three-course, soup to proverbial nuts. But I don't have to tell you, your French cuisine these are definitely not! Naturally, with me it is all in my imagination, right? I am making reference to the true nature of the cuisine of this type. But Cote Basque is where I'd like to go when you and yours truly sit down to break bread and finalize our business. Hey, I won't kid you. When it comes to French, count me in. I mean, I'm no expert, but I wouldn't mind taking lessons!

there I go. It was the mental picture. Meaning, Janet Rose and how she liked to French. It gives me the mental picture of Germaning or Jewishing or something on this order. T.C., for example. Maybe that's what she's into, Saleming or Oregoning. I don't know. It's just that when it comes to French, T.C. says forget it!

Don't kid yourself, Frenching was what Janet Rose was great at. But the next thing you know, she got sidetracked. Let's just say I have in mind the hairbrush.

Face it, up until the change in her, it was my privates which got the attention. Listen to this. One time we squished it back and forth. Do you see the mental picture? From her to me and me to her and so on and so forth, etc., etc. Lo and behold, before you know it, it's all gone from little swallows.

I wish T.C. would stop to think of something on this order.

Hey, you think this subject is off-color?

Believe me, it is not my nature to make mention of things which are things that are off-color. Far from it. Apology: I am sorry if I just said something which lowers myself in your eyes. But here is the reason. You need to have the mental picture. This was another mistake I made with the famous author who lives in Brooklyn. In other words, I did not let my hair down, and maybe he could tell it. Whereas with you, I know I can put my feet up and make myself at home.

But you can see this, can't you? I mean, you can see how with you it's not like it was with Norman.

Okay, I guess you caught me. It's the truth. I'm still a little jumpy. And here is something else where I wasn't one hundred percent aboveboard.

It is about Fourteenth, isn't it? I mean, I made a certain statement. I said I don't go down there as a habit, but I was fibbing, take it or leave it. First of all, it's the buys on all the staples. So number one, it's the savings.

Whereas number two, it's the spot where it happened. Not that there is anything to see anymore. But that's the thing which interests me. Let's face it, even the next day there wasn't.

This is nothing new in Gotham, blood one day and no blood the next one. Come back an hour later and the sidewalk's just the way it was before it happened. Meaning, it's just back to all the filth it was in the first place. People don't care what they step in. Your foot traffic wears everything off. Hey, you name it! One head, you can't believe what came out of it. On the other hand, this was the one exception. But it goes without saying that a person fat as her, you had to expect it to be different. God is my judge, you should have seen it!

I don't know. Maybe Paki touched a kind of clot or something. Or maybe there was some kind of infection. The thing of it is, it kept on bubbling out like it was something which has gas in it.

You know what? I say your average Gothamite would come along and not give it a second thought. You see my line of reasoning? Live and learn. But I'm here to tell you, these individuals will step in anything!

So to make a long story short, Fourteenth was just like nothing ever happened. Whereas suppose the same amount of you-know-what was on the sidewalk in the Hamptons, and you come back a month later to take a look at it. Hey, you would really see something, true or false?

But maybe I'm just kidding myself. Maybe they walk on everything everywhere.

I don't know. If it happened on ice, it wouldn't last no matter where it was. Another thing, maybe there are no sidewalks in the Hamptons. But *you* tell *me*. Isn't this the way it is where the houses are really big ones? No sidewalks, nothing in front, just the road with the limos on it?

Like I told you, I am from the Island myself. Not that present company really is—or even that you are a real Gothamite. New Orleans, right? Hey, I know what the story is. It's no secret. Listen, I grew up somewhere different myself. Who didn't? T.C., for example. She is from Salem, Oregon. You see what I mean? In a manner of speaking, nobody isn't from somewhere else. Look at my dad. Or Janet R. They are not even where you could say they are anywhere anymore!

Hey, from New Orleans to Gotham to your private table at the Cote Basque! You name the individual, and I will take my hat off to him if he can point to something like that.

Much as they like to act big, I do not think the bank officers that come into my zone have ever actually eaten there. Meaning, the C.B., of course. Antolotti's is more their speed. But I am not saying these are your top men. So far as I can see, the top ones you don't know about because they don't show up in Payroll.

I would make mention of their names for the record. But I do not see why I have to involve my employer in my personal business. But listen to this. You come by here, though, this branch. You pass it. It is on the way. I mean, chances are your limo has to pass it when you go to eat your French cuisine at you-know-where.

It was new seven years ago. But I don't have to tell you how run-down it is now. When I first moved into it from a different one, it made me proud to be in this one. But now that's water over the dam. It is ridick, I know, but when a place you're in runs down, you think you did it too. On the other hand, this is Gotham—so that's where your wear and tear comes from. You give it seven years in Gotham, nothing's going to look like new, not even a branch of a top-ten bank.

a writer would not know what I am talking about. A writer does not have a building. He is more like an actor, page here, page there—Gotham, the Hamptons, Palm Beach, Palm Springs—never the same situation day in and day out.

Granted, this is only your top people. You and Norman, for example. Whereas your others, they probably do their writing all in one place. But let's face it, wherever they're doing it, it's not like sitting in Payroll year in and year out.

Listen, let's not forget this. When I was on the radio, it was different. I was in a studio! Or take Bobby R., for instance, so long as we're talking about your top individuals. He used to do what? Eight shows on a good day? Not that we called them shows in that day and age. We called them *programs* or *soaps*, these were your professional terms. God is my judge, Bobby R. was making good money. Fifteen minutes here, fifteen minutes there, time out for commercial announcements. I wonder how much he did. Ann Shepherd too. Don't kid yourself, she must have cleaned up. Well, let's just say it was (joke) Scheindel Kalish who did, *ha ha*.

You remember Mutual—the Mutual Broadcasting

System? Remember when they used to say, *This is Mutual, the world's largest network.* Or sometimes, *This is radio for all America, the Mutual Broadcasting System.* This is what Bill Lido said.

I did all my soaps on Mutual. I'll be honest with you, that's where Bill Lido worked.

Believe me, I was next to the big money once. But let's not kid ourselves, it was peanuts alongside what you and the boy are going to take in on the book of my life and my death. Am I right or am I right?

Hey, I just thought of this. At the bank, I am next to the big money day in and day out, so long as you don't count (joke) weekends and holidays, ha ha.

I have been with this organization seventeen years. I have the highest respect for my colleagues—in this branch and in all the others. But it is not the same as it used to be. Everything is different now. Did I tell you the building is getting run-down? I think I did, but I don't have the time to go back and check.

On the other hand, nothing is so high and mighty it can't come down a peg, bank buildings included. Maybe even all the pegs there are. Picas and inches and pegs. Just wait and it will.

That is a funny mental picture. How many pegs are you? Who is more pegs, you or Norman? Or let's say between the man who made pizzas and the other one in the sport coat, where are the pegs in this situation? In your personal analysis, what do you think, one so tall and one so short?

You take the people which frequent the Cote Basque. I mean, the people in that circle. Don't they have to walk the sidewalks just like everybody else? Do you see what

I'm saying? Nobody can stay off the sidewalk even if they try. So let's say you are on it. Can't it come at you when you are?

This is why you have to stay on your toes in the corners of your eyes, end of discussion, period.

A person could be walking out of a place. For instance, out of the Cote Basque. He could be thinking of his new best-seller. He could be thinking how the money is coming in when the wave comes instead. Take me. I mean, this is how it was last Christmas. I was thinking about the money just the way you could have been. Hey, I am always thinking about it, take it or leave it.

Tell me the truth. Do you make reference to it as the Cote Basque or the C.B.?

You have to get a mental picture of this to believe it. Four youngsters, one with a knife. But meanwhile the one cutting is also the one which is scared! Let's not kid ourselves, this was something to see. I am tall enough. In other words, I can follow the action. Besides, the foot traffic is mainly your Spanish, give or take the same exceptions. In this situation, five-nine to five-eleven is tall enough, okay?

So the wave comes, and it carries me into the middle of the street. The next thing you know, it starts going the other way. This is because they're pushing back to see. It is also because of the three of them which are trying to get away. Meaning, get away from the one with the knife! Do you follow this mental picture? They don't want them to! Meaning, *it* doesn't—it being the wave which switches and starts going back the other way.

Here is something I do not have to spell out for you. Which is that with Paki, it's different. Notice, I am not saying this is how it is always going to be. In other words, we are talking about what? Only twenty-three individuals so far? So who knows with the twenty-fourth?

But meanwhile, here is my theory, and you can take it for what it's worth. Just don't put this in the book unless in your analysis it checks out one hundred and ten percent!

Okay, the thing of it is is this. Let's just say for the sake of argument there are people behind the one I'm going to say the word to, or there are people behind yours truly. You see this mental picture? Granted, there never was to date—but we are just talking for argument's sake.

The question is, do you think if this was the case, pushing would come into it?

My answer is a definite no.

Here's why. One push and that's it.

At least, this is my opinion. Meaning, right in front of her you-know-what.

You see what I am saying? Because with Paki, it's a question of picas.

People want to see. But so far as pushing goes, do they or don't they? I have to stick to my theory and say that the answer is no.

But this is the best I can do on the particulars. In other words, it's guesswork. Granted, I am in a position to speak as an expert. But even so, only as a layman, if you see what I mean.

Listen, I'll be honest with you. I say you will have to go to the books on the subject if you are looking for the reason behind the reason. Or maybe you know a professional individual who specializes in this department. In my opinion, this is the best policy. I just want to get you thinking in the right direction.

So getting back to the people on Fourteenth, even if the wave pushed, it didn't have to. This is because the boys wanted to go. Granted, they were cut. I mean, just look at the blood to begin with. But even so, the boys which are bleeding didn't need any pushing. The thing of it is, far from it. Meaning, they weren't the ones which were scared. Whereas the scared one was the one which was cutting!

Here's something. The shirts is where you saw the blood. On the ice you couldn't see it.

Here is something else—white shirts. As God is my witness, just shirts, white shirts, no sweaters or coats or jackets! Notice, cold as bad as this, but just shirts, all four of the boys which are getting cut and cutting.

I just had a theory. Okay, I haven't made a special study of this, but maybe it is a Spanish thing. In other words, that element, maybe white shirts is what they wear when it's Saturday or Christmas.

The thing of it is, the tails are out. Another thing is, they flop around like they're heavy because they're wet with something. I don't think it's just the blood. Here is my analysis. The cold was what it was!

So what do you think? You think the cold can make you wet like that? Maybe it is some kind of current which goes through the air when the air is cold enough. What I mean is, the dust gets frozen, so things get wet and heavy.

But to make a long story short, it's a thing you can't forget. Also the screaming—the way it doesn't sound like boys their age but small dogs screaming. That's it! Small dogs screaming. Like you stepped on their foot and they start screaming.

Here is something else. It's all of them! It's not just the ones which are cut but also the one which is doing the cutting. Hey, you really have to hear it with your own two ears because I can't give you the mental picture. God is my judge, if you didn't hear it, you wouldn't believe it.

Okay, you go to the movies, but I say forget it! As far as I am concerned, the movies are all wet from the word go. This goes double for the channels which T.C. watches. You see what I'm saying? It's little dogs screaming and shirts which are floppy. But you think they could handle a thing like this on the channels or in the movies? Don't kid yourself, they couldn't. They wouldn't get to first base.

I saw it. There's no comparison. For example, the one with the knife, his arm was like this. Stiff, even when he's cutting, it's stiff. So what's your opinion? You think maybe the cold or the fear froze it?

Hey, I made that up. Okay, I was just kidding. That was just an icebreaker. Forget it. I was just being funny because things were getting too serious.

But this is something solid. This you can put in the book. The knife, I never saw it! I'm all eyes, but where is it? In other words, you know where it is, but you don't see it!

On the other hand, when I found Paki you-know-where, you couldn't miss it. So how come nobody saw it before yours truly? In the final analysis, this is not the kind of item somebody could look at and not know he is seeing it. So it makes you think, doesn't it? Meaning, is Paki waiting for a certain someone to see it? Does this make sense or does this make sense?

Get this. There is brass on both ends of the handle, whereas there are steel rivets in the wood part. Four big rivets on one side, four big rivets on the other. The thing of it is, they curve in the curve which the handle goes in. But maybe you call them grommets. I don't know. The important thing is, they make Paki look bigger. So how could anyone miss it when it's sitting right on the copier?

I didn't.

I took one look and I saw it.

Here is the mental picture. There is this little room right next to Payroll. Which is the room that's just for the copier. So this is where Paki is—right on top of the Xerox!

Time out. Granted, it is telling tales out of school, but the point is it goes to show you. It's what T.C. says when she makes mention of the Xerox they have in the office she goes to in Brooklyn. Like this—Exrox. She goes, "Lord, Lord, I am sick to death of always having to Exrox something."

You see what I am saying? This is what happens when you watch the wrong channels. Let's face it, her and her "Charlie's Angels."

Okay, I for one am not pointing a finger. Meaning, it makes you laugh, granted. But we all have to have something. You name me the individual, and yours truly will show you where there's always something, take it or leave it.

Take me, for example. Let's say I get a call from Nature and I have to you-know-what. So just for argument's sake, let's say this. Whereas the thing of it is, you'd think I'd do it standing up, but yours truly doesn't.

You see what I mean when I say that everybody has something? But when you stop to think about it, what's the reason? Because the thing of it is, there is always a reason. Okay, yours truly sits. So what's the reason?

Here is the reason. If you sit, then nobody can hear when I do it.

So now you know. But you say, What if no one is there to listen? The answer to that one is easy. Which is that I am, end of discussion, period.

Don't kid yourself. You can live and learn when it comes to how someone feels about their feelings!

t ime in again.

So there's Paki. In other words, the copier is what Paki is right on top of. This is why I ask you why I'm the first one to spot it. On the other hand, maybe it's Paki which spots me. Okay, forget it! I guess it sounds to you like I have got a screw loose. The thing of it is, I was only making a suggestion.

Hey, here I am sitting here thinking you go into the Cote Basque and it's no different. So let's just say you go into the famous restaurant which present company frequents. So you go in there. And you know what you see? I say you don't see anything until it's ready for you to see it!

Okay, it's just a theory. So *you* tell *me*. Am I right or am I right? I mean, there it is, and it's fabulous, but what about this and that in particular?

Granted, I am not in a position to say one way or the other. But my guess is you see so much you don't see anything. Listen, do you think you would see a knife? Even if it was one which was where you didn't expect it?

So the same thing goes for the Xerox room next to Payroll. This is why it makes you think. Okay, here is the thought in words of one syllable. *What is the reason nobody sees Paki until I do?* To tell the truth, I would like to hear your personal opinion.

On the other hand, go stand at the door of where I and mine live. You see the difference? Sure, the whole thing comes from stores you don't want to shop in. But do you see all the crap at once? The answer is a definite no. Take my word for it, it's one piece of crap at a time!

But getting back to where I was, I have to take a big deep breath first. I really have to. In other words, I am sitting here and trying to get myself collected.

Okay, so I see Paki, and the first thing I think is Simon's. Then I think, This is a knife but who does this knife belong to? So here is how I answer. The repairman. I say to myself, "The repairman must have been here and he went away and forgot it."

Here is something else I think. Maybe there is a spot in the Xerox and the repairman has to touch it. Whereas the only way you can do it is with the knife. You see what I am saying? Okay, it is crazy, but this is the thought which comes to me. Which is that even a thing like the Xerox has a you-know-what! In other words, it is like with the opposite gender and there's this special little spot inside it. So the man has to come when they call him and this is how he touches it.

Let's face it, it makes you stop and think. Meaning, maybe with everything there is a place like that and you have to reach with something to get to it. But, okay, this is just a thought I have. I mean, don't think I really think a machine can actually have one! First of all, why would it? Second of all, a thing like a Devil's heel, what would be the reason? On the other hand, you never know, do you? Listen, I'll be honest with you. Even if it's a crackpot theory, it couldn't hurt to check it out with the Xerox people. Except forget it!—I mean, who's kidding who? Believe me, not in nine million years would they ever tell you!

I don't know. You sit here and everything makes you stop and think. On the other hand, who am I to tell you about a thing like this? Because who's the expert? But for what it's worth, I'll just go ahead and tell you what I just thought. Which is that with food it's no different!

Tell me I'm crazy, but I say the facts are the facts. Meaning, you swallow something and what do you say? You say it hits the spot or you say it doesn't. Does this make sense or does this make sense?

Hey, here's something. When I was the age the boy is now, everything hit it and the same goes for Davie. Don't kid yourself, we were hungry. But this is as far as it goes. Meaning, in all the other departments, he was one thing and I was another!

Talk about things we were good at, for instance. With Davie it was swimming and dancing, whereas with yours truly I don't have to repeat myself. It was voices of every description!

You know what? This is something else I never thought of. I mean, there I am on the radio with one of my hundreds of voices, whereas out in the audience there's a little boy just like I was! You see what I am saying? In other words, his parents didn't tell him either. So what does he think? The answer is the same thing I did! Meaning, the radio! I mean, he thought I was *in* instead of *on* it!

Hey, believe me, I'm not pointing a finger. Far from it! Let's not kid ourselves, when it came to listening to the radio, I always did it. Let's face it, they were all my favorites. "Young Doctor Malone," you take that one—we used to listen to that one together. Up until the time she went to business, that's the one we always used to listen to together. I mean, see if you can see the mental picture. I'm on the hassock and she's in the chair, and the light is coming in from behind her. Whereas the other things are the needle and thread and "Young Doctor Malone" on the radio.

Except that was back before I was on it. You ask Bill Lido if I wasn't. He's the one which got me on it. It's just that it's too complicated to explain to a beginner. Face facts, it would be like present company trying to tell yours truly about how he writes his best-sellers. True or false, it takes an expert to know an expert, and vice versa?

Bobby Readick, he could get the Nobel Prize in Breathing. If they give a prize for it, he should get it. Because the whole thing of it is how you breathe. You take Bobby R. when he was Doctor Malone. Believe me, this was breathing bar none! Except here's the thing. When it came to breathing, I was the second best there was.

But it's all a question of nobody seeing you when you do it. Whereas take television, the answer is they do.

Let's face it, breathing is a subject by itself. The word *because*, for example. Or the word *with*. You know what Bobby R. could get out of a word like that? Hey, I don't have to tell you! Can a writer do a thing like that, present company excluded?

67

You think Norman could?

Hey, don't make me die laughing.

I'm telling you what Bobby R. deserved. The Nobel Prize for Breathing! Ask anyone. Ask Scheindel Kalish— only don't forget the name she might be using.

I don't do voices in this day and age. There's no call for it in Payroll. "Calling Doctor Malone, calling Doctor Malone!"

I was just kidding. That was just an icebreaker. I know what a bank is. Or a minute, ask me about a minute.

Sure, live and learn. Enough said?

actors are the worst, always making jokes, always thinking so much of themselves. But I say writers are probably no different. I bet you know some it would make a person sick to talk to. Look at the pictures some of them pick. I mean, the pictures they pick for some of their books. Hey, some of them, you can see it sticking out all over them, always thinking of themselves and never anybody else!

It's the same thing with rich people. In my analysis, there are rich people which make you want to vomit. This is why I should get down on my hands and knees and thank you for that story. Hey, you know the one. About the rich people when they're all eating at the fabulous C.B.?

God is my judge, you really gave it to them good! But I say they had it coming. Listen, when a person has it coming, then a person has it coming. Whereas here comes present company and really gives it to them in the chops!

"La Cote Basque." Wasn't that what you called it? What a title! It says a mouthful. Watch out! Here it comes! It's just a person writing, but it's the wave, run for your lives!

I was just wondering. You think I could use it instead of one of them from the calendar? How about instead of *capstone*? "La Cote Basque." So what do you think? You think it would work? You think she would say to herself, "He said *what*?" You think it would open up her eyes?

No kidding, the people you went after in there. Hey, they didn't see it coming, but it came! *Wham!* It was fast. In other words, it was like you yourself were the fellows in Kansas. Hey, you know the ones I mean. Wasn't it you which made them famous? You wrote the book on it, true or false? Let's put it this way. Here they come and everybody gets it. *Wham!* The whole family! But the thing is that nobody really got it last Christmas. I mean, when the wave came on my way to check out May's.

It was just cutting, but that made it worse. Now here's the worst thing of it. The boys getting cut kept going back to get cut some more. Do you see what I'm saying? Is that the worst or is that the worst? Listen, I was there. I heard. It was on the ice, but I heard it all. I mean, like small dogs. And the knife! You know where it is, but can you see it? But maybe this is the reason. I mean, maybe they can't either! Hey, you think they didn't even know what made them bleed?

I don't know. It made me sleepy just to watch. It was like with Ben Bernie back in my day and age. It was like with Ben Bernie coming on and giving you his wonderful sign-off.

You know what else I heard? Someone's yelling "Fight! Fight!" But you can't tell if it means here's one or do it. On the other hand, the paper when they threw it, that was the worst of all. I mean, the boys which are cut keep picking things up. They pick up these pieces of things on the ice. In other words, whatever the trash is in a vicinity of this particular caliber. Do you see this mental picture? They pick it up and they throw it! These are the things when they did it. Matches and newspaper and bags! Which is why it's the worst thing of everything of all. I mean, paper, right? What they're throwing is paper at the boy who has the knife!

Okay, I'll be honest with you. Here is another thing we better get straightened out. But it wasn't that I didn't mean to be aboveboard. It was only because when I'm going so fast, the next thing I know I'm all balled up. This is why at the start we should have had more time out for big deep breaths. Am I right or am I right?

Okay. It's not the *Times* we send him out for Sunday morning. It's the *News*. Enough said.

Let's face it, I didn't want to lower myself in your eyes, end of discussion, period. Is this human nature or is this human nature? It's not something yours truly is going to be ashamed of. So we get the *News*. But the thing of it is, it's only because of the money.

I mean, big deal, so Sunday we get the Sunday *News*, whereas for the *Times* they quote you a quarter additional. Okay, maybe I am just in Payroll and maybe I haven't partaken yet of the cuisine at Peartree's, but does this mean yours truly has to make his apologies for a slip of the tongue back when my mind was on something else?

Forget it. Let bygones be bygones. The thing is, I'm doing my best to let my hair down.

Listen, don't think I take any chances when T.C. sends him out to get it. The bike for last Christmas you already heard about. But long before that I really spent the big bucks. Didn't I already tell you? The walkie-talkies? The seven-watters? Let's face it, you know what kind of range this gets you? So if he goes to the corner to pick up the paper, who's with him every step of the way?

"Red Dog, Red Dog, this is Blue Dog checking in."

Certain persons say this is going overboard, certain persons being a certain somebody's ball and chain. But I say you can't be too careful. You take the question of bodily harm, let's not kid ourselves, okay?

"Red Dog, Red Dog, this is Blue Dog calling Red Dog. Answer, please."

You see what I mean? So say he goes down to the corner to pick up the paper. So even if he went a block out of his way! Hey, come on. Seven watts? Seven watts, you're talking range! I mean, where he couldn't hear me from is a place that's not even on the map! It's like with the vacuum cleaner, all that noise, but I can hear it. *Davie, Davie, Davie, Davie.* You see what I am saying? You don't even have to be listening, but you hear it over the noise. Or *in* the noise. I don't know. Ask her. She's the one that ran it!

The difference is, he hears it from his pocket. In other words, there's all the difference. So the thing is, it's just the opposite. *Davie, Davie, Davie,* it makes you sweaty to hear it. But when the boy hears yours truly coming in, it's like everything's okay because that's what his pocket is telling him!

So *you* tell *me*. Around the C.B., what kind of voices is it? You know what my theory is? I'm just guessing, but I'll bet some of the old greats go in there. Bobby R. and Bill Lido. Hey, how about Ben Bernie? Let's face it, these are your top names. They're the boys with the big bucks, not to mention you yourself and our fine-feathered friend in Brooklyn.

"Good day, Mr. Capote. What a delight to see you with us again."

"Thank you, Andre, I am thrilled to be back."

"Will you be lunching alone, Mr. Capote?"

"Yes, thank you, Andre—I shall be alone today."

"Very good, Mr. Capote. And how is your new best-seller?"

"Just grand, thank you, Andre. If you tune in on Johnny tonight, you shall hear me talking about my new best-seller."

"Thank you, Mr. Capote. It will be a delight to tune in on Johnny tonight and hear you."

Will you just listen to me! I could probably be a famous author myself if I really stopped and put my mind to it. Hey, don't kid yourself. I mean, I know there are professional secrets. Like maybe the Word-a-Day calendar is one of them right there. Just between you, me, and the lamppost, true or false? Be honest with me, is it? Hey, you think I can't keep a secret?

You should have heard me on the radio. I don't know, maybe you did. You probably heard me the time I was Doctor Malone. Sure, Bobby R. was great, I grant you. But what do you think I would have been if things had been different?

On the other hand, nobody called color better than I did. Meaning, when I did it at Fascination. Naturally, I am making reference to the all-important summer. But to make a long story short, I better start at the beginning.

It was the top concession.

h ere is the mental picture.

There's this place that's open at one end, which is where the boardwalk goes past it. So the people walk along the boardwalk, and there are all these concessions which come one right after another. Here are some examples—ringtoss, penny toss, cork poppers, rod and reel. So there are all these choices, right? I mean, I gave you some of them, but those weren't even the half of it!

Okay, so let's say you run ringtoss. Meaning, the people go by, but you don't want them to go by ringtoss and go to penny toss. So this is where your calling color comes in. In other words, somebody has to do it. Which at Fascination is yours truly. At Fascination I'm the one which calls the color.

Listen, I'll be honest with you. Up until now I was thinking about giving you a little demonstration. You know, "Roll the ball, roll the ball, don't hold the ball, don't hold the ball, roll it slow and roll it steady, steady and get ready." This and that and so on and so forth. But let's face it, I'm out of practice. So you'll just have to use your imagination. Because to my way of thinking, it's better if I don't give you the wrong impression. But for what it's worth, they didn't come any better.

The thing is, it was good money. Whereas this was the summer when we really started needing it. Here's why. They took his license away. Something happened. My dad, I mean. Something happened, and they did it.

She was still bringing in something. You know, she had her position at McClellan's or wherever. But my dad, it was different. I was fifteen, but I could see things were in a situation. I mean, he has to get around to sell his liquor. So what is he going to do, take a train?

He didn't take anything. He just went to bed and then he went away.

Hey, we had this house full of samples. I won't kid you. We had your full selection of alcoholic beverage. You name it, we had it! But the truth of it is, in my house we didn't use it. Maybe a little sherry on a red-letter day. Except you can count me out. I mean, even when it comes to your special occasion.

Hey, ask Gary. Believe me, you can go ahead and ask him, it's a free country. You ask Gary if he's ever seen me touch it—and I mean even *once*.

Yours is pink peppered vodka. I mean, that's your drink, fair enough? Hey, I know some things. Listen, let's be honest with each other. How does it make you feel knowing yours truly knows an inside thing like that?

Personally, I don't figure it. I mean, how do you swallow the stuff? Pink liquor with pepper in it, don't kid yourself, that's one for the books!

You know something? Janet R.'s mother! Hey, was she a thirsty individual or was she a thirsty individual?

You know what I say? I say not even Gary himself ever saw anybody thirsty as that!

Wait a minute. Time out! I just remembered. Okay, the facts are the facts. But I promise you, I'm not hiding anything. Granted, I came close once, but you ask Gary if I ever really did it. I mean it, be my guest. You ask Gary next time you see him. He'll tell you how close I came. But when it got down to actually giving him my order, I changed my mind at the last minute. God is my judge. Hey, you go into Peartree's and see if he doesn't tell you!

I guess I don't have to tell you when it almost happened. In other words, it was right after the pigeon-toed one, she being the one I first used Paki on. Meaning, I'm on my lunchbreak with time left over after I do her. Whereas Forty-ninth and First is right around the corner!

To tell you the truth, I think I could have used something with a little more kick to it. So I'm standing there and I'm saying to myself, "Here comes Gary, get ready to place your order." I mean, he asks me, and I say, "Make mine the usual." Granted, I came close. But when the time came, I said, "Make mine the usual."

Let's face it, it's the old story—the liquor salesman's son and so forth and so on.

This will interest you. I mean, how it went the first time.

Number one, I'm going to get my egg roll. Now when it comes to egg roll, you never know what you're getting. This is why you have to know who you're giving your business to. Because you're crazy if it's just anybody. So walking distance from the branch, we're talking about how many different possibilities? Okay, I never counted. But just for argument's sake, let's say upwards of twenty, give or take. Believe me, I'm not saying the other nineteen have anything to be ashamed of. But when it comes to Chinks, I say you can't go wrong near the corner of Forty-eighth and Third!

Listen, don't ask me to mention the name. Because one thing they don't need is the publicity. I mean, you talk about your takeout lines, here's where they really invented it. On the other hand, don't kid yourself, you serve an egg roll where the people really know what they're getting, you'll do business, believe me. You take the clientele at Forty-eighth and Third, I guarantee you they're big enough without any plug from yours truly!

So to make a long story short, I'm fifth in line to get to the cash register. In other words, I've got my egg roll and it's time to settle up. Sixty-five cents, right? Meaning, maybe I've got it in change. This is when I put my hand in my pocket and it's the pocket Paki's in. Except I'll be honest with you. At this stage of the game, I didn't get it home yet and see what's stamped on the blade. So at this stage of the game, let's just say it's just a knife.

The next thing I know, there's this customer ahead of me. To my way of thinking, she is the type of individual a person would notice. In my opinion, a person would. Here's why. Number one, the hair. The reason is, it's hair colored the color of the candy called Turkish Delight. But that's just number one. Long hair the same as the candy. Number two, I could be wrong, but in my opinion she's not wearing underpants.

This is something I always check for.

I walk behind and check for it.

Ninety-nine times out of a hundred, you can tell. So long as it's summer and you're right behind, you can!

Believe me, I'm not saying anybody can. Far be it from me to talk for somebody else. I'm just making reference to my own personal experience. No offense if it's off-color, but the fact is it's a question of the crack. Granted, they all have different types of ones. Take it or leave it, but there are no two cracks which are exactly the same. On the other hand, when they're not wearing underpants, they're all the same in a certain way!

Okay, you say, "What way?" Whereas I say, "What if I asked you how you write your best-sellers?" You see what I'm saying? In the final analysis, let's just call it the tricks of the trade or professional secrets or whatever. You have to have yours and I have to have mine. Enough said?

Okay, so here is the mental picture.

To begin with, I go out the door behind her.

By the corner of Forty-ninth, I've got mine all swallowed. Whereas she is just nibbling on hers. So she turns toward Second. Nibble, nibble, nibble. She's walking slow. Nibble, nibble, nibble. You know what? A person which is pigeon-toed, it's funny when they walk slow. Nibble, nibble, nibble. But don't ask me why. It just is.

The other thing is her shoes.

Like they're white and soft.

Hey, I can hear them, white and soft. Like this. Woof, woof, woof. Only slower. Woof. Woof. Woof. More like that and very soft.

Number three, listen to this.

It's her elbows. You know how some people hold them out like this? So the thing of it is, she is one of those people! Out like this. You see what I am saying? In other words, her crack, right? But also her elbows out like this. So this is where the knobs come in. Most cases, the knobs are definitely hidden, okay? Except here's a time they're not. Most cases, they go in where the waist is, only hers are showing, seeing as how the elbows are sticking out!

I'm speaking strictly for myself. But you know what I say? I say this is interesting. I say you are seeing something you know you are not supposed to! I say you are seeing something they are always trying to keep hidden! On the other hand, let's say you're in the right place at the right time. You see what I am saying? For example, you take the time they came out dancing. Enough said?

Meanwhile, nibble, nibble, nibble, woof, woof, woof. And then she stops. What she does is she stops. But what's the reason? The answer is a window. Pay attention. This is what she's doing—she is looking in a window.

So I don't know. I mean, it's just a store. If you want the facts, let's face it, I don't remember. The point is, she's nibbling. Here's something else. Even standing still, she's still pigeon-toed!

Myself, I wipe my lips and wipe my fingers.

This is another important thing about the place. Okay, it's sixty-five cents, but consider the extras. Which are a little bag of mustard and a little bag of duck sauce, not to mention a napkin and the wax paper they give you to hold the egg roll with.

Hey, you guessed it.

It's because of the extras that it comes to me how to get up close to her.

This is the mental picture. There is a garbage can in front of the store. Whereas she is standing in front of the store. So this is what I say to myself. If I go throw something in the garbage can, I'll be standing right next to where she is.

It is easy. I just go throw the things right in there. I don't say this. I don't say, "Pardon me." I just lift the lid and throw them in. Then I put it down and go like this. You know, brushing the tips of my fingers.

This is smart. It says, "He is all right." It says, "He is a tidy person and clean and you don't have to run away."

But here is the best thing. I mean, here is how the whole thing comes to me—the word and my trademark and everything.

I brush off my fingers, right? So now what? In other words, I have to do something or how can I stand there? Whereas if I look in the window, then that's the tip-off. So I say to myself I have to do something. Because the thing of it is, you have to look like a person which is strictly all business. You see what I'm saying? I mean, in this pocket, there's Paki. But what about in the other one? So this is when I put my hand in and, lo and behold, what's in it?

Hey, I know I don't have to tell you. *Resuscitate*. It's the word for today from the Word-a-Day calendar!

Bingo, the whole idea just comes to me!

So do you get the mental picture? I look at the page and see the word. But meanwhile it says, "He is a person who is taking care of business. He is a person with things on his mind. He is a person with places to go." You see how it says these things?

The next thing is, I put it back. But it goes back in the same pocket as Paki.

Nibble, nibble, nibble. That's her. I mean, she knows it's all right. Aren't I a person with business on his mind?

"Resuscitate." That's me, I just say it. "Resuscitate." Which is when she looks. Like, you know, he said *what*? Which is when they look and their eyes open wide.

ou take somebody who didn't know about the word. He says, "Hello." What happens? He says, "Do you know what time it is, please?" What happens? He says, "Excuse me, is this way east or west?" What happens?

Forget it!

I mean, that's the whole thing about the *word*.

They look!

They open wide and look.

Bingo, Paki goes in the one on the left.

Enough said?

Okay, so where was I? Time out to look and check.

Hey, how about Forty-ninth, the downtown side between Second and Third?

I'm sorry. That was just another icebreaker. It's the jitters. It's the nerves. I was just kidding, no offense intended. Big deep breaths, okay? I know how long a minute is. I'll just take some deep ones. Time out, okay?

All right. All right. Time in again. Time in again.

So the thing of it is, it's no big deal aside from what I said. Except you sometimes hear a click. But you can't really see anything because the goo gets in the way. The fat one, I saw something there, all right. But that one was the one time, and I'll be honest with you—I say, "Thank God." The other times, it's nothing much. At least it's not what you'd expect. It's just some goo and stuff and Paki's handle. I mean, the thing is, the handle's in the way. Whereas so far as what you hear goes, that's a different question altogether. Sometimes there's the click, and other times there isn't.

My own theory is it could be this or it could be that. The click, I mean. Okay, it's maybe she's got on contacts, which is one idea. But I'm not one hundred percent convinced. For instance, it could be you maybe hear a pop and it comes out sounding like a click. So you say to me, "A pop? What pops?" And I say to you it's maybe the eyeball or the brain. But let's face it, this is one for the experts. Myself, I never made a study of the subject. But just for argument's sake, like there could be this skin or shell or something. You see what I mean? Like with a grape maybe. I mean, there's maybe this thing which goes around the brain. So Paki pops it open and you get a little sound. A click. Except you only hear it sometimes. On the other hand, that could be because you don't always stop to think. I mean, you don't always say to yourself, "I better listen close."

Hey, *you* tell *me*. To my way of thinking, this subject is a mystery. Look at it this way—first you think this, then you think that, whereas the next thing you know you're thinking something else. For example, I'm sitting here thinking, and a whole new theory just comes to me. Which is that all the time maybe all it is is bone! You see what I am saying? I mean, a simple thing like that! Except it's a question of you can't see the forest for the trees!

Listen, forget it. Mainly what we're talking is your average midtown Gotham lunch hour. So it's a madhouse, right? No kidding, you're lucky if you can hear yourself think!

So that's it and that's it and that's it—except for getting Paki out and shut down and put away before she falls and the people come to take a look. But don't kid yourself. You don't really have to hurry more than what is reasonable. It's dead. I mean, she is. But if she's set right when you jab her, she can stand and stand and stand. You'd be surprised. I'm not talking minutes, of course. I just mean it's not like you do it and here she comes before you have a chance to catch your breath. In other words, she's going to stay on her feet for maybe upwards of five, ten, fifteen seconds, give or take. But it all depends on how she's set, all things being equal. I don't know. Maybe one with big you-know-whats, maybe one of those would tip over fast. But up to now I don't see where the question of the you-know-whats has come into it. Like I said, there's nothing out of the ordinary so far—so long as you leave that fat one out of it. I mean, the way it just kept coming out and out. Like there was gas pushing it. Or something like that. Like a lump sort of, only with these bubbles in it.

So that's the whole deal right there. The rest is turn around and pick a place and keep going.

I picked Forty-ninth and First. I mean, the first time that's the place I picked. You know, I picked Peartree's. It wasn't so far away and I still had some of my lunchbreak to use up, so this was the decision I made. Except, to tell you the truth, I didn't put a lot of thought into it. What I did was this. I just went over there without thinking, and that's all there is to it.

So there you go insofar as the time yours truly comes that close to asking for one once. I mean, I almost said, "Gary, make mine a pink peppered vodka." But to make a long story short, I didn't. What I had was my usual instead, which is a Coke with a twist of lemon. Whereas the thing is, I think a cream soda or a Pepsi would have been just what the doctor ordered. Only they don't handle those beverages there. Or if they do, Gary is keeping the truth to himself. I mean, my stomach was in a state from when I swallowed the egg roll so fast. Let's face it, it was acting up. Whereas I say your cream soda or your Pepsi has got it all over Coke when it comes to getting something to quiet your stomach. Live and learn, right? In other words, they tell you it's a Coke which does. But believe me, that's just another thing they tell you because they say to themselves, "He was born yesterday."

Like you take what they say when they come in and ask you the three questions. Or when they come in and say, "Drink it." Listen, don't kid yourself! Yours truly was there! I promise you, I know what I am talking about!

So tell me the truth, when I thought of the thing of the word, I really thought of something, didn't I? But forget it. Meaning, believe me, I am definitely not asking for any credit for it. Granted, to begin with, it was more or less an accident. Am I right or am I right? Only who knows? Maybe it wasn't. I mean, look at it this way. Every morning yours truly tiptoes in and tears off the page for the day, which is so that this way I can test you-know-who on it at night. So the day in question is just like any other day, right? So I tiptoe in. I get the page. I blow him a kiss because this way he can keep on getting some more of his forty winks without the kiss waking him up. Then I put the page in my pocket and tiptoe out. Okay, so that's the mental picture. The page is in my pocket and I am on my way to Midtown. Only the thing is, that's the day yours truly spots Paki!

I don't know if I told you, it's a walk-up, five flights not counting the first. But I'll be honest with you, the boy is looking forward to better things. In other words, that was the start of something big! On the other hand, don't think I made the media right off the bat. I mean, with *resuscitate*. Like I said, in this day and age you are crazy if you expect to. Listen, there are no shortcuts. There are no substitutes! You are either ready to work your way up or forget it!

I figure it this way. There's only so much room to go around, whereas meanwhile there's all this stuff which is always going on. I don't care *who* you are, every individual has to wait their turn!

Listen, I paid my dues! Which even the media could see by the time of *scintilla*. You take *scintilla*, this is the one when yours truly starts breaking into print and also on the channels. Let's just say for openers the following. The *Post*! Channel 5! Channel 9! Nothing national yet. But in my personal opinion the *Post* is top coverage so far as your local media goes. Whereas I will be the first one to admit it, the *Times* is your ultra situation. Let's face it, did any of the big ones make it into the *Times* overnight either? Check it out! Did Berkowitz? And how about all those other ones? What about Atlanta! Hey, don't make me laugh.

Naturally, all this is a long way from Channel 13 and "Newsline," Catherine Campion reporting. But I don't have to tell you, they came around. They could see I meant business. So when they see it, they give me the nod over there also. Whereas Sue Cott and her Channel 2, forget it! Meaning, pretty as T.C. says Sue is, let's put it this way— that deal is nothing on the order of your ultra! In other words, you don't exactly have to knock yourself out before Channel 2 can see where it makes sense to give you a tumble. They're in the business. They know what side their bread is buttered on! Hey, in this day and age, who doesn't?

1 isten, I'm no philosopher, far from it. But I say it's all the same deal in this day and age. With your two major exceptions. Which are money, number one, and safety from bodily harm, second! These two are where you got some individuals which are trying to get a corner on the market. Put it this way—certain persons have too many pegs for their own good. Okay, that's just one man's opinion. But let's not forget I know what I'm talking about.

Notice, yours truly is not mentioning any names. On the other hand, I am not saying present company didn't make mention of some of the right ones when he wrote a certain famous story about a certain famous dining establishment on Fifty-fifth Street west of Madison Avenue! Hey, I for one take my hat off to a certain famous author, seeing as how he wasn't afraid to call a spade a spade!

Whereas you take me. I'm no genius. Neither could you say I've got all the answers. But let's face it, there is a certain party in my household, right? So considering this certain party, you know what I say? I say he's going to get his share of the pegs, end of discussion, period!

Okay. Enough said. That's as far as I go with philosophy. I'm just saying it's high time I gave myself a little credit. I mean, stop and ask yourself, who figured all this out? You think I just sat around here waiting for T.C. to think it up for me? Hey, the facts are the facts! She's got her "Charlie's Angels." Which is not to mention some other things I would maybe make reference to if I was the type of individual who talks off-color!

But here's the thing.

The boy.

Just don't make me have to remind you!

On the other hand, let's not forget some other things, which is the question of Janet Rose and my dad.

Okay, they're where?

You see what I'm saying?

Now stop to think for a minute. The book comes out. It says so forth and so on. It says this is the authorized story of so-and-so, the famous you-know-what, the individual who did it forty-seven times, etc., etc., the new Gotham record! Add to this the thing of the eyeball, always the left one. Plus the whole deal is what? The answer is, the whole deal is exclusive! And then you ask yourself this—so *who's* got the exclusive? In other words, is it just some wordsmith who went to college or is it the top man of them all!

You see what I am getting at?

I mean, what then? So they see it and then what?

I guarantee you, wherever they are, they'll be on the next boat! With bells on!

Hey, you think I don't know what I am talking about? Listen, don't make me die laughing.

So when it comes to a title, what do you think? Or am I going too fast for you at this stage of the game? I don't know—in my personal opinion, it pays off to think ahead.

Myself, I'm thinking in terms of something short and snappy.

Hey, don't get huffy. So far as the title goes, I would be the first one to tell you this is your end of the business. I promise you, I've got enough headaches already. Believe me, I'm not sticking my nose in where it is definitely not wanted.

Did it look like I was trying to butt in to your department? I wouldn't blame you if you had your feelings hurt! Don't kid yourself, when it comes to between the two of us, yours truly knows which one the wordsmith is! But I am not exactly a moron, okay? I mean, it might surprise you if I told you all the ways I have improved myself. Number one, there's vocabulary, as I don't think I have to tell you. What I also don't have to tell you is this. Yours truly knows himself inside out, and the first thing he knows is he is definitely not perfect. To begin with, I'll be honest with you, I never got all the way through high school. Okay, I had to give it up for professional reasons, but that is another story. The facts are the facts, and I for one am not trying to sweep them under the carpet. Meaning, number one, there are definite deficiencies in my educational background. But in certain departments I have gone as far as you can go in self-improvement. Vocabulary I already made mention of. The bank and radio—here again you don't need reminding. Channel 13 I made reference to when the opportunity came up. Also, my reading material is the highest caliber of it as the day is long. So do yourself a favor and don't count me out. I guarantee you, whatever the situation, two heads are better than one!

In Cold Blood. That's good. I was all for it. But that one you used already. *Executioner's Song.* That one's definitely out. I mean, ask yourself, does it get the message across?

On the other hand, it's got some class. But let's face it, by now it's behind the times.

Son of Sam, on the other hand, here's your real grabber. Okay, I am just a layman, but this is my honest opinion. So maybe you know the individual who wrote it, this Lawrence D. Klausner by name. Hey, no offense. I am just sitting here thinking in which direction I can help you out. So here's my advice. Maybe you and Larry should break bread together and just kick it around. I mean, you never know. The way I see it, it doesn't hurt to spend a few dollars to get the benefit of a person's thinking.

Authorized. It's like *Mutual*, only different. I mean, it's solid, it makes you feel good, but not sleepy and good in how I mean when I make reference to Ben Bernie.

To make a long story short, that's where I got it from. Which is off the cover of Larry's book. Like this. *Son of Sam*, Based on the Authorized, and so forth and so on.

In my analysis, it's this particular word which makes it a hot item.

Authorized.

Listen. *Authorized.* It's like a hammer.

Hey, like *camisole*, right? I mean, talk about your powerful vocabulary, those fellows had it!

You know. "Do you see the thing with the laces? It's called a camisole. Now answer the three questions or we'll put you in it."

Or *paraldehyde*. There's another one that really has some beef to it.

Okay, forget it. I was just throwing *authorized* out to give you something to play around with.

By the way, you know this Larry K. or what? True or false, you and Larry break bread at the C.B. together? No offense to anybody, but I would like to see this Berkowitz match his Larry against my Truman. Let's face it, this is like ringtoss on the same boardwalk as Fascination! Or let's say a certain junior party in my household racing some rich colored on a tenner!

Sure, she beat him. But *you* tell *me*. It's fair—three gears against ten?

Or what about Davie against the whole Atlantic Ocean!

Come on, let's not kid ourselves. I mean, let's not be ridick.

All right, one thing I don't have to tell you is poker is just poker. In other words, so you play it with balls and these lights light up. Meanwhile, the thing of it is, what's the nature of your caller? Let's not forget, it's your caller which gets them in off the boardwalk!

Listen, here's the thing with calling color. It's personality, end of discussion, period. In other words, it's personality and that's it. You think Bill Lido didn't know a good thing when he saw it? Believe me, he was a professional!

"This is the world's largest network, the Mutual Broadcasting System."

That was Bill Lido. He was the best, and don't let them tell you any different!

You know what I think? Let's just say they had let me back on the airwaves. Okay, they didn't, but if they did. You see what I'm saying? That's just one man's opinion, but let's not forget who's talking.

Or you take Buddy Brown. I mean, what if she put up a picture of me next to that one so you really could get a good look at the both of them together!

I don't know. It makes me feel fast inside to get involved with you in a discussion of this type.

I think I better slow down. I'll be honest with you, I think I have been going too fast.

Ben Bernie. Hey, Ben Bernie. There's the one that could slow you down.

Remember? Remember him and his band? Hey, who in his right mind could ever forget the Old Maestro? God love him, Ben Bernie could really slow you down.

The way he used to do his sign-off, it was like this voice which is putting you to sleep and pulling the covers up to your chin. *A bit of a this and a bit of a that*, he used to say. *A bit of a this and a bit of a that* and so forth and so on. Hey, you remember? All these good-byes and good-nights in all these different foreign languages?

Ben Bernie.

He was the greatest thing there ever was.

You heard him, and you could really believe it. I mean, like there was this person right inside the radio on the table. Even his name, for crying out loud. It made you feel like it was back before she went to business, and let you watch her sewing. I'll be honest with you, that's how Ben Bernie made me feel. Ben Bernie made me feel like nothing I could ever tell you. But you know what I mean.

Listen, I'll tell you this one thing where Ben Bernie is concerned.

He was the best friend a certain somebody ever had!

Au revoir, auf wiedersehen, good night and pleasant dreams.

Okay, so I don't remember it exactly how he said it. But don't worry, this is definitely not a permanent situation. Believe me, it is just a question of waiting until it is ready. A thing like this you can't hurry. In other words, when it is ready for you to remember it, it is ready for you to remember it, end of discussion, period!

Hey, Ben Bernie, Ben Bernie. Am I right or am I right? The Old Maestro. All I can say is I never stop missing him.

1 isten, what doesn't come back when it gets good and ready? Take Janet R. or my dad, for example. Believe me, you're wasting your breath if you say anything to the contrary.

Put it this way. You get the book all typed up and give it to Random House. So then it comes out and it's this unbelievable best-seller. The next thing which happens is they hear you on Johnny's talking to Johnny about it. So Johnny asks you all these questions about what they did to me after they caught me, and meanwhile the television audience is listening. In other words, Johnny wants to know the name of the place where they're keeping me. This is when you tell him. But guess who else is listening! They could be anywhere, as it goes without saying, but doesn't everybody everywhere listen to Johnny?

Okay, it's just the mental picture I have. But that doesn't mean you can't depend on it. Hey, can you just see their faces when they see me! First, we kiss and hug. Then when everybody catches their breath, I will give them a little time-out for them to make their excuses. They'll go, "We did not know where to find you, but now that is ancient history." Then there will be some more kissing and more hugging. The only hard part is going to be which one I kiss and hug the most. So what is your thinking on this, my dad or Janet R.? I don't know. I am going to have to think about it some more. The thing is to think it through enough.

"Do you read me, Red Dog? This is Blue Dog calling, come in."

Here's something. I just thought of this. Yours truly is more or less the same as Ben Bernie so far as the boy and his pocket goes. Okay, so let's face it, Ben Bernie was the one and only. But in a manner of speaking, so am I. Enough said?

The other thing is when I do you-know-what with Paki. I mean, I try to handle it the way the Old Maestro would—slow and mellow and more or less like I am not even doing something.

This is Ben Bernie saying good-night.

Talk about the greatest thing which was ever on radio!

"Effectuate."

"Disdain."

"Resuscitate."

"Scintilla."

It's like the calendar is the script and I am signing them off the way Ben Bernie did—just so slow and so mellow and so dreamy and nice.

Au revoir, auf wiedersehen, a bit of a this, and a bit of a that, and good night.

You watch. I'm telling you it's going to come back to me! Let's face it, the whole deal is out there where everything else is. It's like dust, if you know what I mean. It's like it's only a question of when it gets ready to blow over to where you happen to be when it gets ready to do it.

Like Janet Rose the night she shows up at Fascination with yours truly calling color. You know what? She just stood there. I mean, you had these loops the different callers worked, so I am working mine. Let's say it's nine to ten, eight to nine, somewhere in this neighborhood. So she stands there through my whole loop. I'm not saying she played. You see what I'm saying? I'm saying she just stands there watching you-know-who. You think I'm going overboard, but God is my judge, she was. In other words, she was only thirteen, but you don't know the half of it!

Correction: Not through my whole loop exactly. To begin with, I was into it for a while before I see her. So maybe she wasn't there until I did. And the other thing is this. She goes off for a minute and comes back with a cone. So let's say it wasn't the whole loop. But it was more or less the same difference!

Did I tell you your frozen custard was just coming in that summer? It was like your cha-cha-cha. This was when they were both coming in. At least on the Long Beach boardwalk they were.

Hey, but what did a frozen custard cost in that day and age? A nickel? Tops, a dime? You see what I mean?

She Frenches me the night I'm telling about. She Frenches me just the way I see her French her frozen custard.

You think her mouth was still cold from it? I don't remember. Maybe it was. I don't know. But this is not why I will never forget it any of the times she did it, first time definitely included!

I heard somewhere where some of your opposite gender put ice in their mouth before they do it. But let's face it, with Janet R. you wouldn't need it. I'm telling you, she was in a class by herself. Whereas I'm not saying ice isn't interesting. Except yours truly can't see it in this particular connection.

To my way of thinking, ice makes whatever it is

worse. Like those boys in your best-seller who killed the family. Just stop to think about it. They did it indoors. But let's say they didn't. I mean, just for argument's sake, let's say they took them outside and did it on the ice. You see the difference?

It's different on ice. I don't know, but it is.

In my analysis, your movie people and your television people are all wet in connection with this particular department. They don't know what the real thing is—how it's fast and slow at the same time and looks floppy if you look at it right. But let's face it, your average individual is a total layman in this department. According to my theory, your average individual thinks the movie thing or the television thing is what he is going to see when the wave comes. Am I right or am I right? Whereas the mental picture they are waiting for is all wet from the word go. This is why the real thing looks so funny to them! You see what I am saying? They don't know how to see it because they never saw it before!

This is the thing with Janet R. In other words, when we get on the beach. What I'm saying is, it was funny because it was real! Just take the way she took her shoes off and how she moves her legs and arms when she's doing it. I mean, this wasn't anything anybody ever saw before.

Here's another thing. Which is how her head goes when she gets going with the Frenching. It's like your you-know-what is the microphone and she is trying to get in the right position to talk into it!

It is a question of things being where they are supposed to be—this I don't have to tell you. If something is a pica off in any department, forget it!

Listen, only Janet R. could fill you in on this. Myself, I

94

am not the expert. But for what it's worth, it's how you breathe. Let's face it, everything is. The whole thing is this. It's getting the deep breaths and holding them in!

I'll be honest with you. If anybody could breathe better than Bobby R. could, they'd have to name Janet Rose the one person which could do it!

Okay, this was the thing she could do better than anybody, and don't let anyone tell you different. A girl who could do what Janet R. could is a girl in a class by herself!

And let's not forget something else. She says she's fourteen, but she isn't. Whereas you and I know she is thirteen the all-important summer I am talking about. God is my judge, thirteen!

But what's the diff one way or the other? I mean, suppose she was the same age T.C. turned last birthday. You think age is your factor here? Believe me, when it comes to Frenching you, age is definitely out of the picture. Whereas let's face it, you haven't even heard about the mirror yet!

Okay, time out. I made a mistake to wait so long to get to this particular subject. It's this thing of ages. So the question is, how should you handle it when you get down to typing it up? Time flies, take it or leave it. This is why I say there is no time like the present.

Let's not kid ourselves. The minute I mention it, I start getting hot under the collar. But at this stage of the game, do I have to pull any punches? Let's put it this way, I am really beginning to feel okay with you. I'm here to tell you, I don't know how you did it, but God is my witness, you did. Do you see what I am saying? Because at this particular stage of the game, I am beginning to feel I can let my hair down with you. Let's be honest with each other. I had my doubts. But that's all water under the bridge.

So it's time to talk turkey, okay?

What I am doing isn't nice, and I know it. But so far as present company is concerned, I know I don't have to explain myself. End of discussion, period.

On the other hand, so long as we understand each other, I want you to know I am not afraid of criticism. In other words, I've got a lot to learn, and I would be the first one to admit it! But there is one particular item which is definitely out-of-bounds. And for your information, I don't want to hear one more word about it!

As regards this particular item, let's not kid ourselves. You have already heard the media's personal opinion. Fair enough. But before you say one word on the subject, I think it is simple decency for you to give me a chance to tell my side of the story.

To begin with, I am acting within very strict guidelines. I have nothing against anyone personally. So far as I am concerned, business is business and everything else is out of the picture.

Okay. So far, so good.

Now, to my way of thinking, forty-seven makes sense as regards the cutoff on the total. Whereas in the same vein of thinking, it also makes sense to establish a lower limit with regard to the age of any particular individual.

This I did. Right off the bat, I said to myself, "Let's establish a lower limit with regard to the age of this or that individual."

I promise you, this was my policy from the word go. Do you follow me so far?

All well and good.

Now I don't have to tell you, what I am working with is guesswork. That's just for openers. Number two, factors enter in.

Okay, so live and learn. So a handful of times because of this, that, and the other, I maybe guessed a little wrong with regard to the age factor. In other words, the media comes out with the actual statistics, yours truly sees where sometimes the individual was still in her teens. So like I said, live and learn.

Naturally, it goes without saying, yours truly is accepting the media's word at face value.

Enough said.

So now to get down to cases. You read the papers. You watch the channels. What they are saying is no secret. But I say don't jump to conclusions until you give me an honest appraisal.

Do you want my personal analysis?

This is what Norman didn't do. I could have talked myself blue in the face, but the man's mind was made up on the subject, end of discussion, period. All right, it's a free country. To my way of thinking, the man was entitled to an explanation, whereas no one can say it wasn't forthcoming. Meanwhile, if he holds it against me, then he holds it against me. So if this is the price you have to pay for being aboveboard, I for one am only too happy to pay it.

I just want you to know my thinking is clear as regards this particular item. Number one, it's raining. Number two, the word's *cellulose*. Number three, was she really fifteen or is this just what the media is saying? My recommendation is this, *maybe the media has its reasons for lying.*

But one way or the other, let's go back to the beginning. Like I said, there are factors. The particular word for the day, to begin with. What it's doing in there I couldn't begin to tell you. To my mind, it doesn't belong in the boy's calendar in the first place!

Second, it's a Friday. So why is a Friday special? Number one, it's the day before I get two days all alone with you-know-who. Number two, it's the deadline for handling the time charts and for posting the paychecks for the Friday following. Number three, it's the traffic. Meaning, your smart money beating it out of town for the weekend.

And did I make mention of the rain yet? Hey, forget it!

Okay, so all this adds up to pressure.

Not that yours truly can't handle pressure.

But think of it this way. One of your best-sellers gets delivered to the printer. It's a cinch it's another classic. Still and all, in your heart of hearts, there are these pressures, etc., etc. Am I right or am I right?

So here are certain factors to begin with. Granted nothing major—but you still cannot just go ahead and sweep them under the carpet.

Okay, so next we come to the biggest one. And in this connection, there is no getting around it. In other words, we're talking about a subject which is definitely off-color. Meanwhile, I promise you, I will try to give it the once-over-lightly.

Wednesday night is the night per usual. Meaning, this is the routine night for you-know-what in my particular household. Whereas you take the week in question, it turns out Thursday I have to make an exception. The result is that T.C. and me make amends, granted, which is the point of the thing in the first place. But the other thing is my tongue. Do you see what I am saying?

Correction: Not the tongue, but the thing which is underneath it. Meaning, the thing which keeps it attached to the bottom.

So Wednesday I do her per usual. This means front and back to the best of my ability. But then, lo and behold, come Thursday, T.C. has one of her outbursts. So the upshot is, the thing which is underneath doesn't have time to get back to normal.

Okay, here is the mental picture.

These teeth down here, these little ones down in front, no way you can do what I have to do and not get the thing under there all torn up from getting rubbed over the little teeth at the bottom! Let's face it, it takes a week for it to get back to normal. I guarantee you, a week minimum!

Okay, now listen to this and see what you think. It's Thursday night. The TV is going right here in the kitchen, Channel 13 doing the honors. Meanwhile, I and mine are putting supper on the table. The picture is this. The boy is washing the forks. T.C. is getting the milk out. Whereas yours truly is shutting off the oven because the timer says the Swansons are ready. The way I see it, everything is copacetic. This is a happy American family getting ready to eat their supper. But the next thing you know, T.C. is going, "Lord, Lord, I am sick to death of you and everything about you!"

I go, "Sweetheart, little pitchers have big ears. We will have a discussion of this subject later."

She goes, "Let's not and say we did!"

I go, "Chicken dinners, everybody. Everybody get a

nice fresh napkin and sit down at your place at the table."

She goes, "We ain't sitting nowhere! Him and me are clearing out right this goddamn minute!"

To make a long story short, T.C. has these outbursts. Granted, they are nothing to get in an uproar about. To my way of thinking, it is just a question of holding your breath until the whole affair blows over.

Meanwhile, the Swansons are getting cold, you-know-who is missing "Newsline," and T.C. is getting worse by the minute. So as it goes without saying, when all is said and done, there is only one way you can get back into her good graces.

Just between you, me, and the lamppost, I say the thing of it with T.C. is too much nervous tension. For what it's worth, this is my personal analysis. Number one, the job she has to go to Brooklyn for, and also the fact that the subway scares her. Number two, whatever she says to her way of thinking, I say she still misses Salem. Number three, the State of the Union and the thing it's been doing to yours truly's budget. Number four, the question of the boy's education and training—because so far as this question goes, let's face it, T.C. and me are on two different planets.

So let's not kid ourselves. Meaning, yours truly says to himself forget the condition my tongue is in. In other words, marriage is a give-and-take situation. So first it's the front and then it's the back, but not until she says,

"Hold the phone." Which is what she says when it's time to roll over and get her finger down there.

Enough said?

But like I said, the upshot is, come Friday morning, when a certain person feels what his tongue feels like, he could scream bloody murder. You see what I am saying? Marriage is marriage, but the thing under there wasn't ready for another situation!

I'll be honest with you, the thing of it is this with T.C. As regards either side, you have to reach with your tongue all the way in there. In words of one syllable, you either get it all the way in there or forget it, end of discussion, period. The thing you have to do is keep doing it until she says it. Like this. "Hold the phone." So then she rolls over for you to do the back while she goes at it with her finger.

Hey, believe me, yours truly is definitely not complaining. It goes without saying, the mother of the boy deserves every consideration, first, last, and always! But meanwhile, when the teeth which your tongue gets rubbed on are thrown into the bargain, a week is what it needs under there between episodes of this description!

So getting back to the Friday in question, the toothpaste is where it begins with. Add to this, I make my tea and forget to leave out the lemon. Third, I get to the branch and it hurts too much to even say good-morning.

Now, do I have to go back and go over all of these factors or was a word to the wise sufficient?

Forget it, I already talked myself blue in the face with Norman!

So where are we? Friday of the week in question. In this pocket I've got Paki and *cellulose*—whereas in the other, there's the seven-watter per usual. Meanwhile, my co-workers have a right to expect an iota of courtesy. But can yours truly open his mouth to give it to them? On top of this, there is the rain and the time charts and this, that, and the other.

The next thing you know, it's the lunchbreak.

So here is the part you are entitled to hear from my side of the story, irregardless of versions to the contrary. I am not saying that everyone does not have a right to his or her personal opinion. But let's not forget something.

Yours truly was the only (joke) eyewitness, *ha ha.*

hey, hold it, hold it, hold it!

Hey, that was way out of line and I know it. God is my judge, I'm really sorry. Honest, I really deserve Hail Columbia for that one. But okay, it was just a slip of the tongue. I mean, forget it, I'm just jumpy again, and that's what happens—I get too speeded up and I start saying these things which sound like a crazy man. Hey, blame it on Everett. It was Everett which taught me about the icebreakers.

You'll see. I'll get to Everett.

I don't know. I felt good just a minute ago. You know, hot under the collar, granted, but comfy more or less. Hey, now I'm getting the jitters again.

Okay. Okay. Deep breaths, deep breaths. Time out for yours truly to take some big deep ones. Okay. The thing is to get calm and collected and stay that way!

Ben Bernie. Hey, Ben Bernie. *This is Ben Bernie saying good-night and pleasant dreams.*

It's just this thing of having to tell you about the one I did which they are saying was fifteen and not years and years older. I mean, stop to think. You know what was going on under my tongue all that morning? Do I have to make mention again? I mean, two nights in a row? Listen, when I say you have to reach to get T.C. to have her finish, I am saying you really have to!

But okay, okay. Getting back to the one that was *cellulose*, it's raining cats and dogs. So maybe it was the umbrella which made me notice. Meaning, she didn't have one. Second, she has these shoes you just step into—clip clop, clip clop, like a horse, you know?

In other words, I am coming out the main entrance and there she is, clip clop, clip clop, cutting across Lex right through all this Friday craziness, not using the corner and the walk sign in accordance with the lawful regulations. Granted, the traffic is not budging, which it never does in Gotham when there is something by way of a little precip in the picture. Whereas the Friday in question, it is coming down like you-know-how, as I don't have to tell you.

So yours truly crosses right behind her.

Did you ever see a lassie go this way and that way and this way and that way?

I don't know. This is what she makes me think of, how she is moving her you-know-what this way and that way to get through the vehicles. So I ask you, does a person of what they say her age is have a right to walk like that? Janet R. herself aside from the picture, *you* tell *me*, fifteen years old and she has the gall to go this way and that way and so forth and so on?

In your heart of hearts, *you* tell *me*. I mean, to my mind, there is absolutely no question.

Meanwhile, don't forget my tongue!

In other words, wherever you turn, there's a different factor. Four aspirin but, let's face it, am I getting any relief? Oh no, clip clop, clip clop. Post the checks, do the time charts, pressure, pressure, pressure!

I guarantee you, it's a madhouse! The rain is just to begin with! You want the mental picture? Here is the mental picture. Umbrellas, umbrellas, umbrellas! And meanwhile clip clop, clip clop.

So first she goes into a shoe repair and I watch through the window.

Hey, you know my favorite thing to do? Hint: Don't forget the Plymouth!

It's just I get so hot under the collar. Hey, I don't mean sweaty. In this case, I am talking about *hot under the collar!*

To make a long story short, she takes off her belt and she hands it to a colored behind the counter. Then she stands around and stands around, and then she goes and sits down in one of those special seats they have in those places for when you're getting heels or something.

Maybe you're forgetting this. Did I have anything on my stomach yet? Could I even eat it if I tried? So where was my egg roll this particular Friday! And do I have to tell you I am standing in the rain while a certain person is sitting down where it is dry?

The thing about her was she had a good hairdo.

She goes to the Pathmark next. Hey, you know the one! At Third and Fifty-second?

I say to myself, "She is in there buying Maybelline." But I can't see her through the glass. Did I tell you she has got this hair that is like there is a fuzzy ball on top? I say to myself, "How come it stays like that when it is raining cats and dogs?" This is interesting. I wish I could have found out how. But bygones is bygones.

Listen, I'll be honest with you, the rain is making everything go fast.

It's just a face when I get a good look at it. Meaning, here she comes back out and it's nothing special, except she looks twenty if she looks a day! Meanwhile just clip clop, clip clop, on up to the corner with you-know-who taking care of his end of it and staying right up there behind her.

This is when I switch the umbrella over. You know, like from this hand to the other one.

Guess why.

Hey, it's a madhouse, all the horns and the splashing and nothing really moving but everything going faster.

To my way of thinking, there's maybe two dozen on this side, and ditto on the other, waiting to cross over. She's this far away. I mean, yours truly could reach out his fingers and put them in the ball of fuzz. But forget it! One thing I don't do is something which is crazy. Let's face it, touch the ball of fuzz?

I say to myself, "When the walk sign changes."

You know, it's broad daylight but this is Midtown and who notices? Whereas with the rain, they wouldn't notice even if you sent them an engraved invitation! Hey, let's not kid ourselves. It comes down like this in Gotham, all they're thinking is, "Don't put my eye out with all your umbrellas."

I put Paki in hers.

I didn't even have to turn her around with *cellulose*. In other words, I didn't have to.

Here's why.

The sign changes. Then there's all these Gothamites

crossing over, all this crazy honking and splashing because of the puddles. But you-know-who is not budging!

So neither does yours truly!

I say to myself, "Stay put." I say to myself, "Stay right where you are because a certain person is changing her mind and she is going to turn around." Which, bingo, is when she does it and I say, "Cellulose."

Then it's just a question of this, you've got two handles and you've got to hold on to the both of them!

1 isten, I was just as perturbed as anyone else when I read she was the age they said. But live and learn, okay? I mean, at this stage of the game, it's ancient history. Am I right or am I right? Believe me, in my dreams I still get the picture! You know, clip clop, clip clop. You think I don't hear it right this minute? But can yours truly wave a wand? So what am I, a magician or just a person which has a position in Payroll? Even if it happens to be in one of your top ten banks!

Cellulose. I mean, forget it! If I had half the brains I was born with, I would have skipped that one for the next one.

But with my luck, it would have been a worse one, right? Take it or leave it, not even Bobby R. could do a thing with *cellulose*—and let's not forget who he was!

Hey, I just thought of something.

True or false, Mason Adams was Pepper Young?

Remember when Pepper used to say, "Aw, heck, Pegs"?

Pegs was Pepper's sis.

You know what? It would be nice to be in Pepper Young's family. I mean, let's just think about how nice that is.

It would be like Ben Bernie talking all the time—the Old Maestro saying good-night to you morning, noon, and night.

"Aw, heck, Pegs."

That's nice.

God, how I loved all those programs! But you take in this day and age, where are they? I mean, it's like with Janet Rose and my dad. So *you* tell *me*, does it add up or does it add up?

I don't know. I get so sleepy when I think a thing like this.

So long as I made mention of sleepy, you might as well know that's how it was back in the days of Janet R. Except it was different because it was all these opposite ways at once. Hey, you're the expert, so *you* tell *me*. In other words, you have these people and there they are, far off. Whereas when you look, they're close up! So the question is how it happens—and I say glass is the reason it does.

Look at it this way. Glass is just like water. Here's the only difference—water doesn't break.

Hey, skip it. I mean, this is really crazy. God is my judge, I'm just sitting here making it all up.

"Darn it, Pegs, what the Sam Hill is the poor sap saying?"

Question: Who did that remind you of?

Here's something. Think of Pepper Young saying *custard*. You see what I am saying? Think of Pepper saying that!

She just licked and licked it. Meaning, first the frozen custard and then my you-know-what. The thing of it is, there wasn't any talk or the rest of it. Let's face it, we didn't have to. Not that there wasn't your usual per usuals—how old you are, what school you go to, what your parents do for work, and so on. But all this is for is to keep things going while you get from up on the boardwalk to under it. In other words, keep talking so you can keep doing something else. Which is to get down on the beach and get busy.

Here's the thing with Janet Rose. She lets you see her thoughts! She doesn't have to say things. But she just shows you with the things she does. I don't know. These are dirty thoughts. But they are not what you would call off-color. Do you see what I'm saying? Granted, Janet Rose was dirty. But it's not the kind of dirty you ever thought of.

Forget it. It's too hard for you to understand.

Hey, I'm getting a boner just trying to explain. I'm sitting here and really getting one.

The thing of it is, her tongue—touching it and touching it to the top of the cone and saying these things when she does. But the words don't have anything to do with it. Which is what makes them even dirtier. Do you follow what I am saying when I say this?

Listen. You know the words someone just says to say something. So the thing of it is, those are the words which are the dirtiest ones!

She never says, "Let's go under the boardwalk and I will put it in my mouth." She knows that dirty talk isn't talk like that. Don't kid yourself, it's all the difference, what kind of talk is dirty or not. Hey, skip it. It goes without saying, you either know what I am saying or you don't!

This is what happens next. The cone is all gone.

Now watch this.

She dabs her lips with the little napkin and then she dabs her lips again.

So here is when yours truly asks the all-important question.

"You want me to put it in the trash over there?"

You see how this is really the thing of it?

Meaning, there are the stairs. Whereas there is the garbage can just before you get to them. You see how this makes it even dirtier? In other words, it's the reason you said it, but you really didn't say so!

It's like this. It's like saying to someone you'll just be a minute, and then really being it!

It's dark once we get down the stairs. But what's the big deal about seeing a face? I'll be honest with you. As faces go, they're all fakes. It's just that who can really help it?

Here is what I remember next.

She says she is fourteen and yours truly says he is sixteen so as to make a big enough difference. I don't know. Is this when I say my brother is a very good dancer and he dances at one of the hotels? Let's not kid ourselves, who can remember from soup to nuts? It's just it gets hard to remember when I start getting one of my big boners.

This is when she takes her shoes off. This is when I see her do it. Take it or leave it, but it's not like a thing I ever saw before or ever saw since.

Here's something. It's like this is how a girl really

does it. It's like this is what she does when she thinks no one is around to see it. But here's the second thing of it— which is she knows there really is!

Does this make sense or does this make sense?

I mean, it's like seeing something secret. It's like there's the glass, but you don't have to ask when you need to look through it because she really wants you to.

Hey, it's how she lifts her legs up or reaches down to get them off!

Janet Rose's shoes! Janet Rose's shoes and feet!

And let's not forget the other thing, which is Janet Rose's hair.

In words of one syllable, Barbara Luddy!

How's that for a name from the Golden Old Days! Is that a name from our day and age or is that a name from our day and age? Don't you remember week after week— Barbara Luddy and Olan Soulé?

"Mr. and Mrs. First-Nighter." Am I right or am I right?

The thing of it is, this is what you think of—Barbara Luddy's name and Janet Rose's hair. Don't kid yourself. I couldn't give you a better mental picture—the kind of hair I mean. In other words, it's brown and bouncy just like Barbara Luddy's name.

You know what? Go look at "Newsline," Catherine Campion reporting! Whereas for the story on Sylvia Berman's, check out Channel 2 and Sue Cott!

Let's not kid ourselves, these two are the only two types which are even worth mentioning. Whereas faces, forget it from the word go! If anything can throw you off, a face is the first thing which can do it!

But take feet. Or take shoes.

Shoes is something you can always count on. Not that

you also can't do it on feet. So as regards this question and the individual we are talking about, do I have to sit here and tell you? Believe me, the answer is Janet R. is bar none in both departments!

So let's just start with her shoes, just to begin with. It's summer, but the color is what? White like everybody else? Forget it! Meaning, they're not! But the color is not the best part. It's the thin little strap which is!

See if you can see this, this little glass window the strap gives you when you look at her feet. In other words, the toes are covered but the beginning of the cracks aren't! It's like these tiny you-know-whats and you can look through the little window to see them.

To my way of thinking, it's shoes like these which make you think of naked. But do me a favor and don't ask me to tell you why it's this which is the caliber of my thinking. I mean, it could be a question of this or it could be a question of that. Not to mention it could also be the bones and the veins along with the toes and the creases between them!

Hey, am I getting a big boner! I guarantee you, yours truly is really getting a big one.

Okay, okay, big deep breaths for everybody involved!

She puts her arms down. She lifts her legs up. The elbows go in and then the elbows go out.

Did you ever see a lassie go this way and that way and this way and that way?

Sometimes I think of it like this—like the thing on Fourteenth or the one where the man who made the pizzas jumps up. In other words, it's a thing which is real, and this is why it doesn't look it! You take a thing which is real like this, and you know what? You say to yourself somebody is making it up!

111

et's face it, creases, cracks, whatever—just don't make me have to spell it out for you. These are the words and that's that. I mean, guess who just got a boner only from writing them down and not even saying them out loud.

Here's another thing. She already had you-know-whats. Granted, there's this blue dress with white dots on it. But I could tell even in the dark.

Not that I get to feel them or see them—or do anything else in this particular department. As regards the all-important summer in question, I don't. On the other hand, I don't have to tell you what happens when the summer is over!

Meanwhile, it's still the night I am talking about. In other words, it's the beginning of August.

The thing of it is, she only takes her shoes off. Also, as it goes without saying, there is no feeling anything of hers, end of discussion, period. Do you see what I'm saying? It was okay to give her little kisses. But it wasn't okay to hug her or feel her you-know-whats.

Here's what she said. She said this was the way to start. She said the thing was to do the thing with her mouth and then she would decide after that. In words of one syllable, the thing with Janet R. was to give you a suck-off and then give you another one after that!

Okay, that was uncalled for. That was definitely way off-base. Forget I ever said it. I know we don't need that caliber of language, whatever they tell you to the contrary. Believe me, it is a caliber which has no place in a situation like this. I guarantee you, my mind is not in the gutter. This is one thing I cannot condone, which is a mind which is in the gutter! You know as well as I do, I am a man who runs a household, not to mention a former show-business person in my own right. So I naturally know things, as it goes without saying. For example, my experience as regards this department could fill up a shirt cardboard on both sides.

You know what size those cardboards are? And I was writing small! In other words, yours truly was not born yesterday. On the other hand, an individual in your circle goes to a French hand laundry, true or false? Whereas your French hand laundries give them back to you on hangers. Fair enough?

Listen, I have been around. I know not everybody and his brother has to go to the Chink on the corner!

All right, you caught me at it again. I mean, okay, I wasn't aboveboard one hundred percent. So big deal, T.C. does my shirts at home and we don't take them to the Chink's. The thing of it is, that's how it is in banks. Meaning, the dress code which says what you can work in. Whereas your writers, they can write in anything they want to. Take Norman, for instance. You think he has to ask his ball and chain to iron him five shirts a week?

Listen, do me a favor and don't make me laugh.

Hey, let's face it, here I am just shooting my mouth off again because I am trying to get rid of this boner. So all right, you can tell, can't you? Listen, if I had half the brains I was born with, I'd get back to where I was about the part under the boardwalk. Am I right or am I right? It's just that where the thing of it is, I start going back to it and I sit here getting a new boner all over again.

Hey! I mean, a boner in your own kitchen?

Okay, so here we go again. So let's everybody stay calm and collected.

These are some things Janet Rose told me.

She says her father does something in the dress business. She says he doesn't live with her mother. She says he lives in the city but in a different apartment. She says she's going to go to the Bronx High School of Science. She says she skipped a year so she's going to start with the year after that. She says it's the school for the smartest kids in Gotham.

Listen, check this out before you put it in the book. I mean, about the Bronx High School of Science. In other words, what I'm saying she told me, it was how many years ago? Myself, I am in no position to give you the facts on this, one way or the other. The thing is, we don't want them shooting us down just because a certain famous author didn't do his homework.

I went up there once. It was after I got out of the place the second time. It was the day after that. This is when I saw her walking in the leaves with her you-know-what going back and forth.

Did you ever see a lassie go this way and that way and this way and that way?

I guess you know the place I am making reference to. Naturally, I cannot make mention of either one of them by name. But this is not for the reason you are thinking. Hey, if I tell you the real one, you swear it won't lower me in your eyes or in your personal opinion? In other words, don't say it if you don't mean it! Because I think it did in Norman's.

No offense. Believe me, I am not drawing comparisons.

Okay. The answer is I never asked. Yours truly never asked and no one ever told him!

114

So that's the answer, take it or leave it.

Hey, you think they put a sign up?

She has her shoes in one hand. She's wearing this dress with white dots. There's this belt that goes around the middle. It's thin and white and tight. It's like the thin strap which goes across her feet, only that one isn't white.

Her eyes are brown. They are brown. I can't help it. They make me think of the name of Barbara Luddy. Her name is eyes and hair like that.

I was so excited. Just going under the boardwalk did it. Just going under was like saying you were going to do something—because everybody said this was what you went under there for.

We didn't talk about anything once we got under there. There was only the one thing she said. This is what it was.

"Lie back."

Here is the one thing I said, but I don't know when it came up.

"You should see Davie dance." Or maybe it was this instead. "You should see Davie swim."

I don't know which one it was.

It's nothing big—except I'd like to know which one.

I don't know. She made me want to say things. I wanted to tell Janet R. everything there was—even about Buddy Brown.

It's crazy, but here is the truth. Janet R. was like the

sky was hugging me again. It was like the sky was putting down its arms to hug me, but it wouldn't snatch me up.

Hey, forget it. I mean, I hear myself writing this, but it just dawns on me, what's words with a thing like this?

It's just too hard to tell you when it wasn't your you-know-what in her mouth. Except I'll tell you this. It was like the sky before Buddy Brown came along. In other words, I didn't have to do anything. She just wanted to put down her mouth like it was the sky with its arms. It was like she was all the things which couldn't wait to hug me and I was too small to have to hug back.

She says, "Lie back."

Hey, there I go again, not being one hundred percent. I mean, maybe she didn't say that. Maybe I just heard it coming out, but it didn't have to come out of her mouth.

Listen, you think I really thought the voice in the vacuum cleaner wasn't coming from somewhere else? You think I didn't know it was? And this goes double for the specks! I mean, how could they be little animals if every single one of them went the same way at once? Little animals wouldn't do that! I mean, is that ridick or is that ridick?

Here's the thing of it. I look. I listen. Whereas I don't really do either one. Let's face it, who else on Fourteenth heard and saw the things yours truly did? But did you-know-who have to try?

I could hear the screams. I could hear the shirts. When the boys threw the paper, who heard it crash?

You think I wanted to?

It made me sleepy. It made me get sweaty and sleepy and scared.

Even when the police came, I couldn't stop seeing and hearing.

116

There was the rack with coats on it. I mean, I saw it. But who else did? I can even smell how the boy with the knife was when he backed up into the rack. I can taste it when he did. I can hear his arm come out and stay out and cut them with the knife. I can feel the things which hit him when they did. I can taste the paper! I can taste it in my ears!

Hey, time out. Time out!

So I ask you, when it comes to Paki, where do we stand? Okay, *you* tell *me*. Are we talking about the big bucks or are we talking about the big bucks?

Look who's asking who! I mean, who wrote the book on this particular subject, present company not excluded?

That's why I was way off-base with going to Norman first. True or false, who's the top man in this—him or you?

So what do you think so far, okay? In other words, just for argument's sake, suppose I quit right here. Meaning, at twenty-three, I call it a day, end of discussion, period. You think we're already ahead of the game what with twenty-three to the good? Be honest with me. Let's say we called it a day at twenty-three. So if we did that, then what's the story? You and the boy get to divvy up what? A million? Five, six? Or am I so out of the picture I'm just talking small potatoes? Hey, so *you* tell *me*. Ten? So you tell me what we're in this for, ten big ones just at this stage of the game? Because just between you, me, and the lamppost, I wouldn't mind getting a rough idea. So give me a ballpark. Twenty million? Is this too crazy?

On the other hand, make believe I'm already up to *capstone*. So how much for forty-seven instead of for twenty-three? I mean, let's face it, you're the man who wrote the book, so talk to me. At this stage of the game, am I just knocking myself out for nothing?

Hey, do me a favor and don't make me laugh. *I* could tell *you*. Don't forget, I was *there*. I was the one on Fourteenth! I saw the people coming. You couldn't keep them away on a bet! It was standing-room-only! And nobody even got *killed*! Whereas yours truly is handing you how many? And I mean signed, sealed, and delivered!

Hint: How old was yours truly last birthday?

She could turn you into water. Her mouth was like being in water. She could make her mouth into water. You were water inside of water. And when you had your finish, you weren't even that. You were sky. Not the air the sky is made of, but just the color of it.

It was what it was before Buddy Brown or anything in the Buddy Brown department.

She says, "Lie back."

She puts her fingers on my chest and pushes. She says, "Lie back," and pushes me down.

I feel her getting my pants open. I see the cracks in the boards over my head. I know she is getting ready to do something. But I don't know what it is. I can see the cracks and the people go over them. I can see the shoes go over the cracks. I can feel her breath you-know-where. It's breath where I never felt it before.

I can't help it. It's giving me this big boner. It's terrible having what I am telling about, and then you can't ever have it anymore.

Oh, Mr. Capote, Janet Rose!

118

We swore our love forever and always. We kept saying it over and over. This is why I say to you "Mr. and Mrs. First-Nighter."

You don't know what a person feels. With all due respect, who does? No offense, but not even your greatest genius like yourself can get anywhere near first base!

It's like with Davie—such a swimmer, such a great one. But could he get anywhere with that water? Grady couldn't. Namick couldn't. Whereas Davie was the greatest. But could he, once the water made up its mind he couldn't?

Go ask Bobby R. to stop vomiting when he had to. Or, hey, how about my dad? I mean, how could he carry his samples around if he didn't have a car to do it? So do me a favor and don't tell me about Davie and those waves! Because the thing of it is, it's God which made the Atlantic Ocean! Am I right or am I right? So when God gets ready to punish you, does even a great swimmer stand a chance?

Hey, can a three-speed take a tenner? Couldn't the moron even count?

Listen, I don't have to tell you. So far as any Bronx High School of Science goes, Davie was a dancer and a swimmer. End of discussion, period.

On the other hand, yours truly is such a genius, he was the first one which went in the water!

Okay, so here's the whole thing of it the way I count the picas.

Let's say it's half for Janet R. and the rest for my moron brother. I mean, didn't I owe him a whopper for taking care of Buddy Brown?

Dumbness. Hey, wait a minute. Didn't I already have one that was something like that? Hey, hold the phone a minute, didn't I? I know! I know! It was the one which went with the fat one where all that stuff kept coming out! Didn't I tell you about the one which had the clot? So maybe it wasn't a clot. So maybe it was a growth like, with like this air in it or an abscess like.

So the word was what?

Amentia! Amentia is what the word was!

Hey, how's that for everything coming back!

"Amentia." Then Paki in and Paki out.

She was this messenger. Meaning, she was one of them from this bike service we use at the bank. Hey, for crying out loud, here's something else! Guess where a certain person was in the process of going to at the particular time I'm talking about! Listen, is this a crazy coincidence or is this a crazy coincidence? Because yours truly was on his way over to Peartree's of all places, when, lo and behold, I spot her and like I see she is walking instead of riding her bike! So the question is, so why is she doing that? Sure, she wants you to think she's walking it because she has a flat. But I say that's what they all say. Am I right or am I right? I mean, *you* tell *me*, is she a messenger or is she what? Hey, let's face it, you shouldn't hire a fat person when you want someone on a bike!

Not to change the subject, but I'll give you three guesses what I was on my way to Peartree's for.

Hey, go ahead and give up. I promise you, you'll never guess!

Hint: It was to ask Gary something.

Now do you get it? Because it was to ask Gary how they get it pink when they make that type of vodka!

Not that I would ever touch the stuff with a ten-foot pole. It's just I wanted to know how they did it in case it ever came up. Like suppose you-know-who was to ask me what are those little things flying around? The thing is to have the answer at your fingertips, right? So does this make sense or does this make sense? In other words, I'm ready to say the answer is dust! Whereas was anybody ever ready to say it to me? Listen, do me a favor and don't make me laugh! All they ever said was they were dancing. But I say dancing in a closet?

Listen, check me out on this, okay? True or false, I have or haven't told you how the word works? I mean, the thing of it is, it makes no sense, which is why it does!

Like this. "Somebody said *what*?"

But let's face it, did Ben Bernie? Just ask yourself, when the Old Maestro said what he said, didn't you say to yourself, "He said *what*?" But that's what made it so wonderful! *A bit of a this, a bit of a that*, and so on and so forth. Whereas wasn't it why you listened so hard? Don't kid yourself, when it doesn't make sense is when everybody starts listening!

Like you take your youngsters of today and their songs. So am I right or am I right?

On the other hand, it's all a question of keeping up with the times. Like if you took the best-seller about the boys in Kansas and then you took the best-seller about you-know-who in Gotham. So you see how you have to keep up with the times? I mean, look at your own situation, a handful of farmers and they're all in the same family and none of it happened on ice! Whereas look at me and my forty-seven, even granted it's only twenty-three of them so far. You see what I am saying? Don't kid yourself! I don't care who you are, a person has got to keep up with the times!

Not that I envy your youngster of today. Far from it. The streets, for example—whichever way you turn, here comes something, and chances are it's bodily harm!

"Red Dog, Red Dog, answer, please!"

a *bit of a tweet-tweet!* That's what Ben Bernie said!

Hey, it just came to me—*a bit of a tweet-tweet.* God is my witness, it came to me just like that!

And then there's something else. It's like *yes sir, yes sir, yes sir.* Or it's something like that.

Don't worry. It's coming back. It all comes back from wherever it is. You name it, it'll do it!

God, how I loved to hear it! It was like how I felt when Janet R. got busy with her mouth. Ben Bernie swallowed you, every last drop!

She always did it once a day minimum. But mostly three or four. She did it all that all-important summer— and even more when the summer was over. It didn't matter where we had to. Janet R. would find a place and then we'd go ahead and do it.

Nights it was under the boardwalk. But days we had to look around—parked cars and telephone booths and the ladies' room at the Texaco. She just had to get down somewhere or find a place to lean over.

Let's not kid ourselves, this was the summer of summers!

122

Number one, here comes Janet R. Number two, there goes my dad, and then Davie right behind him.

Pay attention. This is the mental picture.

Yours truly is making good money. And she is still on at McClellan's or whatever. I don't know. So maybe it's a Woolworth's or a McCrory's. What's the diff so long as it's a dimestore? The thing is, she says she is sick and tired of going to business. She says she is fed up right up to here with always having to bust her chops for every kind of colored. She says good riddance to bad rubbish because he never brought in enough to begin with.

These are all quotes I am giving you.

You don't have to bother to check them. They're okay, I guarantee it.

Ask Davie.

Hey, no offense! I just thought it was time for another little icebreaker.

Blame Everett. He was always doing these little icebreakers. When they would say "Drink it," and yours truly wouldn't. Or answer the three questions.

Okay, so you can't ask Davie. I mean, I know I don't have to tell you forget it.

Hey, how about ask Grady or ask Namick instead of the moron which thought it up?

Money was why he thought of it. Money was why him and me always thought of anything. In other words, Davie wasn't a lifeguard, but he had an idea how to make money off it. Grady and Namick were. Meaning, they were the ones in charge of the beach which was right across from Fascination. There's beach here and there's beach there, but that was the part of the beach where all the big business got handled.

They were older individuals than Davie. But they were

not as fabulous swimmers. Okay, so here's the part you have been waiting for. Here is how it happened.

Late August, early September, this is when the beach shuts down and the lifeguards put on the raffle. It's just a stunt, the raffle. It really isn't a one hundred percent thing, just to begin with. Let's face it, everybody knows what the story really is, which is to take care of the lifeguards as regards their tips for the season. In other words, this is what they get extra, seeing as how they're supposed to get it as part of the regular deal.

Do you see what I'm saying? So there's this raffle which really isn't a raffle. I mean, a raffle is just what they call it. Okay, it's like *camisole*, right? Except it's really the thing with the laces.

So to make a long story short, the prize is a bottle of liquor. So maybe it's worth five dollars. Whereas what does a ticket go for? Let's say double.

Okay, actual figures I can't give you. But let's not forget, we're talking a different day and age. Some things you can wait for to come back, but some things what's the percentage of waiting?

Number one, Davie gets the bottle from the samples. So if Davie gets the bottle, then he gets a cut on the take from the tickets. But that's just number one. Meaning, there are certain other factors! But let's just say where money is the first and foremost of all the factors.

Let's put it this way. I am pulling down thirty-five from Fascination. Whereas Davie is getting good money from his lessons. So this is what the situation is as regards the household economics. Meaning, you add in her forty-five from McClellan's or Woolworth's, you've got all told something to think twice about when the summer is going to be over.

This is when she says we better start thinking about where we are turning next, seeing as how she has done all the waiting on the colored she is ever going to, end of discussion, period.

I can understand this, her saying what the story was. On the other hand, this is not the policy I myself practice. I say, the less my own particular household knows, the better for all parties. Let's face it, I am making reference to T.C. and her outbursts. With this in mind, here's the answer. She already has enough of her nervous tension.

Here is my analysis. There is too much pressure to begin with. So if you start talking certain factors, what happens to the pressure? You see what I am saying?

I say this is no way to deal with the nature of the situation. I say dissemination of information only does what to the pressure? Whereas if it's T.C.'s outbursts which are the question, the best policy is not to make mention.

Do you see the thinking behind my thinking? Because that's what it is, take it or leave it.

Dissemination.

Like this. "Dissemination."

But don't waste your breath and ask me which number it was when I did it. Time out. Did I say something about a fat one where these bubbles keep coming out around Paki? So did I or didn't I? Because I don't want to forget to tell you about that one. A real tubby! So what was she doing with a job as a messenger? Hey, she's a messenger and she's walking her bicycle! Like she wants you to think it's because her tire was flat, but I say was it?

Forget it. I don't have time to take it up now. Except here's the thing. How do we pin down what it was coming from? Like a tumor couldn't do that, could it? Unless there's a type you get and gas gets in it. I don't know. I guess this is one for the experts.

We don't have time for it now anyway. You think Norman is just sitting there and twiddling his thumbs down in Brooklyn? Do I have to remind you what makes a bad situation worse and the fact that I already did it? Let's face it, there has been too much dissemination of information, as it goes without saying!

So getting back to the discussion of the raffle, which is the one we were already involved in. So with this in mind, reviewing the facts so far, the raffle is a phony, true or false?

Granted, it costs you ten to take a chance on something you only get half as much for. Whereas chances meanwhile are you won't get even that to begin with. So Davie says this is where you have to have your rescue. On the other hand, you say to me, "What's the rescue?"

Okay, fair enough. This is a perfectly legitimate question.

So let's say for argument's sake, a certain somebody goes in the water. Let's also say this certain somebody goes out where it's too far out for his own good. So then the next thing is this individual, whoever it is, starts drowning. He's screaming, "I am drowning!" So then the people on the beach scream too. They scream, "Lifeguard, lifeguard, a person is drowning!" So do you follow this mental picture?

Grady and Namick are ready and waiting! Don't kid yourself, they know from the word go the whole deal is a setup. Is anybody really drowning? Hey, forget it! It's just a patsy! It's just the individual they get to go along with the whole situation. So this is how come they look so good when they go out to get him. You see what I am saying?

They go in and they look good and they go out and get him!

Hey, the thing is to do it up. The thing is to sell tickets! Whereas what is Davie's cut going to be for getting the bottle and also thinking up the rescue?

The answer is one-third of the action, but that's only depending.

So you say to me, "Depending on what?"

The answer is only if he also gets the patsy.

I say, "You be the patsy. It's your idea."

But he says he can't be because everybody knows he's too great of a swimmer!

So like I said, wasn't the whole thing of it the money? Don't kid yourself, ask anybody. Meanwhile, the next thing you know, it's the Sunday in question because this is the last Sunday of the season. Whereas what does the city put up the night beforehand? The answer is a sign which says NO SWIMMING. Do you see what I'm saying? In other words, yours truly comes out and he sees it says NO SWIMMING. But meanwhile a certain someone came with him. Hey, are you kidding? You think I was going to let Janet Rose get the wrong impression? Listen, I know I don't have to tell you, forget it! So I've got my trunks but before I can get them on, you-know-who gets down on her knees behind Fascination and gives me a big send-off. The next thing is yours truly goes out to deal with the situation.

Listen, I'll be honest with you, the water looked like it was whipped up with an eggbeater!

I don't know, I have this crazy feeling like they're all waiting. You know what my theory is? They really are! Not just Janet Rose but everybody! They're waiting for somebody to come along and be the one to do something. Hey, for what it's worth, I'll give you my analysis—which is if somebody didn't, they'd probably make him, take it or leave it.

So I go past her where she's sitting on her blanket and I say, "This is for Mr. and Mrs. First-Nighter." Then I get to the lifeguard station, and I say, "Get ready." But they don't say anything. Grady, I don't have to tell you, is up on his chair per usual. Whereas Namick is on the catamaran flipping around his whistle. As regards Davie, I don't know, he must have been somewhere even if yours truly couldn't see him.

Hey, don't forget Everett's favorite icebreaker—"Everybody's got to be someplace."

You know what? I think that was his best one.

"You ready?" I said. "I am going in."

Grady says, "Hey, can't you read, asshole?"

Namick says, "Get the fuck away from here, kid—the deal's off."

I say, "It's okay. We need the money."

Grady says, "Shut him up, somebody."

This is when I take a good look at them. But I'll be honest with you. What if I didn't see their sunglasses and the zinc salve on their noses? So then I look at the ocean. But it wasn't a thing you could look at either. This is when everything gets to be different. Because now all I am doing is running. Whereas when you do it, that's all you can think about, which is how the sand can see you going.

Hey, let's put it this way. It's like I just jumped into the worst thing a person could ever jump into. Listen,

I won't kid you. I made maybe three yards tops when I already can see it's a foregone conclusion. It's like I jumped into something and I'll never jump back. You know what? You know what is going through a certain person's head? The answer is the sky reached down and really did it!

I was screaming. But it's just bubbles because the ocean keeps going in my mouth. So I say to myself, "Keep breathing." But then I can't remember what I said. I mean, one minute you're running and you're thinking about who's watching. Whereas the next minute you're drowning and they can't even see you do it because the waves are in the way!

Three yards in and there's no bottom. And that's a fact and you can check it! Then the first backwash hits me and it takes me out what? Let's say another twenty or thirty, just for argument's sake. Meanwhile, I know I am trying to scream, but is there anything coming out? Then I know forget it, just breathe is the only thing left.

The beach is where? I can't see over the water to see it! But I don't know. Maybe I was facing in the wrong direction. Here's something. I can't even see the water I'm in! I just keep smacking at it and trying to catch a breath. But here is when another wave gets me on its way back—and when this one is through with me, I am out past where the jetty is! Hey, everybody's got to be someplace, right?

Listen, don't make me have to tell you, yours truly was praying. You know what? I was even praying to Buddy Brown. No, forget it, that wasn't one hundred percent. What I was really doing was thinking something instead. Which is that my dad will come back when they tell him I'm dead—and when I am, will I have to see Buddy Brown?

It's Namick and Grady who pull me out. Except I never see them until they're doing it. I don't even feel them yanking my hair. In other words, I thought it was the water which was. Even though it's the two of them and the catamaran is knocking my head and my hair hurts and my crotch does because Grady has me by the trunks.

I'll be honest with you. I was crying. I was crying and screaming and making no sense. You know what I screamed? I screamed, "Where's Davie!" I was screaming, "Where's Davie! Davie made me do it, I swear!"

I'll tell you where my brother was. You want to know where the moron was?

He was swimming!

And you want to know why he was?

The answer is because he figured it out that the catamaran was a two-man boat!

How's that for the world's foremost moron brother!

I just thought of something. I mean, let's say you make one up. In other words, for argument's sake, you don't have a brother. So you go ahead and decide to make believe you do, okay? Fair enough.

Now here is what I just thought of. Which is that if you stopped to make one up, you couldn't make one up as dumb as the one I had!

On the other hand, God paid him back. But do me a favor and don't put this analysis in the book. Naturally, the time came when I had to tell Janet Rose. But just between you, me, and the lamppost, the whole theory should have stayed under my hat. In other words, if it's not water under the bridge, then it is water over the dam! Am I right or am I right?

Meanwhile, it goes without saying, you're fifteen and

130

you say things. So let's just say I said things to a certain Janet Rose! Meaning, it's after I get to Gotham with her and her mother. Whereas the next day Janet R. has to go to school. I don't have to tell you, with a thing like this you start thinking out loud. I mean, one thing leads to another, right? So before you know it, there you are and what you are doing is you are talking about your philosophies. Okay, so there I am in Gotham and the leaves are changing color. Number two, I am talking to my one true love. Who I don't have to remind you has also been through the proverbial mill in her own right! So we are talking to each other and telling each other what our philosophies are—fathers and so forth and everything changing and the meaning of life and so on. Let's face it, Janet R. and yours truly have certain things to talk about—fathers gone, mothers going crazy, this, that, and the other. So that's when I say, "Here is something I can't tell anybody."

She says, "Tell me."

So I say, "God punished him for what he did to Buddy."

She says, "Who?"

I said, "My brother."

She says, "I didn't know you have a brother. But that's a nice name, the name Buddy."

h ey, that's what he said! Not *yes sir, yes sir, yes sir*, but *yowsah, yowsah, yowsah!*

Oh, Mr. Capote, Mr. Capote, I got it! *Yowsah, yowsah, yowsah.*

Hotdog! I told you it was coming back!

This is Ben Bernie, ladies and gentlemen, and all the lads in the band, wishing you a bit of pleasant dreams, a bit of a tweet-tweet, a fond cheerio from the Old Maestro, yowsah, yowsah, yowsah.

It's coming, I knew it would! That's not it yet, but it will, it will!

Yowsah, yowsah, yowsah.

You see what the Old Maestro did? He took *yes sir, yes sir, yes sir* and made it *yowsah, yowsah, yowsah.* That's because the whole thing of it with Ben Bernie was to make it easy and sleepy and nice!

He said *dree yums.* You see what I mean? For *dreams* he said *dree yums.*

Oh God, that's nice.

It was so sleepy and nice. Just listen. See if it doesn't make you feel easy and sleepy and nice. *This is the Old Maestro saying yowsah, yowsah, yowsah, au revoir, a fond cheerio, a bit of a tweet-tweet, and pleasant dree yums.*

Not like today. I don't have to tell you what it is all like in this day and age. I should get down on my hands and knees and thank God that I am not in the show business of today.

Hey, let's face it, I don't envy you having to write best-sellers for the kind of people you have today! The people of today wouldn't let you get to first base with something sleepy and nice. You take the great American classics like the ones you always write. They don't mean a thing to the caliber of people you have in this day and age! Believe me, these individuals, they're not laying out good money for one Kansas family all inside the same house!

Don't kid yourself, everybody's got to keep up with the times! You blink your eyes, and there it goes, getting out in front of you, a ten-speed all the way! But *you* tell *me*, isn't this where yours truly and Paki come in?

Yowsah, yowsah, yowsah.

Tonight, for example. In other words, "Newsline" comes on. So what's her top story, your latest best-seller or Paki's latest you-know-what?

Time out. It's time for a correction! Correction: It's Kathleen, not Catherine.

Can you believe it? I mean, it just suddenly dawned on me how I had it all balled up. It's Kathleen Campion on Channel 13. Meaning, the individual with hair like Janet R.'s—except if you think of Barbara Luddy's name, you get the same idea. Am I right?

Oh my God, as God is my judge! I mean, I just had this second thing with names!

Norman and Truman! Truman and Norman!

Do you see what I am saying?

It just hit me like a ton of bricks, where the both of them have the same word in it! Whereas guess which one it is! Hey, is this one for the books, or is this one for the books?

It's like everything's the same thing! It's like the things with the laces is Buddy Brown, whereas Ben Bernie is what it is when they say, "Drink it and you'll fall asleep."

I don't know. You think there is something in this? Or is this just yours truly making mountains out of molehills again? Hey, let's not kid ourselves, there is something in everything, you name it!

For instance, there is something in the air, true or false? In a pica, true or false? In a minute, true or false?

Listen to this. Here are some quotes.

"Step on it before it has babies."

"Let's not and say we did."

"Hold the phone."

"Lord, Lord."

The boy can tell you how long a pica is. Or a minute.

One thing I can tell you, T.C. said he would. In other words, you can't stop a boy from racing, this is T.C.'s thinking and this is what she said. But it goes without saying, he didn't have a chance! Seven watts to the good, but seven gears underpowered! Let's be honest with each other, a girl and a colored on top of it!

For what it's worth, here is my personal analysis.

This is why the boy is not riding it on Sundays anymore! On the other hand, he says it's the streets. Meaning, you never know what's out there, bodily harm just to begin with!

T.C. says he needs the air. But I say there is plenty of it upstairs. Listen, I am the one which breathes easier when he is you-know-where and the door is locked and bolted.

You think I don't know what I'm talking about?

Do me a favor and don't make me laugh.

I mean, let's not forget when yours truly was seven and we moved to the second house. I knew what could happen when you went outside in the air! And don't kid yourself, it did! Just for openers, they kept building new houses. Am I right or am I right? But even when they got them finished, wasn't there one they never did?

Hey, I guess I don't have to tell you which one that one is!

It was November, or it was March. It was a month like that. What I mean is, the weather was the way it is in a month when everything is always muddy and dark. Let's face it, any way you looked at it, the new block was mostly muddy. Meaning, it just had this muddy look to it. To my mind, it looked like somebody just came along and put it where it was. It looked all dug up! It looked like the Japs and Germans were bombing it even if they really didn't!

You know what? It was mud instead of grass!

The other thing is, the boys were new just the way the houses were. Davie was the only one which wasn't. But Davie wouldn't stay inside and play. He went out. He was out there in it all the time. And when he came in, he was all covered with mud! He had mud on him everywhere! He even had mud on him in his hair.

Here is a question. So *you* tell *me*, can you be a picture-book boy with mud in your hair? Listen, do me a favor and don't make me laugh, okay?

I am talking about the new block. You don't understand what it means when I talk about the new one. Don't you see that I was seven? Hey, you want to know something? *Pulmotor.* So the thing is this, did I have to get it off any Word-a-Day calendar? Believe me, everybody has to live and learn!

Listen, I respect your second-rater as much as the next one does. But I am here to tell you, it is going to take more than some second-rater to pull a thing like this together. With all due respect, who else but you could handle a subject on this order? You know what? I say Norman knew he couldn't! This is my personal analysis. Face facts. Norman could see how this was over his head! The block, for instance. In other words, when it comes to telling about the block, it's going to take a genius to do it. Am I right or am I right?

Balloon! That's what you call those fat tires—balloon tires. Hey, look at that. I mean, the thing of it is, I was trying to remember the type of tires which the messenger

was acting like they were going flat. Let's not kid ourselves, it was her head (joke) which was, ha ha.

You see? I guarantee you, there is nothing which does
not come back. Balloon, for just one example! Believe me,
you are never going to have to say, "And then what happened?" Where yours truly is concerned, I guarantee you,
it all comes back. I know what happened next and then
the next thing after that!

So one wasn't enough of an example? So here's another one if you want proof. The puddle! I even remember
my shoe when I stepped in the puddle. I even hear the ice
when I stepped and it broke. But let's not forget who
pulled me! I mean, if she didn't, would we have to turn
around and go home?

Here are some other things. Fourteenth Street! How
about the pizza maker when he came out of the doorway!
Let's face it, it's things like these. It is your breath when
you can't breathe. It is your breath when Janet Rose says,
"Look in the mirror." It is your arm when Paki goes
through the socket and touches the thing where the brain
begins!

Your average person, this kind of thing goes right
over their head, good-bye and good luck, forget it. Your
average person, all they want is the highlights, end of
discussion, period. In other words, your average person,
where's the percentage? Like the salesperson at May's
when yours truly finally gets upstairs to ask about a
miracle.

Do you see what I am saying?

I was shaking like a leaf. I was green around the gills.
I was a person which was just outside there where everything was one hundred percent different!

I said, "Guess what I just saw."

136

He says, "What? Somebody get killed?"

You see what I mean? I mean, is this your average person or is this your average person? God is my witness, it makes me sick. Leaving present company and Janet R. out of it, wherever you turn it's just one more average person!

gotham was the next big step. I just went with Janet R. when she went with her mother. I didn't go home after Davie went down to Davie Jones's locker—to use a certain manner of speaking.

Nobody said anything when yours truly got off the catamaran. Nobody even looked at me in particular. Just think, all those people there, but aren't they all average? I mean, does anybody stop to think? Forget it! They're all too busy being average.

I was freezing. It was just like with the puddle. Whereas the difference was, that was just my foot! The thing of it is, there wasn't any reason to think about anything except to think about being cold. Here's something. I keep opening my mouth to yawn. I keep opening my mouth to get it wide enough open so I can get a good yawn.

To tell you the truth, I never took another look at the ocean. The next thing is, here comes Janet Rose. She says, "Baby." She puts her blanket around me. She says, "Oh, poor baby." She says, "Let Mama come and take you and go get your clothes."

It's like *yowsah, yowsah, yowsah*. It makes me want

to sleep just to think of how she said it. Oh, Mr. Capote, I'm so sleepy all the time even if I can't really do it.

Should you ever send in your requesta—why, we'll sure try to do our besta—yowsah, yowsah, yowsah.

It's the truth. I won't kid you. It's so hard for me to sleep. But, hey, don't get the wrong impression! Believe me, it's not what I think you're thinking. It's just where all my life I was a bad sleeper from the word go. Let's face it, I'm talking ancient history! But the thing of it was, everybody was always sleeping—whereas a certain person couldn't. Granted, it made me sweaty, not being able to when they could. Hey, you know how it is, how you go from bad to worse. I mean, you go this way and that way but nothing works. And then you start hearing things in your ears. You hear this type of crunching noise. But does anyone tell you what it is? I mean, it was the same difference as the vacuum cleaner before she went to business. But you go ahead and you make mention of it, dissemination of information just makes a bad situation go from bad to worse. Like if you make reference, your average person just laughs.

So yours truly just stayed awake with the radio by his bed. Meanwhile, I'm saying to myself if they hear it they're going to be mad. Hey, forget it! They were always sleeping so they never heard a word!

He didn't say *request*. He said *requesta*. That's what the Old Maestro did! Just listen. He took *request* and what did he make it? He made it *requesta*! So stop and think a minute why he did it. The answer is just listen. Isn't *request* the wrong kind of word? I mean, it's like I said at the very beginning of this letter. It's all a question of the right word in the right place. But the right one has to start out being the wrong one!

I don't know. Ben Bernie just did it.

Do you think this was because he was a bandleader? I have to think about it. Maybe it was because he led a band on the radio.

"Baby, baby, baby." That's what she said. All the way back to Fascination, that was Janet Rose's word. So what is your opinion? Did she start with the wrong one or did she start with the wrong one?

We went to the concession and got my clothes. We went from there to Janet R.'s hotel. We sat in the lobby. This is because this is what she said we had to do. She said we shouldn't go up until her mother came back from wherever her mother was. But when she didn't, we went up the stairs to the room.

Here's something.

Did you know this was another first for Mr. and Mrs. First-Nighter? In other words, we were in a room. And here's another one. I told her it was the same. Can you believe it? It was the hotel where Davie did his dancing! But who knows, maybe it wasn't. The thing is, it was hard to tell. I mean, yours truly wasn't seeing things as sharp as he is normally used to. It's like they took away the glass, so your eyes get full of dust. It's the same thing as when you look through the see-through ruler. You see what I'm saying? It's like you either see the scale or you see the thing you're measuring.

Forget it. It's just like with *requesta.* You either see it or you don't. Let's just say I am in a chair next to a chest of drawers and Janet R. is saying, "Baby, baby, baby." But so far as a certain person goes, I don't do anything but just sit there.

You think it was my act or wasn't it? I mean, was I just doing this to look like I was a boy who couldn't do something? True or false, was I acting or was I acting?

In my analysis, I think I was. But let's face it, who really ever really knows? Believe me, you think you yourself are the expert? Hey, let's not kid ourselves. In this department, nobody's got the last word nohow!

You want to hear the payoff? When I was a little boy, I was always faking. You name it, my face and my voice! I even did it if nobody was there! Correction: Even if nobody was, things were and I was.

It could be for anything. It could be for the paper I am writing on. It could be for the water I was drowning in. How about for the chair or for the chest of drawers?

What I am saying is, you put on a face for something—even if it's got no eyes. And the same thing goes for a voice and ears!

Hey, this is an opinion I just thought of.

Isn't everybody always doing just like I was?

I guarantee you, their faces are not the faces they let you look at.

So think back to when I told you I couldn't fall asleep. So here's the thing! Sometimes I think it was only because I wanted the bed to see me not doing it! And the same goes for why I didn't run up the block when Buddy Brown fell. It's crazy, right? But the thing of it is the same thing! I mean, I wanted the house I was in to see me sitting alone in it and scared.

So *you* tell *me*. So which was I? Was I really scared or was I just scared for the good of where I was? When I can't sleep, is it just so the bed will see a person which can't? I don't know. And you know what I say? Yours truly says nobody else does either!

You take the people which come to you and they ask you the three questions. You think they know the answers? Granted, they know the answers to the three questions. But let's face it, that's only because they were the ones which made them up!

Lanuginous. How do you like this word? Now watch this. "Lanuginous." Number which one on the list I can't tell you, because nobody can remember them all! But the thing is, you think the face she showed Paki was the real face she had? Hey, do me a favor and don't make me laugh! I mean, you got one second left before it's good-bye and good luck, but you think the face you show Paki isn't just a big act? Face facts! It's just the face you put on so that you are putting on the right one for a knife!

Like you take the one which Janet Rose put on when the hairbrush was up her you-know-what. Don't kid yourself it was just an act! Whereas suppose you were watching her toes! Hey, or better yet, her you-know-what! You see what I am saying? Believe me, that's where your real story is!

Me, I say you're better off with the one which is made up. Number one, just imagine what it would be like if you had to be the other way all the time. You know what? It would wear your face out! You would use it up! You'd get old a million times as fast! So to my way of thinking, fake faces is just this thing they say about self-preservation. I mean, it's just Nature helping you live a longer life!

Like Scheindel Kalish, right? She makes believe she's Ann Shepherd, she adds years and years to how long she keeps Scheindel Kalish alive!

Listen, as one friend to another, take my advice. You let Nature take her course. She makes you unnatural, sure, but for whose good is she doing it?

I'll bet you never thought about this before. Let's face it, nobody does.

You see what happens when you think a thing all the way through? It comes out backwards! Take anything and keep on thinking it through. You know what you get? You get the opposite of what you took.

Take me, for example. You name me the individual which is more perturbed when he is in the vicinity of some bodily harm. Whereas stop to think what yours truly is doing when he makes them stop and look. You see how it comes out backwards? Hey, the whole thing of it is, stay large. You get small, where's the room for all the contradictions which keep on getting inside of yourself? So take it or leave it, but this is my philosophy in a nutshell.

On the other hand, you take the salesperson last Christmas, okay? In other words, I am making reference to the one which sold me the three-speed and which also tried to sell yours truly this bill of goods about no factory warranty and so forth and so on. I mean, the thing of it is, what did he want to know? *Did anybody get killed?* End of discussion, period! But I ask you, isn't this the type of thinking you get when you don't think a thing through?

Because nobody got killed! Nobody! But do I have to tell present company this is what makes it worse than if somebody did?

Did anybody get *killed!* It really makes you want to vomit, a person with this kind of thinking.

Listen, I'll give you another example.

T.C. and yours truly have this tiff, okay? It is the usual thing. In other words, it's household economics or it's the boy's education and training, whatever. So the thing is, it's an outburst, but what about my tongue? So to make a long story short, it was a Thursday after a Wednesday and I figure my tongue has had enough. For all concerned, I say to myself the thing is to make myself scarce. Meaning, be it as it may that it is not my regular custom, yours truly takes his leave of the premises, okay? Listen, I promise you, for me the marriage vows are the marriage vows irregardless. So that means in sickness and in health. Which I say goes double on a Sunday! But let's be honest with each other, it was a Thursday after a Wednesday and I just couldn't take it.

Listen, when T.C. is in a state, T.C. is in a state. So even if you talk yourself blue in the face, there is only one way to make amends. Besides, isn't you-know-who hearing every word of this particular outburst? Hey, forget it! They can hear it five floors down!

I say, "Sweetheart, little pitchers have big ears."

But does T.C. take the hint? So I say to myself the way they used to say on the radio, "It's time to take a powder." Whereas the next thing I know, I'm over by the river and one thing leads to another. In other words, I see a certain someone and she sees me. So to make a long story short, we take a little walk over to her place together.

Believe me, it's like I told you, I still have my looks. So if I don't have all of them, then I still have some of them, whatever Janet R. said irregardless!

She wasn't much. One thing is, she gets herself so full of alcoholic beverage, when it comes time for what is on the agenda, she's just meat. But is this the reason I made mention of this? Far from it. Here is the reason I raised the subject to begin with. Which is when later on she comes in and gets busy shaving.

Sit tight. This is the mental picture.

It's dark out, okay? So yours truly is getting ready to

get out of there and get back to you-know-where. But before I can go, I see how I should use her place to empty out my water. So I am sitting there, right? I mean, this is the way I do it, as I already told you. When in she comes and starts rubbing the stuff on and getting out her razor!

I'll be honest with you, even this was good. In other words, it's watching someone do the things they do when you are not supposed to be there. And I don't have to tell you, this is how she is acting—like I am definitely not, end of discussion, period.

First thing she goes is, "How come you do it like that? You got something busted or something?"

I go, "It's quieter. I like it better quiet."

She goes, "Yeah, yeah, honey—you got something busted, and you don't have to tell me."

She keeps rubbing the stuff all over, getting everything covered.

Next thing she goes is, "Jesus, honey, make room—I ain't got all night."

This is when she puts her foot up. In other words, on the seat! I mean, her toes right there in the middle of where yours truly is sitting and doing his business. So then she wobbles her knee back and forth. It's like she's checking for the best spot to get the razor started. It's like the boy who backed up into the coat rack. It's like here is where you are, so where do you go from here? Meaning, everybody's got to be someplace, right? So the same thing goes for things as much as for people!

Meanwhile, here is the thing. There is this view I am getting of her privates the whole time when she is shaving! And when she really gets going with it and it's getting harder to get to places, what I see is even more secret.

Which is because I can see her privates changing!

You don't understand. It's not seeing it which counts. Doesn't it go without saying you can always see one when you want to? T.C.'s, for instance, she lets me look at hers. Whereas that's the whole thing of it! If they let you, then you never see what's secret! Whereas the thing of it with the one which was shaving was seeing it when there is something going on which has nothing to do with you seeing it! You see what I am saying? I mean, *you* tell *me*. Do I have a theory here or do I have a theory here?

Let's face it, this is something to really stop and think about!

You know how when you shave your face. You know how when you do, you keep moving it to get the right part of it. So get this. It is the same way with one of them! Meaning, she is making all these little movements, the leg lifted to reach it, the leg turning this way and that way to get at all the places. She pulls the skin and pushes the skin, doing all these little things to it, her toes meanwhile doing their own things into the bargain. Whereas each little thing brings her you-know-what into play in a new way—and guess who can see every iota of the whole deal! I mean, here's the mental picture. Her privates are acting like I am not even there. And even if they really know I am, they're showing me the things you show when you show secrets!

You see the thing I'm saying? It's like "Somebody get killed?" In other words, the thing which was really something wasn't the thing when she was meat. It was the thing when she put her foot up on the toilet seat! But is that the thing your average person wants to hear about? Hey, would your average person even stop to listen? Don't kid yourself, all they want to know is did somebody get killed! Believe me, they don't ask you, "Did somebody throw paper?"

The man at May's, for instance, did he listen after yours truly said nobody did?

n ow here's another thing, and it's the same night. I get my clothes back on and follow up with Paki per usual. Maybe *iota*, maybe *scintilla*. I think it was the first one, but don't hold me to it. But for argument's sake, we'll just say this is what I said. "Iota."

The streets are almost empty going home. Which is the part where this new thing comes in. So when this wave hits, it's just the two individuals. I don't have to tell you I am making reference to the pizza maker and the other one. Like a person in your circle would spot this other one right off. I mean, the way he is tall and has a sport jacket and the right type of hair. In my analysis, this is how your top bank officer looks when he is not at his branch.

To make a long story short, yours truly is proceeding with all due caution. For example, you walk on the curb and you watch the doorways which keep coming up on the one side you've got to watch. In other words, it's times like these when you have got to get all the way up on them. I mean, on the toes in the corners of your eyes. Also, don't think I am not listening for what could be moving in at me from behind. Let's face it, a wave can come at you

146

from anywhere, not to mention from behind. Which is just what yours truly is thinking about when here it comes. But it's just the two of them, the pizza maker and the tall one in the sport coat.

Don't kid yourself, maybe it's just the two of them, but it was the fastest wave of all! Where it starts from is from the door of the pizza place and from there it goes tearing across the sidewalk, all this speed and all this power, but no noise. Except for this jingling sound.

Like this. Tinkle, tinkle, tinkle.

See if you can see this, the thing going across right in front of me. Number one, it comes out from the door of the pizza place. Number two, it goes across the sidewalk right in front of my face. Number three, it comes to a stop in the middle of the street, which is First Avenue, just by way of giving you the whole thing the way I see it. First, there's the pizza maker, which is this very wide but very short individual in a candy-stripe shirt. Pink and white, to give you the whole thing one hundred percent! So that's the first one, whereas the second one is way up there and skinny and has this hair you see which is the hair of your really top men.

So the short one has a hold on the tall one. He has him in a hold around the waist. I mean, *you* tell *me*. Isn't it a funny place to have a hold on someone? Don't kid yourself, it is! So that's how the short one's got him and he's running with him into the street. But then when he gets him there, he lets go and climbs and jumps. Do you see what I am saying? The one in the candy-stripe shirt? In other words, he can't hit the other one where he wants to hit him unless he climbs up to reach it or stands there and jumps! So he climbs and he jumps. And this is where more tinkle, tinkle, tinkle comes in.

147

Also the smacks you hear when the pizza maker smacks him on the head!

Up there, all the way up. Right up there on the top!

Smack, smack, smack.

It's got the sport coat all bunched up.

Did I tell you there is flour all over them? It's on their faces! So you see how this makes the eyes stick out? Not to mention the tall one's mouth when he opens it up. But here's the point. Nothing comes out! I mean, all you hear is the pizza maker jumping and the smacks. And way off, this tinkle.

Tinkle, tinkle, tinkle.

Here is something else. The tall one isn't doing anything. He just stands there letting the other one jump up. To my way of thinking, this is the worst part. Except for the tinkle, tinkle, tinkle. That and the way their faces are all white and there is no other sound except the smacks.

Listen to this. For yours truly, it is the same thing as the time when I got off the catamaran. Meaning, as regards me, the people were screaming, I think, but did I hear anything much? It was quiet. I mean, if there was really screaming going on, there was a muffled sound which was covering it up. So *you* tell *me*. Is this crazy or is this crazy? In other words, there's this jingling when the pizza maker jumps and the tall fellow just stands there and lets him hit him on the head. Right on the very top. Up here in the middle—smack, smack, smack. But it is like there is no noise even though there is! I can't explain it. It's like you're watching somebody get it, but it is happening way off—so the things you hear don't go with the things you see. On the other hand, they're how far away if

148

you actually stop to measure it? Let's face it, maybe only double what it is from here to the sink!

It's floppy and also gooey. Here is my analysis for what it is worth—it is always floppy and gooey. I mean, make believe you are watching the television and someone's shaking it and the tube is going out. You see what I am saying? I mean, how do I explain it to you about a thing like this, floppy and gooey at once? Like the pizza maker's shoes when he's climbing up! Or how the other one's jacket is all bunched up and coming off! So this is the floppy part, just the way it was when the boy with the knife slips on the ice and then the next thing you know, he is all balled up in the coats on the coat rack. So that's gooey and floppy, but both things at once!

Hey, forget it. You just have to see it like you saw those boys in Kansas.

So the whole deal is what? Five seconds? In other words, from start to finish, it's like Simon's, in and out! Meaning, the wave comes and the wave goes. The pizza maker is back in his place, whereas the other one's right where the pizza maker left him, and he's just standing in the street. So this is when it looks the gooiest, the one with the nice hair just standing there with his mouth open but nothing coming out.

Hey, *did anybody get killed!* Don't they see it's worse than that? The pizza maker climbed on him and hit him on the head! Sometimes he had to jump and he was wearing a candy-stripe shirt! And their faces, so white, and the tall one letting him do it like he is something you're supposed to climb up on!

So go ask your average individual! All they want to know is did anybody get killed! But do they care about the tinkle, tinkle, tinkle? Hey, don't make me laugh. Like with the salesperson at May's asking me what he did instead of asking me about the shirts! You see what I mean? This is what's wrong with your people of today! All they know is what's fake. But then you go and give them something real, don't waste your breath, you won't even get to first base! They'd say, "Tinkle, tinkle, what's that?"

You know what? It just breaks my heart how you only have a handful of individuals which know what the story is.

So there you go. I mean, that's the deal right there. The pizza maker goes back in and the other one keeps standing in the middle of the street, whereas yours truly runs all the way home.

Listen, I have to tell you something. I said to myself, "I better run before the tall one sees me." In other words, look at it this way. Suppose you are there watching and Buddy Brown turns around and looks up at you when he is already halfway down? You see what I am saying? Meaning, he's halfway down the shaft where the chimney is going to go, but then he looks up and sees you when you're looking down! So if that happened, *then* what? Which is what I keep on trying to tell you!

This is why I pick a different way and start running and run all the way home. It's also why it is a piece of cake when I get there. Meaning, there is something to tell T.C. before she can start asking about something else. Like for instance, what was a certain person doing before he got good and ready to come home like a decent American citizen?

To make a long story short, she isn't even a little bit interested anyway. She just says, "Lord, Lord, look at what the cat dragged in," and goes back to watching something.

I don't know. Maybe it was "Charlie's Angels." If it's not Channel 13, then it's not Channel 13. In other words, the rest of it, whatever it is, they all look the same to me.

I'll be honest with you, I went ahead with it anyway. I mean, the situation with my tongue irregardless. I figure make amends and be done with it! Look, in sickness or in health, enough said? So I do the front until she says you-know-what, and then she rolls over and gets her finger down there to get her finish, it standing to reason yours truly is meanwhile going to do the back as good as can be expected.

This is what the thing of it is. It's not that I am just doing my duty. Because the facts are the facts and you can't get around them! Meaning, when it comes to T.C., the facts are I love her! On the other hand, I won't kid you. When they come and visit wherever they've got me, Janet R. gets in first! Even if it's T.C. which is the official missus!

hey, I can talk to you like this, true or false? I mean, it's okay if the conversation gets a little off-color? Norman you couldn't warm up to in this particular department. I'm here to tell you, with Norman you always had this feeling you better not let your hair down. Let's face it, I kept trying to. But in my personal opinion, you couldn't get close to the man if you stood on your left ear to do it! My theory is this. As soon as I opened up my mouth to him about this, that, and the other, it comes to me that he is saying to himself I am getting lower and lower in his eyes. To tell you the truth, I think he holds it against me. Meaning, doing T.C. both sides. But I don't know. Maybe this is just my thinking and I am wrong to point a finger.

Listen, when it comes to thinking, don't think you can't go overboard! I mean, strictly for the sake of argument, some thoughts you are better off without! Like would I be wide awake all night if I thought of something else? On the other hand, the answer is what? In other words, you're in a bed. So doesn't it make sense the bed is what you think of? Am I right or am I right?

Lanuginous. This will make you laugh. It's crazy, but I am not ashamed to tell you. It means something about hair, hair being gentle and soft and so on and so forth. So here's the thing. Going back to before I saw Janet R.'s you-know-what, that's what yours truly thought! You see what I am saying? I mean, I used to think girls would be like that if you got a look at their privates. I mean, like that word! Hey, but I was all wet from the word go, true or false? I mean, you take Sylvia Berman's, granted, it was sort of. But so far as Janet R.'s mother's or Janet R.'s, it was nothing on this order, not to mention the nature of the situation as regards T.C.'s herself. On the other hand, T.C.'s is light in color and there's not much of it. Hey, here's something. You look at T.C.'s and you can almost see her Devil's you-know-what. I mean, even if she's just standing there, you can almost.

All right, I won't lie to you. Let's face it, you probably would have caught me at it anyway. In other words, the reason I made reference to this is I was trying to see if I could get another boner! I mean, I was thinking about me and Janet Rose in her mother's hotel room. So one thing leads to another, and the next thing you know, I'm sitting here thinking about Janet Rose in her bathing suit with the hairs sticking out! So I said to myself, "Just wait, you are going to get another boner!"

Granted, it was just a handful of them. But I don't have to tell you this was another first for me, seeing the hairs growing out of the you-know-what of my beloved Janet Rose!

But getting back to the situation, I'll put it this way. This is how I went away. I didn't take anything but the clothes I had at Fascination. I didn't have any money except for what I got when I got my clothes. It was what they owed me, twenty dollars, two fives and ten singles.

I think that's something—how you remember a thing like that. But let's not kid ourselves. I always remember money.

I tried to go to sleep in the basement of the hotel. Naturally, I am making reference to the night before I went away with Janet Rose and her mother. But I couldn't do it. Number one, I knew I was supposed to be thinking about my brother. But all I could think about was going to Gotham and the hairs I saw when I looked. I kept thinking what it would look like if you could see all of them. Listen, I'll be honest with you, I kept thinking if I would ever get to have a look at Janet Rose's privates.

Number two, it was the all-important basement. Meaning, wasn't this the Traymore or the Broadmoor or whatever? So I don't have to tell you it's where Davie gave his lessons when he was dancing!

On the other hand, I am not a sleeper on my best day, as I also don't have to tell you. I said to myself, "Somebody should call her up and tell her." I thought of all the different things to say. Like this. "Lady, are you the mother of the boy who pushed Buddy Brown?" "Lady, did you ever stop to think before you moved?" "So you had to move, lady, but did you have to leave a certain hassock?" "Lady, it's his own fault, but your dumb son drowned." "Hey, just you wait, lady, you'll see how long a minute is."

Listen, you can see it for yourself! Her with her shoes, soft and white, except they never really were because they were dirty the day she brought them home! Wasn't she the only mother with shoes like that? Special shoes for special feet which have to have special support? So *you* tell *me*. You think a person with feet like that was a dancer, true or false? Hey, do me a favor and don't make me laugh! They said they were dancers, they were dancing. But I say don't make me laugh. She had veins popping out! They came out of the closet and she had veins popping out!

Hey, I just thought of something. *Did you ever see a lassie go this way and that way and this way and that way?* It really makes you think, you know? I mean, me seeing her standing around in her shoes for Davie to come home and me to show up. But it's somebody else instead and he says, "Lady, he's dead," or "Lady, he come and got his money and he left."

I was on my way to Gotham! This was the thing of it and the rest was nothing nohow! Janet Rose said it was the answer to our prayers—Mr. and Mrs. First-Nighter! She said here's the way to think about it, and that's the way I did! She said it's just Nature taking its natural course!

I'm here to tell you, Janet Rose was smart.

Let's put it this way, I had twenty dollars, minus what it cost for the two frozen custards which got me through the night.

154

You're laughing. But this was good money in that day and age!

It's like an inch and a pica. Okay, the inch is bigger, but what happens when you put the inch next to a mile? You see what I mean? You're not laughing so fast now, are you? Whereas, granted, an inch is plenty when it only takes four of them to get through your eyeball and jab you in your you-know-what! Hey, that's as far as anything ever has to get! I mean, is there ever going any farther than a foreign object in your brain? Nothing has to go any farther than that! Am I right or am I right?

Time out. I looked it up. The boy has this book, so I took a look. Here is what happens according to the experts. The optic chiasm! It gets into something called that! And that's just for openers, right?

Hey, the optic chiasm! Is that one for the books or is that one for the books? Check it out! *Your Body and What Is in It*. Whereas they don't give the name of the author, but big deal, what's the diff? I don't have to tell you, whoever he is, he is not eating any hundred-dollar lunches at your fabulous Cote Basque. I mean, *Your Body and What Is in It*, did you ever hear a title with less punch to it than that?

And where's *Authorized*? Or even *Mutual*?

Forget it.

Twenty-three optic chiasms!

And guess what's in back of all twenty-three once Paki gets enough picas in!

"Red Dog, Red Dog—please call in, please."

Listen to this. You know what he's got in his pocket down there under the you-know-what?

A dollar!

End of discussion, period.

Okay, you can laugh your head off over that one, but that's what he's got. And the reason why is this. It's another major rule!

So okay, here's the deal. There are these two major rules yours truly inherited from his father, that and the one about brown paper. Like this—"Always have a dollar in your pocket!" "Don't ever go anywhere *anywhere* without a dollar in your pocket!" "Whatever happens, check to see you have a dollar in your pocket!"

Hey, the jingling! The tinkle, tinkle, tinkle! Hold the phone! You think what he had was lots of change in his pocket?

Lord, Lord, all it takes is waiting till it's ready, *yowsah*, *yowsah*, *yowsah*. I mean, *you* tell *me*—let's say yours truly stayed right there in the Plymouth. In other words, strictly for argument's sake, let's just say that's what he did. You see how there's all the difference in the world? Whereas just picture me in Janet Rose's mother's car, jumping up and down every minute. You think I could sit still for two seconds? I mean, I know I was supposed to be a boy with a dead brother, but I'll be honest with you. So far as I was concerned, I was a boy on the way to Gotham!

It made me lean forward. It made me look around. It made me ask Janet Rose's mother lots of questions.

She says, "Where do we drop you?"

I say, "I don't know. You do what you think is best."

Janet Rose says, "He can decide when we get there. We'll go home and he can decide from there."

So this is how I moved in. In other words, you just had to leave a thing to Janet Rose. You left it to her, whatever it was, and Janet R. took it from there.

I helped them up with their stuff. By the time supper-time came, I was still there and they said stay. The mother gave me a plate. We ate at a table in the kitchen. I'll be honest with you, it wasn't such a wonderful place. But it was much nicer than the one I'd come from, not to mention the one where I and mine are keeping residence as of now.

Did I say her father did something in the dress business? So this is my analysis, dresses pay off better than liquor. Even if he didn't live there either, you could see this was the case.

After supper we go sit in the living room. It's like being a family more or less. The mother keeps asking what's to be done with me, whereas Janet R. keeps saying the thing is to let Nature take its course. Meanwhile, here's the thing I notice. Which is the mother keeps drinking from a glass. I loved it in that living room. I loved it, just listening. I loved it, just sitting and watching their mouths.

Hey, and let's not forget. Janet Rose's. I keep thinking to myself, "That's the mouth which does it."

I didn't do any of the talking. I liked it better with her talking. Here's what she said. She says the truth is I was running away. She says I had every reason in the world to. Then she starts listing what they are. But let's face it, they aren't anything I ever thought of before. To make a long story short, I think I stopped listening. I don't think the mother was either. Here's why. She gets up in the middle of it and goes off somewhere. She gets the bottle she's been pouring out of and just goes off.

This is when Janet R. makes a place for me on the sofa. It's just a blanket and a pillow. But I say how she did it was very, very nice. Then she says to lie still—that when it's all right, she will come and get me.

I want to be aboveboard with you. Mr. Capote, this was the greatest night of a certain person's life! I say this to you in all honesty—even though I did not see anything. But there was nakedness! Let's face it, we were afraid to turn on the light. On the other hand, you-know-who took her nightie off. Or maybe it was her pajamas. I don't know. It could have been just the top.

I won't kid you, I was too excited. We were naked lying down. She let me hold her. She said I could not touch her places but I could hold her if I want. She said, "Baby, baby, baby." She said it was okay to hold her, but no touching anything private.

It was wonderful! It was the most wonderful thing there was!

We whispered how I loved her and that she was my beloved. I said that we were Mr. and Mrs. First-Nighter. She said, "Oh, baby, am I making it hard for you?" She said, "Baby, baby, baby, love is just so hard."

Hey, you guessed it! I made myself get a big boner again.

Big deal. So you get it and then you lose it, big deal.

To tell you the truth, it's like trying to remember what Ben Bernie said. One minute you have it and one minute you don't! I mean, let's be frank. At this stage of the game, what's the point in not being honest with each other? I can't be expected to remember everything! You take the

158

one whose eyeball was like a cork stuck in a toilet. You remember a thing like that, it's hard to remember everything else!

Enough said? I mean, at this time of the night, let's not kid ourselves! Rome wasn't built in a day, you know. Besides, the other thing is I'm getting tired! Did I tell you I'm tired? God is my judge, I am! My arm, my hand, my fingers, not to mention my you-know-what from sitting on it here in the kitchen like this!

Okay, the one with the muck which comes out, I'm trying to think. Was she *lanuginous* or was she *interim*? Because I know it wasn't the colored in the can, because with her there wasn't any word at all. Only don't think that one was any picnic either!

Listen, I wasn't born yesterday, you know? In other words, you don't have to send me a telegram, okay? Believe me, nobody has to tell me nothing nohow. I guarantee you, I know as well as the next one I don't deserve any medals. Far from it. In all humility, you should get your head examined if that's what you think I think!

You think I'm cut out for this kind of thing? You think a thing like this comes easy to an individual of my type? You think when I am lying there my first night with Janet Rose that I am thinking how in thirty-odd years a certain person is going to have to sit in his kitchen with Paki in his pocket, which God forbid I don't get sharpened before this one or that one wakes up? You think anybody ever stops to think a thing like this? Don't kid yourself, we all got a lot to learn. That's all I can say. Live and learn, believe me, that's the whole thing of it right there!

You know what I was thinking then and there? I was thinking here I am naked with a girl in Gotham and a grown-up could walk in any minute! I was thinking look at all the things which are happening to me and what is going to be the next thing which does?

I said, "Without you, where would I go? You are my beloved."

She said, "Hush, baby, hush."

She got down between my legs. She did it with her mouth. She did it right up until the time you have your finish, and then she took it out. She says, "Baby, baby, baby, baby." Then she puts it back, and then she took it out. She says, "Baby, baby, baby, baby."

It went on and on. It was better than anything. It was the best thing which ever happened to me until the next thing which Janet Rose did.

She says, "Hush, baby," and gets up off the bed. She pulls the covers up and smooths them over me. She says, "Hush," and pats me on the head. Then she goes out and comes back. She pulls the covers down again. She gets up on the bed. She puts her lips against my ear. She whispers, "This will make him better." She says, "Hush, baby, sleep."

She gets down again and gets between my legs. There is this sound of something—like three sounds, the first and last ones opposite, but the same, okay?

She goes, "There, is that better?"

Oh, Mr. Capote.

She says, "Is that too cold?" She says, "Is that too cold for baby?"

Oh, Mr. Capote, please.

She says, "Is it better now?" She goes, "Oh, Noxzema is just the thing." She says, "Baby, baby, baby, does it sting a little bit?"

Just the fingertips. Just the fingernails. Just the tippy-tips of everything!

I said, "I love you. Oh my dearest, dearest."

She says, "Hush, baby, hush." She says, "Now you just go to sleep."

She pulls up a piece of the sheet. She gets it wrapped around my thing. She pats it down. She goes, "Oh, baby, he hurts all over. Oh, oh, baby."

She unwraps my thing. She says, "Shame on me, he's too hot. Oh, I made him so hot. See what I did? His little bandage is too tight. Oh, oh, let Mama fix it nice."

She gets it all off and she says, "How's this?" She says, "Oh, yes, Jergens is nice." She says, "Now, now, don't you dare let Mama hear you say that Jergens is making him sting."

I said, "Oh, Janet Rose."

She says, "Is he cold?" She says, "Oh, I have to make him warm again." She says, "Look what Mama did."

She puts it in her mouth. She puts it all the way in. She goes this way and that way and that way with her head. She says, "Oh, he's so tired." She says, "Did Mama make him so tired he can't sleep?" She touches my thing with a finger. She says, "Oh, oh." She touches it with a fingernail. She says, "Can't baby go to sleep?" She goes around and around with her fingernail, and then she goes around and around again.

Oh, Mr. Capote, don't you see what I mean?

She says, "There, there, can't he go to sleep?"

She says, "I know what he needs."

She says, "Let Mama put more medicine on him." She says, "Baby is so sick."

She says, "There, there."

She says, "Now hush, hush, and go to sleep."

She puts it in her hand and she gives it these little squeezes.

She says, "Oh, oh, he's so cold again. How could he get so cold?"

She puts it in her mouth. She moves her mouth all around.

She says, "Now hush-a-bye." She says, "Now go right to sleep right this minute." She says, "Shame on me, the doctor said give him his medicine." She says, "He needs more Noxzema." She says, "Now just you hush and be brave."

Oh, Mr. Capote, don't you see what this is? It's the same thing as Ben Bernie. Only it's Janet Rose instead!

Oh, I get such a boner remembering. I can't help it. I just have to have these boners.

She makes rings with her fingers and puts the rings on.

She says, "There, there."

She says, "This is what the doctor said." She says, "Did you ever see a lassie go this way and that way and this way and that way?" And she goes this way and that way with her fingers like rings.

She says, "Hush, hush. Go to sleep."

And then she makes the rings again.

She says, "Did you ever see a lassie go this way and that way and this way and that way?"

I said, "Oh, my beloved, you are the most wonderful thing."

She says, "Hush. Now you just hush now. Make him a good boy and hush."

I said, "Oh, my beloved, my beloved, please."

She says, "Please? Please? Can't the bad boy behave and go to sleep like Mama said?" She says, "Now roll over on your tummy and hush."

I said, "Oh, my beloved, please."

She says, "There, there, just you hush and go to sleep."

I said, "Please, don't make me, please."

She put it in her mouth. She put it in and took it out. She says, "There, there. Shh, shh."

She touched it with a fingernail. She says, "Now be a good boy and go to sleep." She touched it with a finger. She says, "Now let me see what's wrong here." She made it bend the wrong way.

She said, "Oh, I know." She said, "I know why baby can't go to sleep." She said, "You can't go to sleep because he can't go to sleep." She says, "Do you want me to make him go to sleep?" She says, "If you want me to make him, you just have to say so." She says, "Oh, he's such a naughty boy. He won't go to sleep." She says, "Do you want me to make him?"

I said, "Oh, my dearest beloved, please."

She says, "Oh, look!" She says, "Look what a full tummy he has." She says, "Does he have a tummy-ache too? Is that why the bad boy can't sleep?" She says, "I know what." She says, "If he had an empty tummy, then he'd go right to sleep." She says, "Is that what you want Mama to do? You want Mama to empty his tummy?" She says, "Oh, the naughty, naughty little dickens, his tummy is just too full to sleep."

I said, "Oh, Janet Rose."

She says, "But then Mama will have a full tummy instead of baby." She says, "Is that what baby wants?" She says, "Shame on him, the bad, bad boy."

She took it with her hand and went this way and that way and this way and that way. She took it with her hand and did it hard.

"Oh," I said. "Oh."

"Oh," she said. "Look what he did. Oh, the nasty, nasty dirty boy, look what he went and did, throwing up all over Mama. Shame on him. Shame, shame."

She held it and squeezed it. She licked all the you-know-what up from wherever it went. She came and put her lips on my lips. She squished it from her mouth into mine. It made a little sizzle sound. Then I squished it back into hers. That's what we did. We squished it back and forth. We just kept on doing it until there wasn't any more, until it was just spit and kisses—and we fell fast to sleep.

O h, you see what she was? She was the most wonderful thing anyone could ever think of! I mean, even if you think of T.C., could you ever think of Janet Rose?

You know something? Hey, this is really one for the books. I mean, you know what Janet Rose could do? She could do it just with talk!

God is my witness, with talk! Now is that one for the books or is that one for the books? Janet Rose, all she had to do was talk and yours truly would get his finish, end of discussion, period.

You take the last time I ever saw her. Meaning, when she says let's stand and look in the mirror. In other words, this is the mirror which is on Sylvia Berman's brother Arnie's closet. Hey, a person in your circle, I know I don't have to tell you this is a thing which well-off people have, mirrors on the doors of closets. Be honest with me, how many houses do you have? So be honest with me, they all have mirrors on the closet doors, true or false?

Listen, I guarantee you, I wasn't born yesterday. I know what people have.

So okay, this is when I last saw her and I was staying at the Berman place. She says, "Look at us in the mirror together." This is what Janet R. says. She says, "Look at us naked in the mirror together. You're naked and I'm naked and we're looking at each other in the mirror together. Do you see my boobies? See my cunny? You can't see my hole when I'm standing this way, can you? Do you want me to show you my hole in the mirror? If I get down and I squat and pull my knees out with my hands, then you could see my hole in the mirror. Do you want me to do it? Maybe we'd have to get up closer. Maybe you won't be able to see my hole from this far away. Do you want to go closer and I'll squat and pull my knees out wide and you can take a good look? Then you can tell me what it looks like. Do you want to go closer to the mirror now? Or would you rather stay here and just look at my boobies and my cunny from where we are? Do you like my cunny better than my boobies? If I touched them, would you like my boobies better? Do you want to look in the mirror and see me touch my boobies? What do you like to call them? What's your favorite word? Look in the mirror and tell me what your favorite word is for everything you see. Or do you want me to turn around so you can see my other side? Do you want me to turn around and bend over and touch my toes? If I bent over like that, do you think you would see one hole or both holes at once? Do you like my other hole as much as you like this one? Tell me if you're tired of this one and want to look at my other one now. Go ahead. You can tell me. Which hole? Do you want to look at the other one or this one? I'll touch this one to show you what it looks like when I touch it. I'll put my finger in to show you. Which finger? You want me to use this one? Or this one? You tell me which one you want me to use. Do you want to see me do it to myself? Look in the mirror and tell me if you do. It's different when you see in the mirror, isn't it? Tell the truth, isn't it different when you look in the mirror? Look, see me touch it with my finger? Is this the finger you want me to touch it with? Do you want to lick it after I do it? What if I put it in my other hole? Would you lick it if I put it in that one? Tell the truth. Would you? Would you really lick it? Look in the mirror. What if I went and got a hairbrush and put the handle in? What if I did it with a hairbrush? Do you think you'd like to see that? What if I went and got Syl and asked her to come in and do it to me with a hairbrush? Which would you like best, seeing me do it or seeing Syl do it to me? Or what about seeing yourself? I know. What about another boy? Would you like to see another boy do it? Make believe there's somebody else and he's watching you watch me in the mirror. Go ahead and make believe that's what's happening, somebody watching you watch me. What if it was Syl watching you watch? Make believe you're somebody else watching yourself. Put your thing between your legs. Push it down and put it between them and hold them together like this. See? You see? See how we look the same? But my hair's different. See how different it is? Look. Look in the mirror and tell me how it's different. No, I know, tell me about Syl's. What do you think Syl's is like? Do you want me to watch you touching Syl's? I'll go get her and the three of us can look in the mirror together. Do you want me to do that? Does it hurt like that when it's back behind you? If I had one, I bet it would hurt if I did that. Does it hurt? Do you want me to kiss it and kiss it and make it stop hurting? If I kept on kissing it enough, would it shoot off if I did? I know what. Make believe I'm doing it. Look in the mirror and make believe I'm doing it. Can you look in the mirror and make believe? Make believe. Look at my lips. Look at my lips in the mirror. See my lips in the mirror when I talk? When I put your thing in, I go like this. Can you look in the mirror and make believe you feel it? Look at my cunny in the mirror and make believe I'm doing it. How does it feel? Can you feel it? What do you think it feels like for me when your thing is in my mouth? Look in the mirror and tell me what you think it feels like for me. Look in the mirror and tell me. If I went and got Syl, would you tell her? Tell the truth, would you like me to go get her so you can? Would you like her to put your thing in her mouth? Would that be something you'd really like? You can tell me. Look in the mirror and tell me. It's okay to say it if that's what you want. You want her to do it and me to watch? She could get down here in front of the mirror and do it and you and I could watch. Is that what you'd like? Would you like to see me watching you while you're watching Syl do it? Look in the mirror. Make believe. You see all the things you can make believe if you have a mirror to help? You want me to get Syl? If we had Syl in here, think of all the things we could do. Make believe she is. Make believe she's back behind you and she's got your thing and I am watching her do it to you. Look at me. Look at me looking at you look at me in the mirror. Watch my lips. See me doing it to myself with my finger? I'm using the finger you want me to. It's going to make you shoot off, isn't it? Go ahead. You can shoot off if you want to. Do it. Do you want me to hold it and do it? I'd do it but I want to do it to myself. Shoot off.

You have to shoot off because I said so. I think I'm coming now and I want you to shoot off when I do. Oh, I am. Oh, I think I really am. Look in the mirror and look at my eyes and you can tell I really am. Look in the mirror. Look at my cunny. Look at my eyes. Look at me, I'm coming, I'm coming, I'm coming. Shoot off, shoot off, oh God, I'm coming, shoot, shoot!"

It's the truth. I mean, I did it just like she wanted me to, and then she laughed and said she was only making believe.

She said, "Good boy, good boy—look how he does what I want him to do."

Oh, Mr. Capote, don't you see how wonderful it was?

Listen, I'll be honest with you, it just happened from me sitting here and saying what I did.

I can tell you this, can't I? Did it lower me in your eyes? It didn't, did it? I mean, I have to let my hair down before we call it a day! Hey, wait a minute. You think I'm going too fast? You think I need some breaths? Okay, if I'm out of line, I'm out of line. But what can I tell you except Janet Rose!

Let's face it, she knew things. She knew everything. Janet R. knew things which nobody ever thought of! She always had a new one. She could talk you to your finish. And then she could give you another boner right after you just got through having one. And let's not forget something. She was thirteen! End of discussion, period.

Okay, correction. Okay, you caught me on a little one, correction, correction! The thing is, she was fourteen the time I was just making mention of. Which was the last time that I saw her, time out for the interim when yours truly was you-know-where.

So do you blame me? I mean, she was mine and the next thing she wasn't. I'll be honest with you, these are the things a certain person will never forget!

Hey, I just remembered. *Interim*. This one was definitely one of them!

"Interim." I just remembered. "Interim." Except I don't have to tell you, I only said it once!

Whereas you take the three questions or when they came in and said, "Drink it." Don't kid yourself. Yours truly was no pushover! I promise you, they could have talked themselves blue in the face or stood on their left ear. But let's face it, that's water under the bridge. You know what I say? I say you take the thing with the laces, that's water under the bridge! Forget it! Bygones is bygones. Hey, put it out of your mind.

"Red Dog, Red Dog, this is Blue Dog calling, please come in!"

I miss him when he goes to sleep.

Here's something. You know what else?

I miss the people on the old block. I miss the way they used to look at me. But I don't miss Davie or you-know-who. They changed. I don't miss someone who does. I just miss what they changed from and keep on wondering why they did it. But what's the percentage? Myself, I don't understand why everybody can't be like yours truly, which is all these different ways at once.

That was the thing about Ben Bernie. He never changed.

You could always count on the Old Maestro. He was always the same. That's what Ben Bernie was— something which never ever changed. *Au revoir, pleasant dree yums. God bless you and pleasant dree yums.*

t's where I stayed for a little while when I first got to Gotham. Meaning, Janet Rose's mother's. She didn't care. She didn't pay any attention to me. She didn't pay any to Janet Rose either. She just got her bottle and sat there, and then she'd take it and leave the room. If I was somewhere and she came in, she didn't see me or she didn't look.

As regards yours truly, I didn't go out. I just sat in the apartment and did whatever was quiet. I played the radio. It was dark in there. It was nice. It was always like five o'clock the season when the leaves come off. Then when Janet Rose came home, she'd make the supper. It was just like she was the mother. She makes this, that, or the other, and we sit in the kitchen and eat it. Then you-know-who would come in and get more ice from the refrigerator. She'd drink a little and watch us wash the dishes. She'd say, "Look at the little homemakers," or "Look at the little mister and missus." It's true. We were Mr. and Mrs. First-Nighter.

Sometimes I'd worry a little about a certain person. But not so much when you really come down to it. I'd say to myself, "Call her." But then I'd say to myself, "Let's not and say we did." Besides, I'll be honest with you. What if she asked me did I go in the water so Davie would have to come after me? Or what if she said she'd kill me for making my brother get killed? Hey, you know what? I could have used one of Everett's icebreakers. But let's face it, I didn't know about any of them back then.

Mostly what I did was sit around and get boners from

thinking about Janet R. coming home from school, that and what we were going to do when the mother had enough and fell asleep in her bed.

Here's something! This is how yours truly got on the radio. In other words, just from being where I shouldn't. Or maybe it was vice versa. Hey, if we had the time, I would stop and think until I had it all thought through. I mean, the thing of it is, wasn't where I was all to the good?

You'll see.

It starts with the time the mother got up and walked in when yours truly was with his beloved and they were naked in the bed.

She didn't turn on the light. We didn't hear her open the door. She was just there in the room suddenly talking. She was sitting and talking in Janet Rose's chair. To tell you the truth, it was like she was just there but you couldn't say how.

Here's the other thing. You couldn't tell who she was talking to. Or even what she was saying. Maybe she thought she was just talking. I don't know. But to my way of thinking, it was like a crazy person was there. I mean, you are there and it is dark and you are scared. Listen, I'm not ashamed to say it. I was lying there thinking she is going to kill me because it made her crazy when she caught me in the bed.

But she just keeps on talking. She just keeps saying all these things. Except you can't figure out what it is exactly, even if you can hear every single word. Do you see what I am saying? You hear these words, granted, but you can't tell. So in a manner of speaking, it's just like the Old Maestro all over again. Except the truth was, it really wasn't.

We just laid there shaking like two leaves. But maybe it was just me. Maybe it was only like one leaf. Listen, let's not kid ourselves. When it comes to Janet Rose, nothing ever made her scared.

So to make a long story short, Janet R. squeezes my hand and gets up.

This is when I start hearing her say, "Mother?" But I don't hear the mother answering.

Janet Rose says, "Mother?"

But the mother goes on talking.

What's next is Janet Rose comes back to the bed and whispers for me to get up and go get in the living room and don't do anything.

I did. I went back to the sofa and got under the blanket. I was really shaking. Then I see the light come on and I hear Janet Rose going like this. "Mother? Mother? Mother?" Listen, I won't kid you, it makes me too scared to be by myself. So far as I can see, it's just like the Plymouth all over again and somebody said, "I'll only be a minute." I mean, I held it and I held it but I couldn't hold it anymore. So this is when I get the blanket around me and go to the door to look. It is also the first time I see Janet Rose naked!

Oh, Mr. Capote, you should have seen! Little titties and everything! And her privates with the hair on them. Take my word for it, you don't know what you missed!

I say, "What's wrong? Is something wrong?"

But she just shakes her head. She says, "Mother?" And then she says it again. Then she comes into the living room and turns on the light by the telephone. She starts calling somebody and acting like I'm not even there.

I don't have to tell you, I can see everything now, all the parts where she is white because she didn't get a tan. But I don't know if I got a boner or not. I mean, to my way of thinking, maybe I didn't because I was scared.

I say, "What's wrong? Is it my fault? Don't you think I better get my clothes on and find a place to go?"

But she just waves her hand for me to be quiet and leave her alone.

She starts talking on the phone. It's her dad. I can tell it's her dad she's talking to. The other thing is, I can tell he doesn't care. You can always tell from somebody's face when somebody else doesn't care. So then she hangs up and calls somebody else. Granted, I got a little more scared. On the other hand, there's her titties, you know? Not to mention her backside and her you-know-what with the hair. But here's the best thing, which is her feet! Meaning, they are twice as good when you can see how they go with everything else she's letting you look at.

Hey, I almost forgot! The thing of it is, this is how I got to be friends with Janet Rose's mother's brother. It's also how I go from that stage of the game to being on the radio as a professional performer! In other words, Bill Lido.

Bill Lido took over.

Picture an individual with hair just like Janet Rose's. Except it goes without saying, he was as big as they come. In other words, this is the mental picture of Bill Lido. But just between you, me, and the lamppost, I say this was his name for strictly professional reasons. Meaning, like Scheindel Kalish and Ann Shepherd. Whereas I am just giving you my personal analysis. So don't quote me, okay?

Listen to this.

"This is the world's largest network, the Mutual Broadcasting System."

Here's another one.

"This is radio for all America, the Mutual Broadcasting System."

These are two of the station breaks which Bill Lido did. Enough said?

So the thing is, I'm there in my blanket when this individual comes over. This is interesting. Which is that no matter what the story is, Bill Lido is always smiling.

First thing he does is get out of his raincoat and start rubbing his big hands together. You can hear it, the noise he makes doing things, like this wind which comes with him. It's like a person who can't wait to get at something. It's like a person who comes in the door and brings the outside in with him.

God is my judge, I didn't notice how dark and quiet it was until Bill Lido came over and took over. This is the thing. You can see he is a person which takes charge. I'll be honest with you, yours truly felt better right away when Bill Lido was there. You know something? I'd give anything to have Bill Lido here right now. Hey, could I give Bill Lido a list of things to take care of or could I give Bill Lido a list of things to take care of? I mean, how about starting with a ten-speed?

Okay, so the first thing he does, he gets the doctor for Janet R.'s mother, and after the doctor goes, he gets Janet R. and me in the kitchen and says we have to have ourselves a chat. He says, "Binny, how is school, how was Long Beach, you got a nice tan, just calm down, I'm going to get a practical nurse, everything is going to be all right." In other words, this is not a quote but it is the nature of his conversation. The other thing is, he never stops smiling, even when he says, "Binny, who is this young man and what is he doing here and I am warning you, I am not your mother, so be careful, young lady, and don't you dare try anything cute." That wasn't a quote either, as it goes without saying.

Let's face it. What Janet R. couldn't handle they didn't invent yet, end of discussion, period!

She folds her hands and sits up straight and says it happens that I am a nice boy and an orphan and I am running away from the Orphan's Home on Long Island. She says I had my reasons, but they are too horrible to repeat. She says did he ever see Fascination? She says if he's seen it, then he knows where I was working, and that's because I needed the money to eat.

You see what I mean? This is how a certain person could handle a thing. Let's not kid ourselves. Was Janet Rose in a class by herself or was Janet Rose in a class by herself?

You want to hear something? Listen to this. When yours truly was you-know-where the second time, you know what they came and told me? They said Janet Rose came to visit. They said she came all the way up from Gotham by train. They said they couldn't let her see me on account of my condition, because it was for everybody's own good in the first place. Then the one who is telling me this says this is his personal analysis when it comes to Janet Rose. He says for what it's worth he thinks she is some girl, take it or leave it.

Listen, feel free to use this in the book. What he said, that's a quote, I guarantee you. And I don't have to tell you, these are the people which everyone says are the experts.

Maybe yes and maybe no. But when it comes to the theory of your average individual, these are the people which wrote the book!

But let's face it, Bill Lido wasn't born yesterday either.

So Bill Lido says, "The hell with it. I don't want to hear about it. I have got my hands full with enough as it is."

To make a long story short, he throws all the bottles out and goes to sleep on the sofa—whereas I just stayed where I was in the kitchen. The next thing is, he wakes up smiling and makes Janet R. stay home from school. Me, he takes over to a hotel called the Ansonia. This is a hotel which is maybe three blocks from Janet Rose's. I won't lie to you. This was the first time I was ever really outside in Gotham. So it stands to reason I would get a little sweaty, right? But Bill Lido says, "Don't worry, you'll be fine, a fine big boy like you?"

It's true, I was. Worried, I mean. But it was more like those times when I get sweaty and sleepy both. You see what I am saying? It's a feeling like you are going slow and going fast and going more of it in both directions at once.

Listen, don't think I can't tell he wants to get rid of me. But I promise you, I personally am not pointing a finger for him wanting to do it. Bill Lido had his hands full, just the way I quoted. I mean, let's face it, he said he did, didn't he? To tell you the truth, in my personal opinion, Bill Lido was as good as they come, take it or leave it. Even the time he held me against the building and got mad about the towel, he was just doing the best he could. Fair enough?

So getting back to the Ansonia, he gets me a room and pays for a week and gives me twenty dollars. The other thing is, he says it is okay for me to talk to Janet R. on the telephone, but not ever to go back where she is. He says, "I am taking care of everything, son. So you just look after yourself."

I don't have to tell you how I felt. I mean, it made me cry a little when he called me that. Also, this was my first time out of anybody's house. I don't have to tell you how it is in Gotham when you're only fifteen and you're from somewhere else. So I just stayed in the room all day the first day. I just stayed in there and felt lonesome for Janet Rose. I didn't even go out to get a little bit of food. What I did is I kept calling a certain person on the telephone and asking her if she could please come over. But she says she has to stay where she is because the nurse is there—and if she didn't, the nurse would tell her uncle. This is when I said why couldn't she talk to me the way she used to do it at night. But she said the nurse would catch her at it, whereas the thing to do was just to make believe she was doing it and spit in my hand and do it myself, unless I had some Jergens.

It goes without saying, I did it. I did it about five times the first day and more times the second. This is because the second day I went out and negotiated the purchase of some you-know-what. I got two bottles just to be on the safe side. But I guess I don't have to tell you I didn't get any Noxzema.

Meanwhile, Bill Lido keeps on taking charge. For example, when the week is up, he gets me this other place, which was a room on West Eighty-fifth. It was really nice. It was in the apartment of this woman which had a son away at school and who was a widow. I say widow because that's what I think Bill Lido said. But maybe he didn't, so don't quote me.

She said it was eight dollars a week, and this was with breakfast every morning. She also said I didn't have to pay her for two weeks because Bill Lido already did.

It was very educational. She was a singer, I think. Or maybe she was just someone who wanted to be. I don't know. I never found out. In my analysis, it wasn't something you went ahead and asked. But the thing was listening when she practiced. In other words, scales and other things. The way it worked out at the start, I was always there to listen. Here's why. I didn't see the point in going out yet. Number one, breakfast was enough to hold me. And she was always giving me more things besides. Number two, it was nicer inside. It was even nicer than Janet R.'s was. There were books, just to begin with, books and things like that—you know, pictures on the wall and so on and so forth. It was the first place I had ever seen which looked anything like it did. You know what? To my way of thinking, it looked like the type of place where Buddy Brown would live if he grew up to have a place where he did.

I was very neat about taking good care of my room. These things weren't my things. But yours truly made believe they were. I liked to tidy up. I spent a lot of time just making everything tidy and looking at the job I'd done. Also, I looked at the books in the room. Guess who the famous author of one of them was.

Hint: He wasn't a certain person who doesn't know better than to make his residence in the borough of Brooklyn!

I liked to touch the furniture, the wood and all that. There was also a little statue of somebody. To my way of thinking, music had something to do with it—but this is just yours truly's educated guess. The thing is, I moved it from where it was to where the light from the window could stay on it longer. Another thing I did is look at it a lot and try to have slow thoughts. Here's the one I tried the hardest to have. Her sitting in her chair sewing, me sitting on the hassock watching, the light coming through the blinds behind her the special way light comes through a thing like that.

The woman gave me some clothes her son used to use. She says they are too small, so feel free. Also, she tells me about the furniture and the pictures on the wall and everything I was always asking her about.

It was wonderful when she talked to me. Then she'd start practicing again, and yours truly would listen and sit there and make believe. You know what I would think to myself? I would think to myself, "Guess who is back on the old block back when he was a picture-book boy!"

Her name was Hirsch, Ruth Hirsch. Doesn't it sound like a woman like that? She was tall and had short brown hair. You want to hear something really crazy? She looked like my idea of how Barbara Luddy looked, even though I never saw Barbara Luddy. I mean, let's face it, Barbara Luddy's name! It makes you think of Janet Rose's hair and Janet Rose's feet to hear Barbara Luddy's name, not to mention all of Ruth Hirsch.

I guess I don't have to tell you I was there only two months more or less. Meaning, I suppose you know that now is when everything starts to go about nine million miles an hour too fast! You don't understand yet—one minute listening to Ruth Hirsch sing, the next minute trying to listen to about a billion different things. I don't know. In here is the hardest part to tell you about. But now that I am up to it, I think maybe I should forget the whole deal. It's just that I'm so tired already and I'm just getting to the hardest part.

I'll be honest with you. I don't know how much longer yours truly can sit here and keep on doing this. I mean, maybe this one is the wrong start too. Maybe I should have picked one of the other ones. Remember the first one—shake, rattle, and roll? So *you* tell *me*. You think I should have stuck to start No. 1? On the other hand, if I go back and start over again, what about Norman? Believe me, that's what yours truly keeps asking himself. *What about Norman!*

Hey, but let's not kid ourselves. I mean, if I went back, maybe I'd get here and it would be the same place all over again.

Listen, you know what I say? I say let's just get some deep breaths and stop to think a minute. Don't forget the time with Simon's, right? In other words, what if way back then I took the time to get some deep ones? Face facts, if a certain person took the time to breathe, he'd be right there in the Plymouth and not in front of knives. On the other hand, don't forget what Everett says. Doesn't everybody have to be someplace or doesn't everybody have to be someplace? Look at you, for instance. You could be in Gotham or the Hamptons or Palm Springs or Palm Beach. But you still got to be in one of them. Am I right or am I right?

Okay, deep breaths. Deep breaths and sharpen Paki and get up and walk around the kitchen.

Hey, I'm just kidding. You can't really walk around this kitchen! False alarm. Yours truly was just having a little fun for all concerned. Maybe you can walk around yours, but I can't walk around mine! To tell you the truth, you could take my whole household. Whereas you couldn't even say you could walk around that!

Okay, so here's what happens next, take it or leave it. Bill Lido gets me into the show business!

It's like in the place there was this individual named Everett. But maybe I already made mention of him. So this Everett is always saying things, right? So one of the things he always says is this. "Sometimes I think it is better not to be born. But who is as lucky as that? Not one person in millions and millions of people!"

So here's the point. It's like what Everett says goes for me and the show business. I mean, it's like yours truly is the one person in millions and millions of people. Enough said? What I am saying is, you have to give credit where credit is due. So I say the credit goes to all concerned. Unless you want to say it goes to Janet R.'s mother on account of the time she walked in.

Believe me, the answer is what's the diff when you really come right down to it. Because how can you give the credit to one individual in particular when if you really stop to think about it, you see where everybody pitched in? I mean, don't forget Bobby R., okay?

The thing of it is, Bill Lido gets his day off, and he comes over to Mrs. Hirsch's and he says for me to get ready, he's going to take me over to Mutual and show me how the radio works.

So he takes me over to Mutual and I meet these different people. Some of them do this and some of them do that. You know what? I was so excited, I couldn't even tell.

181

So then he takes me downstairs for a malted, and he says, "How did you like it? Did you have a good time?"

I said, "It was the best time I ever had in all my life." I said, "You won't believe this, but I thought the way it worked was different."

He says, "Really? Different how?"

I said, "I don't know. I just thought it was different."

He said, "How did you think it did?"

I said, "I was little then. Forget it. Do you know Ben Bernie or Barbara Luddy and Olan Soulé?"

He said, "First you tell me how you thought it worked."

I said, "How come you call her Binny—you and Mrs. Rose?"

He said, "All you have to do is stay away from her. Do we have an understanding? I've done some things for you. Now you do that for me."

I said, "Oh, sure. She's only thirteen."

He said, "I'm glad you're cooperating. You just keep on cooperating, and I'll do my best to work with you. Do we have a deal?"

I said, "I am doing my best to cooperate."

He said, "Good. Now how would you like it if I got you a job around here? Do you think you'd like a thing like that?"

So there was the whole thing of it right there! I mean, just like that, Bill Lido popped the question. All yours truly had to do was sit and nod his head. On the other hand, let's not kid ourselves, there was more to it than I am actually saying. In other words, you don't get to be a star on the radio without somebody pulling some strings! I'll just put it this way. Let's just say if you know the right people, you know the right people! Meanwhile, to make a long story short, one thing leads to another. You see what

I'm saying? The rest is inconsequential. Yours truly could talk himself blue in the face, and you still wouldn't get all the ins and outs of it! Let's face it, it's like present company trying to tell me how he got to be a famous celebrity! You had to be there, right? Your layman doesn't understand this! But speaking as one professional to another, the less said the better! I mean, it would be way over the public's head to begin with. In all modesty, when it comes to the complicated parts, the book can live without it! So this is why yours truly will just skip to what you've been waiting to hear about. Which is that the first program I was on was called "My True Story." Naturally, the star of this was Bobby Readick, not to mention Ann Shepherd.

True or false, Ann Shepherd was really Scheindel Kalish?

So the thing of it is, yours truly's voice goes out to the radios all over America. Which means also to the ones in Long Beach!

But let's not kid ourselves, that was just for openers. The next thing I know, yours truly doesn't know whether he's coming or going. Believe me, that's how fast Nature was taking its course. "Big Sister," "Stella Dallas," "Bulldog Drummond," "Dr. Christian," "Boston Blackie," "The Romance of Helen Trent," "Portia Faces Life," "Our Gal Sunday," "Hilltop House," "When a Girl Marries," "Lorenzo Jones," "The Guiding Light," "Hop Harrigan," "Mr. District Attorney," "Counterspy," "Captain Midnight," "One Man's Family," "Jack Armstrong," "Grand Central Station," "Inner Sanctum," "Suspense," I was on all these different programs. And that's not the half of it! But I'm not here to tell you how famous I was. In all humility, I was. Whereas the all-important one to make mention of is "Young Doctor Malone"—starring, you guessed it, Bobby Readick until he vomited, but yours truly when he did.

Did I make reference to the fact that Ann Shepherd was my co-star? Except to me she was really Scheindel Kalish!

It goes without saying, I was making good money. Granted, we don't want to get into a discussion of the dollars and cents of the situation. Let's just put it this way. I was making enough of it to take some of it and send it to a certain someone back in Long Beach!

What I did was I wrote a letter which said, "Here is some money. I am fine. Everything is fine. Turn on the radio and I will say hello." Then I folded the whole thing inside some brown paper before I put it in the envelope and sent it. Which is a thing my dad taught me to do back when he taught me to always make sure you have a dollar in your pocket. In other words, you don't want the people which deliver the letter to know there is money in there!

"Red Dog, Red Dog, do you read me, do you read me?"

I had some left over for this, that, and the other. Don't think I didn't know about getting ready for your rainy day. This is why I put it under the box which Mrs. Hirsch had on the floor in the back of my closet. You know what I always say? I always say better safe than sorry! Enough said? Here's something. I mean, it goes without saying, put it *in* the box is what your average individual would say to himself. Whereas you know what your smart money does? Your smart money puts it *under* the box, take it or leave it! Besides, I kept my Jergens *in* the box. You see what I am saying?

I remember it was a holiday when I did it. This is because I remember all the time I took making up my mind about in or under, and how I kept looking at the little statue when I did it. The other thing is, this is the same day when you-know-who and a certain person get back together again, but only in a manner of speaking. How it worked was this. I waited until Mrs. Hirsch went out to get the shopping done. Then I got the Jergens and called Janet Rose.

First I give her all the news, and tell her what to listen for. Then she says she is making a note and she will if she's not in school when it's on. Another thing she always says is how she can't believe it's me even though she knows it is. So then it's my turn to tell her all over again it's because I disguise my voice this way and that way and so on and so forth. Then she says she can't listen so much in the first place on account of school and homework.

Next thing is I tell her that's okay, that she is my beloved, and how the day will come when we will be together again, Mr. and Mrs. First-Nighter. Whereas that meanwhile I cannot go back on her uncle, seeing as how I gave my word and everything I am today I owe to him.

She says, "Okay, now put some Noxzema in your hand and do everything exactly how I tell you."

I said, "I don't have any. Can't I use Jergens?"

She said, "Do you love me or do you love me?"

I said, "I was just kidding. It was right here all the time, a nice fresh jar of Noxzema."

I'll be honest with you. I didn't really have it. Let's face it, I thought about going out to get some, but then I had this other thought, which is Mrs. Hirsch is coming back!

She says, "Okay, now get your thing out and get ready."

Oh, Mr. Capote, I'm getting a boner again!

She says, "The nurse might come. You have to hurry."

She says, "Do you want me to do it to myself while you

185

are? You can tell me if you do. But I can't. I can't because I don't want to. But you can do it for the both of us. Will you do it for both of us? Do you hear me whispering in your ear? Are you touching it? Did you go ahead and touch it before I told you to? He's sticking up, isn't he? Tell the truth, he is, isn't he? Look at it and tell me how it looks— does it look all red and veiny? Put the Noxzema on. See how shiny it looks? Put it all over. That's right, that's right. Oh, God, I can feel you doing it. Can you feel me feeling you do it? Can you hear me? Oh, oh. I have to whisper softer. Hold the phone tight to your ear so I can whisper soft enough. Oh, oh, it feels so good. Do you hear me? What should I say next? You have to tell me what to say next. You tell me and I'll say it. It's all right—you can tell me to say anything you want and I'll say it. Or maybe you want Mrs. Hirsch to. Or my mother. Did you ever notice my mother? Oh, I've gone and wrecked it, talking about my mother. Did I make it go all saggy? He was all stiff and trying to be big and look what I did. I made him get tiny again, didn't I? Tell me the truth, didn't I? Oh well, have to fly, Latin and geometry, duty and honor. Good-bye, my passion, good-bye. I'll be with you in your dreams."

Did you hear that? Dreams? Didn't the Old Maestro always say the same thing? Except he made it *dree yums*.

Oh, Mr. Capote, I'm so tired!

I have to be honest with you. I'm too tired to be cute with you anymore! I mean, at this stage of the game, what's the percentage in playing footsie? Norman, he definitely held it against me because with him I let my hair down. But I know that where you are concerned I definitely can do it. So here's the thing. In other words, speaking as one professional to another, here is the question.

Do you think you-know-who really loved me or do you think she was just making believe?

Stop and think a minute, and then tell me what you think. It's just that that's the question, so don't make me repeat it! I mean, if she really did, then how come she goes out and buys Scotch tape? Because I ask you. In all honesty, yours truly wants to ask you this question. Was it to stick my picture on the refrigerator or his? Whereas didn't she say it was yours truly which was the picture-book boy?

1 isten, let's stop kidding ourselves! No offense, but I don't exactly have all night, okay? You see what I'm saying? So *you* tell *me*, when do we get to wheel and deal? Believe me, I am not pointing any finger. But who's kidding who? I mean, with Norman, you could talk turkey right off the bat as regards your terms and your general what-have-you. On the other hand, I can see how with present company it's not strictly a question of business is business. In other words, you are an individual with feelings. I promise you, this is something I take my hat off to you for, letting me let my hair down and not making me stand on ceremony! But let's be honest with each other, some things we definitely have to go over, whereas some things we don't need in the book on a bet!

For instance, there's the call I make after the one I just told you about, which because it is long-distance, yours truly goes out to do. So is this what you want me to tell you? I mean, is this the part you couldn't wait to hear? Okay, here is the mental picture.

Number one, I put the Jergens back in the box and get out my money from under it. Number two, I walk over to Broadway and go into a telephone booth.

I say, "It's me. Guess what. I was Young Doctor Malone on your favorite program. Bobby Readick had to vomit, so I was. I love you and I miss you and I am sorry to God for everything. Did you hear me? If you were listening, you did. I was Young Doctor Malone."

She says, "That's nice. I am the Queen of England." She says, "So this is where you have been, in the crazyhouse."

I said, "I am on the radio. Sometimes the stars get sick. He was vomiting. You said it was your favorite. You know who Bobby Readick is. He had to vomit. He couldn't catch his breath."

She says, "He's not the only one who has to vomit." She says, "Where are you?" She says, "I want the truth."

I said, "It's okay. Everything is all right. I am on the radio. I'm on everything." I said, "Didn't you used to say it was the one you liked the best?"

She says, "I want the truth." She says, "I have had it up to here with you." She says, "Do you realize you are as crazy as you-know-who?"

I said, "Write down what I am going to be on. You can listen to me whenever you want." I said, "I miss you. I love you. What do you think about me being Young Doctor Malone?" I said, "Did you get a pencil? Because I am sorry Davie died. Do you have the pencil yet?"

She says, "What died! What is the crazy person talking about?"

Naturally, I hang up as fast as I can. But then I figure live and learn. So I put more money in.

I said, "I didn't do anything. God punished him for Buddy Brown."

She says, "What him! Buddy Brown? Listen to me, do you know you are crazy? For your information, do you know?"

I said, "You know what Davie did."

She says, "As God is my judge, when he was a baby, I knew." She says, "Is this the punishment I get for you-know-when? Two adults, but the child is still trying to kill me for it, is that what?"

I said, "I was making it all up. I never heard anything in any vacuum cleaner. You're crazy for thinking I did."

She says, "I cannot believe my ears. I hear him, but I cannot believe it."

I said, "Please, oh God, please."

She hangs up. I put more money in.

I said, "Please."

She says, "Are you finished? So are you finished with your pleases?" She says, "So what is it you want from me? You want to hear me scream?" She says, "Is that it? You want to hear your mother scream? Because here is what you can do with your pleases." She says, "Do not call me. Do me a favor and do not call me with your pleases and your Davies and your Buddy Browns. Call him. Tell him."

I said, "Him?"

She hangs up again. I call her back. But I just listen to her listening to me wait. You think she wanted me to wait a minute?

She says, "You want his number? You didn't know I had his number? Listen, dummy, you think I did not have it from the word go? So for your information, he is in Atlantic City. So you tell me, Mister Doctor Malone, you have heard of Atlantic City? Because that is where the son of a bitch is dancing in the streets. You want the number? Here's the number."

i 'll be honest with you. I just stood there in the booth trying to think some slow thoughts. Then I went and got more change and told the operator the number to call. But it just rings and rings. So then I call Janet R.'s. But it's busy. This is when I get the operator again. But it's no use. It's just like always, somebody saying they'll only be a minute, but forget it when it comes to what they think one is.

Listen, I won't kid you. I don't remember the bus ride. To tell you the truth, the same thing goes for getting from the phone booth to where the buses leave from. But to my way of thinking, it is not such a big deal if you don't. Let's face it, does yours truly remember all of the Ben Bernie thing yet? Okay, so what I remember next is calling from the depot in Atlantic City and this woman that goes, "I don't care who you are, you got a lot of nerve calling at this hour."

I said, "Is my father there, please?"

She goes, "Who's this?"

I said, "His son."

She goes, "You sure you got the right number?"

I said, "It's the one they gave me. It's the right number. May I please speak to my father, please?"

She goes, "Honey, the poor man is out like a light, honest. You think you could call back in the morning? Where you calling from, honey? I'll have him call you, all right?"

I said, "I can't stay here. I'm where the buses come in. Can you give me the address?"

She says, "You have your sisters with you, hon?"

I said, "I don't know anything about any sisters. Just tell me what the address is."

She says, "You promise you won't ring the buzzer until eight?"

I don't even want to tell you what the cab cost. Let's just put it this way, an arm and a leg. The other thing is, I couldn't really see much until it started to get light. But when it did, I could see it wasn't a house or anything like that. Let's just say it was more like a motor court, except the cabins had long numbers instead of short ones. Also there was this tiny little window to one side of the door. In other words, it's like this little house in a picture book. Except here is the thing—they wouldn't really put one like it in it.

You will not believe this, but I wasn't sitting there thinking what you think. I mean, it sounds crazy to say it, but I was just thinking about the curb. Also, how he was probably looking out the little window watching me sit on it across the street. But you know how thoughts are. Let's face it, when all is said and done, thoughts are just one of those things. You take right now, for instance, what my thoughts are. You see what I'm saying? I mean, I just had a million more of them the minute I stopped to tell you. Hey, forget it. Like just for openers, get this—the Maybelline and the hairbrush and the click. On the other hand, it makes sense to think about a curb. In other words, I was thinking about him looking out the window and seeing somebody who was thinking about what he was sitting on. Here's the thing—I wanted my dad to see I was a boy waiting!

The other thing is, it was cold. It was getting light, but it was cold. What makes it even colder is this pink bird which is up on one leg in front of his place. I don't know. It was like one of the things they give you at Fascination if you got a good enough score. So naturally I kept thinking to myself did my dad win one of those? I kept thinking maybe he did it when yours truly wasn't there to see. You know what? I even thought he maybe made a deal where he wasn't supposed to ever let me know, and that's why he went away. Forget it. I just thought I'd tell you one of the thoughts I was having while I was sitting there waiting for it to be eight o'clock.

But let's be honest with each other, I don't think I waited long enough. I mean, number one, a watch is something I more or less didn't have on me at the time. So the thing is I just said to myself, "Okay, it's eight o'clock." This is when I got up and went across and pushed the button under the number.

You know what? I think it was a little like the number that's on Paki. But I can't say one way or the other, so don't quote me.

The door opens just like that. But it's not my dad yet. It's this woman with frizzy hair instead. She has a bathrobe on and frizzy slippers. She just looked frizzy to me all over.

She says, "Harry, your kid's here!"

I am just standing there. I am thinking about the name she said and about when I heard them in the closet.

I was thinking about how you open the door and there you are in Simon's!

Then there's this man where I can see him and he can see me.

It makes me stop and think when I stop to think about this.

He says, "That's not my kid."

She says, "He's not? How come he's not?"

He says, "Get rid of him."

She says, "All right, get out of here now. You got the wrong people."

This is when the door closes. But I am just standing there, take it or leave it.

Then it opens up again. He puts his head out. He says, "You heard her! Beat it!"

But God is my judge, I couldn't! You want to hear the whole thing of it? I couldn't!

So *you* tell *me*, you think yours truly was just making believe he couldn't? I don't know. Maybe it was me just wanting the door to see a boy which couldn't move. You think that's what it was? Listen, if that is your honest opinion, I would be the first one to tell you maybe yes and maybe no. In other words, a thing like this, it could be six of one and half a dozen of the other.

Meanwhile she's tapping on the little window and waving for me to get away. Then he opens up the window and says, "Come on, you heard me, punk, scram! We don't want any trouble with you! Get the hell out of here before you get your ass in a sling! You hear me? I'm not fucking around anymore! Beat it, you hear?"

But I was just somebody standing and thinking how I am somebody who can't move.

The police come. An ambulance comes. There is all this noise! There is the door opening, the door closing, people moving, people talking, the little window going up and down and me going up onto this thing which rolls. Then there is this man which has what you feel is a wind with him just like Bill Lido did.

He says, "We'll just get this tight here."

Then somebody else says, "Okay, fellas, upsy-daisy."

C an you beat it? I mean, God is my judge. Because it just dawns on me about at lunchtime today. I mean, the fatty with the bike. Remember the one which was walking it and this thing kept coming out? So it just comes to me, it was on the way to Peartree's, right? In other words, this is the direction she was going in, true or false? Whereas do I have to tell you it is also the direction of where a certain famous celebrity lives when he is at home at his residence in Gotham? You see what I am saying? I mean, is this one for the books or is this one for the books? Talk about your small world! Talk about one thing always leading to another! This one is one for the books! I mean, the envelope in her basket! Granted, I didn't stick around to check it out. But it was this big official envelope! I mean, talk about your crazy coincidences! But didn't I tell you everything connects? So what was it, something for you to sign or something like that? Because I promise you, it's a top-ten bank. Hey, you know as well as I do, whatever it was, my branch will get right on it, don't kid yourself. Let's face it, I'm probably wasting my breath. They probably already sent it over via somebody else. You know what? I wouldn't be surprised if you told me one of the officers handled it themselves! On the other hand, there's no telling. Put it this way. One of the authorities maybe said to himself, "This is evidence." But here's the thing. So what if it is? Is it fair to take it out on a certain famous celebrity?

Listen, let's just for argument's sake say this. It is a question of time. Okay, time is money! Fair enough. So this is why yours truly says forget it, he will make it up to you in so many dollars and cents. In other words, you figure up what it comes to you in so many dollars and cents, and we'll just take that figure at face value and deduct it from the boy's end—no arguments, no discussions, no explanations, period! Believe me, I wouldn't even say to you how you should maybe get down on your hands and knees and thank me for keeping her away from you. I mean, let's not kid ourselves. What came out after Paki came out, it could have been from something which is catching! I'm not saying it was. I'm just saying better safe than sorry.

So are we talking about letting bygones be bygones? I promise you, as far as yours truly is concerned, it's all ancient history at this stage of the game. You watch. Believe me, it will make your head spin to see how fast I meet a person halfway and make amends! So be honest with me. Am I back in your good graces or am I back in your good graces? Because, number one, I can't wave a wand! Whereas, number two, I don't have to tell you what time it is and what the conversation was when this thing came up and it got us off the proverbial track. Enough said?

To make a long story short, the next thing you know, they take me out and roll me in somewhere. Then this individual comes over and asks me what my name is.

Okay, so it's crazy. But you know what I said? I said, "Young Doctor Malone." So then this other individual comes over and he looks down and he gives me this look. He says am I ready to say who I am. I tell him he won't believe it because it just goes to show how everything fits.

He says, "Try me."

So I say the same crazy thing.

But all right. Here's the truth. I promised you aboveboard, and aboveboard you'll get.

I think I was making believe.

I can't tell you the name of the place they took me to next. I just know it was somewhere in Jersey and it was up high on a hill. The second thing is, people kept saying hello when I got there. Everybody was very polite. You know what? I thought they were just checking to see if I had good manners—and if I did, they'd let me go.

I said, "Hello." I said, "Good morning."

Then this fellow came over and undid the straps.

He said, "How do you feel?"

I said, "Fine, thank you."

He said, "Good, good. Now on your feet, you little prick."

h ey, I just thought of something.

T.C.'s Devil's heel. You think Paki could reach it better than my you-know-what could? Not that you should ever stick a knife in a place like that. You take Janet R. sticking the hairbrush handle there. Was there ever anything crazier than that?

I'll be honest with you. The worst face I ever saw is

when she's got it up there and she says she's going to keep it there until she has her finish. But the thing of it is, you think it was her real one?

I was making all these different kinds of faces. I mean, when yours truly was sitting there waiting on the curb. I kept trying out these different faces to get ready for the right one for my dad. Hey, you know what? I used to love to sit like that, on a curb just being quiet. It was something I never got tired of. Tell the truth. You did too! Am I right or am I right? In my analysis, you look like that when I see you in Peartree's. Meaning, you look like someone who likes to just look but not at anything in particular. Answer me this. Is it the same way with you as it is with me? Because with me, it makes me feel funny just to sit and look. You know what I am saying? It gives me a funny feeling, just looking but not really seeing what I am looking at.

I miss him so much. I never missed anything the way I missed my dad. I miss him right this minute. Listen, a certain somebody is going to be forty-eight next birthday, but all he does is miss his dad the same way he always did! Face facts, it's him and Ben Bernie! Not to mention you-know-who when he has to go to school or to sleep.

"Red Dog! Red Dog! This is Blue Dog—answer, please!"

So this was the first place. I was in it for sixty days. They said I was in it for C.O., which is Constant Observation. In other words, it's like C.T. for Constant Touch.

"Red Dog, Red Dog, please come in!"

These are some of the things which happened to me where I was.

The cell, first of all.

It's under the roof and there is a leak in the roof, so the rain comes in if it rains. The other thing is, it's mainly just big enough for the bunk and they come in and belted me to it with belts. So then they come in when you-know-who gets out of them, and this time they use manacles instead. Let's face it, it's just like in the comic books! Except this means I have to do my business right the way I am. Hey, that's not something they would show you in a comic book, okay? Meaning, the number two goes under me. But as regards the number one, it runs all over and burns.

The next thing is, they come in sometimes. They come in and feed me with a big spoon and give me some water sometimes. Hey, it's oatmeal and it's only once a day. But I say big deal! I'm no sleeper and I'm no eater.

The last thing is, they come in at night. They put a blanket over me and they tell me not to cry.

So that's it and that's it and that's it. In other words, what I just told you is the whole story right there. The sixty days is over and done with and they give me back my stuff. Then they take me downstairs and hand over my money and tell me to call someone to come get me. So I look at the Yellow Pages and call a taxi. The first one says it's too far. But the second one says he's on the way.

Listen. I have to be honest with you. When the driver asks me where to, I give him the same address.

his time there is a Christmas wreath on the little window, not to mention there is also one on the bird. The other thing different is it's him which opens the door and not the woman. But when I see the one which comes up behind him, it's not the same one the first one was.

This one you can see everything, even if she's got her underpants on and also her you-know-what. God is my witness, you could! You can see all this wet hair sticking out around her underpants just the way I once saw with Janet R.

He says, "What's the matter with you? You didn't get enough the first time?"

I said, "Do you know where my father is, please?"

He says, "You get the hell away from here! I'm warning you! Turn around and beat it or I'll split your head wide open for you!"

She says, "For Christ's sake, Harry, take it easy, he's just a kid."

He says, "Get back in there! Kid, my ass! Can't you see he's looking at your twat! He's a fucking nut! He's out of his fucking head, goddamnit, and I want him the hell away from here!"

I say, "If you see my dad, tell him I was here looking for him. Tell him if he wants me, just check out the Mutual Broadcasting System any day of the week. The other thing is, tell him Davie's dead."

She says, "What?"

He says, "Didn't I tell you the kid is blitzed? He comes around here a couple of months ago with the same crazy shit."

She says, "You feel sick, sonny? It's cold out there. You want me to call you a doctor? You want to come in here while I get somebody to help you?"

He says, "Doctor! You touch that thing to call a doctor and I'll rip your fucking arm off! Call the cops or the fucking nut brigade if you're in such a fucking hurry to run up the fucking phone bill!"

Here's something. All the way back to the bus station,

I keep telling the driver how I can't get over it, Christmas and I didn't get anybody any presents yet. But don't kid yourself. I was just fooling around. It was just to get some practice talking again.

Whereas take you, on the other hand, you could talk the arm off the proverbial Chinaman. Am I right or am I right? Hey, who's kidding who? Yours truly has seen you on Johnny's and I say more power to you!

Listen, if I could talk like you and Norman, you think I wouldn't go on the channels and do it?

But forget it, okay? One thing a certain person would never do is try to horn in when you and Norman are talking to Johnny on that particular channel.

Okay, so you caught me again! Face facts, they sign off on 13 what? Ten, eleven, something like that? Meanwhile yours truly is no sleeper, so where do I go from here? So I watch it a little bit, is that a crime? On the other hand, you take T.C. and what her theory is. Which is that if it's not "Charlie's Angels," forget it!

Hey, time out. I was just wondering something. I mean, for argument's sake, when you go on Johnny's with Norman! I mean, like beforehand or afterwards, I was wondering if you two ever sit down and break bread together, things being what they are. I mean, it just dawns on me how Johnny always says the stars are all old friends of his, so I was wondering if one thing leads to another. But let's not be ridick, okay? You and Norman breaking bread together? What with the way things are? Hey, I really had to be some kind of nut to come up with a nutty one like that!

So level with me, after Johnny's, or beforehand, when you fellas have to go to a place to party, do you give the nod to the C.B. or do you give the nod to the C.B.? Not that you have to tell me if it's something you have to keep private. Believe me, I have plenty of my own private things too. Let's just put it this way. If yours truly started telling you all of his, you'd go through the proverbial roof! No offense, but you would.

I did a lot of talking going back on the bus. But it was more on account of being cold than on account of practicing anymore. The thing of it was, the temp had changed on me without me being ready for it.

But when I get to Mrs. Hirsch's, forget it so far as clothes go. This is because it's not Mrs. Hirsch which comes to her door. It's another woman altogether, and says Mrs. Hirsch moved away. So I tell her I have to get my things. But she says there aren't any to get. So I tell her I have to get my statue. But she says no dice, no nothing, she cannot permit entry to run a check. So I tell her she should tell me where Mrs. Hirsch moved to so I can see her and ask her about this and that. But she says she is not at liberty to offer this information to every Tom, Dick, and Harry. This made me stop and think. You know, the name Harry? So then I take a deep breath and tell her she should call Mrs. Hirsch and ask her if she can do it. But she says she does not have the authority to call long-distance.

I say, "Give me the number so I can."

She says, "Not without permission of the party in question."

I don't know. I just couldn't think of any more things

after that. But maybe it was because you get out of practice when you have been in a place.

Granted, I didn't want to go against Bill Lido. But look at it this way. Where was the choice? The other thing is, it wasn't so far away and I was as cold as I ever was.

The mother's the one which answered the buzzer when yours truly buzzed downstairs. But do I think to myself she'll tell Bill Lido? I just said, "It's me." I was too cold to stop and think of anything else. I go, "I know I'm not supposed to be here, but I have to be."

She didn't say anything back. The buzzer buzzes and I go in and then I go up the elevator. She's got the door open when I get up there. In other words, she's holding the door open like she can't wait for me to get there. But I could see she changed her mind as soon as she saw me.

"So it's you," she said. She says, "You sounded like somebody else."

You know what? She just had on a robe and it was mostly open! You want to hear the other thing?

I could smell it! Meaning, your alcoholic beverage!

She says, "So how come you didn't say it was you? I was expecting somebody else." She says, "Look, if you want Binny, she's not here, she went out with some friends to the movies." She says, "You know my brother was looking for you? Didn't he get you a job as a messenger somewhere? I thought he got you some kind of a job like that over at Mutual. So you just walked out on it, is that nice? After Billy knocked himself out for you, is that nice? Don't you have a coat or something?" She says, "Wait a minute, did you ever lay a finger on my kid? Answer me, how far did you go with her? Do you want to tell me or would you like to explain it to her father? Answer me, didn't Billy warn you not to come around here

202

again? If you want to do it to somebody, go pick on somebody else." She says, "You dope, don't you know what you could get for messing around with a girl underage? You want to spend the rest of your life behind bars? If Billy knew you were here, he'd kill you—do you know that? Is that what you want? Do you want it so bad you wouldn't care if you got killed for it? You must want it awful bad to get killed for it. Is that how bad you want it? You're a lulu, you know that? You must be some kind of fruitcake to come around here after what my brother said to you. What's the matter, you all hot and bothered and there's no little chippie to play house with? You hear me? The cat got your tongue? What are you, all little birdie and no mouth? Boy, could I teach you a thing or three, a cute little fucker like you." She says, "What's the matter, sweetie, the gals making it hard for you? Is that what it is?"

The next thing is she reaches out for me and it makes her robe come open some more.

She says, "Let's just see what he's got there." She says, "You call this something?" She says, "I call it nothing." She says, "Take my advice, sweetheart, you've got to get it a lot bigger and meaner than that if you want to get anybody interested." She says, "Is that as hard as you can get it? Don't tell me Binny got herself all excited over a little baby birdie like that." She says, "Jesus, you're some fruitcake, you know? You're cute but you're a real fruitcake, aren't you?" She says, "Boy, could I teach you a few things it wouldn't hurt to know." She says, "I've got just the thing for a cute little fruitcake like you."

She takes her hand away and goes back inside the door. She says, "Come on. You want to come in and take a bath? I was just going to take a bath." She says, "Come on. You could come in and take a bath and get warm."

I said, "If I could just get warm."

She says, "Sure, you can. A bath will get you good and warm. A bath will get you feeling good. There's nothing like a nice bath to make a human being feel good."

It was something, seeing the room again, the sofa I used to have to wait on. I just stood there giving everything a good look. But she took me by the sleeve and yanked.

She says, "Come on. We'll get warm. You'll like it. You come with me and we'll get good and warm."

The next thing is, she gets us to the bathroom door and then she gives me a push.

She says, "Go on in. The water's fine. You'll feel so good once you get in a nice warm tub."

The steam was the main thing. Do you see what I'm saying when I say it was the steam? And the smells! Like perfumes and things! It was so warm!

She says, "Oh, look what's here."

It was a bottle on the back of the toilet. She took it and sat down on the toilet. She says, "Now this is what I call cozy." She says, "Here, have a little sippy-poo. It'll warm you up inside."

She says, "Oh, come on, a nice strong boy like you?"

She puts her head back and holds the bottle up. I could see the things in her neck! It's like these little things which are under the skin when she drinks!

She says, "Oh, come on, it won't kill you," and she pushes the door closed with her foot.

She says, "Okay, you've had a bath before. Start taking a bath."

I said, "You're here."

She says, "That's all right, you just make believe I'm not. You just go ahead and get warm. There's a nice tub of water and it's good and hot." She says, "I've seen people take a bath before."

She tips the bottle up and gets herself some more.

She says, "Come on, lover boy, let's see what you've got to be so shy about." She says, "You're not ashamed of it, are you?" She says, "Let's see that little birdie of yours." She says, "What are you, shy or something?" She says, "Life's too short to be shy." She says, "You think I'm shy?" She says, "I can't stand a shy human being."

She reaches her hand over and puts her fingers in the water.

She says, "Oh, does that feel good." She says, "You get those things off and get down in this nice warm tub." She says, "Come on, sweetness, we don't have all night."

I can't tell you how I got on the floor. My theory is it was the steam. I don't know. I don't know what to think. I think the steam made me want to fall asleep.

Here's something. The fuzz of the bath mat! There was a bath mat! There was fuzz in my mouth. Then there was her foot! She has her foot on my head!

She says, "Look."

She jiggles her foot and says, "Look." She says, "It's okay, you can look." She says, "Everybody likes to look."

She says, "Look."

I look and her robe is wide open and so are her legs.

She says, "Look, look, don't be afraid." She says, "Go ahead, just do what you feel like, it's okay, I swear." She says, "Here, here, you touch it here." She says, "You see where my finger is?" She says, "That's right, put your tongue on it right there." She says, "That's right, that's right, now you've got the right idea."

Yes, it's like a little heel where the Devil jumped in and he left his heel sticking out. But I didn't think that then. I didn't think anything then. Except maybe I was thinking the song. You know.

Did you ever see a lassie go this way and that way, did you ever see a lassie go this way and that?

I don't know. Maybe I wasn't. Maybe it's just what I think when I do it to T.C. I probably wasn't thinking about anything except how it felt to be in the steam. I don't even remember when she started screaming. I mean, was it before or after when Janet R. walks in? But then they both were screaming at once. It was worse when I started too. But here's the thing of it. They stopped. But I couldn't.

You think that's why she cracked me with the bottle? In other words, you think that's why? On the other hand, I'll be honest with you. I don't know which one did.

I said, "I am going to fall down." But I didn't.

Someone said, "He's crazy, can't you see?"

I said, "I have to stop and get my breath."

Then I got down by the toilet. But I couldn't catch my breath. So this must be when they left me there and went out to turn everything on. The faucets, the radio, the vacuum cleaner. I could hear the motors that run all the machines.

b ill Lido had me when I woke up. I don't mean he waked me. I just mean he had me with him when I did. I mean he was holding me up.

I could tell I wasn't in the bathroom anymore. But I didn't know we were outside until I felt how cold it was. But then I felt the cold and how he had me up against the building, so I knew I was outside and something was wrong.

You know what? In my opinion, there was snow coming down. But maybe it wasn't. Here's something. There was this towel on my head!

Bill Lido put my hand up there to feel it. He kept putting my hand up there and telling me to hold it there so it wouldn't fall off. The other thing is, I can't. This is because the sleeve of the coat they've got on me is too tight, and I can't get my arm up high enough.

It's crazy, but I smell Jergens Lotion. It's what Bill Lido's breath smelled like, like he put Jergens Lotion in his mouth. You know what I thought? I thought to myself that maybe people on the radio have to do that! Meanwhile, he's holding my head and pushing his shoulder into my chest. This is so I stay up against the building. But it doesn't hurt. I'll be honest with you. It felt good with him pushing me like that!

I said, "How come you call her Binny?"

He says, "You just keep your hand up here like this."

But let's face it. I just couldn't feel what he wanted me to.

He goes, "Now hang on to it, for Christ's sake, so I can get my hand free."

Did I tell you the other thing is it's hard to hold my arm up because of the sleeve?

"Here," he says. "Just close your fingers and grab it so it doesn't fall off."

Be honest with me, you think there are some people in the show business who put Jergens in their mouth for something? You think maybe Johnny does? I know it sounds crazy, but there's no telling unless you're in the know. Listen, it couldn't hurt to ask around. I mean, you know what I always say. Live and learn, okay?

He says, "Grab this goddamn towel." He says, "Can you hear me? You want to bleed to death?" He says, "Stand up and grab it." He says, "Well, fuck it, goddamnit." Then he picks me up and carries me over to the curb. He shouts, "Taxi! Taxi!"

This is when I can see that the snow is really coming down. Then the next thing is we're in one. In other words, I know I'm sitting in a seat.

Guess what. I bet we went by your place on the way. I mean, for what it's worth, I think we did. On the other hand, now that I stop to think about it, you probably didn't live in Gotham then! Hey, you know what just this minute dawned on me? The building where you hang your hat when you're not hanging it someplace else, maybe it wasn't even built back when Bill Lido and me were going downtown in a cab! Whereas don't kid yourself, when it comes to the tallest building in New York City, I could tell you which one it was back in that day and age.

I remember I said, "It's snowing." I remember thinking everything's getting white and how soft everything feels. But I don't know. Maybe I was sleeping. On the other hand, I think I said, "It's snowing." But I know what Bill Lido said. He said, "There's paper and pencil in your lap. Write down your family's telephone."

Then I said, "I want to thank you for all the things you are doing for me. I want to thank you for getting me on all the programs I like to listen to."

He says, "For what?" He says, "What's with you?" He says, "Just write what I told you and do it now."

I said, "Is this on account of Buddy Brown?"

But I don't know. It makes me cry, remembering. I mean, how he had his arm around me and had the towel on my head.

He says, "You'll be okay." He says, "You just need a little rest." He says, "Binny and her mother are a handful even for a kid that's got his head on straight."

It made me cry, the way he was holding me. I think I was still doing it even after he wasn't holding me anymore. There were people getting the coat off, and I think Bill Lido wasn't there.

Somebody says, "Lift up."

Somebody gets me by the wrist and bends my arm out.

Somebody says, "This youngster."

There's light. It's like there is all the light there is.

Somebody says, "That's right. That's good."

Somebody says it again. Somebody says, "This youngster."

Somebody says, "That's good."

Y ou know what I say?

I say, "Maybe yes and maybe no.

For instance, let's not kid ourselves—they like to tell you this, that, and the other, okay? But do they tell you the name of the place you are in? I mean, just for openers, do they tell you something as simple as that? Or, hey, how about how long you have been in the place when they come and tell you you are not even in Gotham anymore and it's time to pack up and go away?

In other words, here is the thing in a situation like this—which is that whatever it is, it is anybody's guess, end of discussion, period! Still and all, in my analysis, it comes to eight months. Meaning, how long yours truly is in the second place.

On the other hand, this is something I can tell you without fear of (joke) contradiction, *ha ha*. Which is that it is definitely miles and miles upstate. How I know this is when she comes to pick me up. Because she says how long a ride it is and what do you do on the train except sit in it and twiddle your thumbs?

I don't know. I mean, I know you have to know about this for the book when you sit down to type it up. But I'll be honest with you, it's not like I am holding anything back. What I told you is eight months, give or take. The other thing is, they come in and ask you the questions. Or they come in and they say, "Drink it." Or they come in and they show you the thing with the laces. That in a nutshell is the whole deal right there.

Except for Everett and his icebreakers.

Like suppose you said to him, "Why are those mats on my walls?" So then he says, "What do you want, tea bags on your walls?" Or suppose you said, "Why am I here?" So he says, "Everybody's got to be someplace." Or sometimes you didn't even have to say anything and he'd say something anyway. Like "Sometimes I think it is better not to be born. But who is as lucky as that? Not one person in millions and millions of people!"

That's Everett. He had all these different icebreakers for you when he brought the thing with the laces. He was what T.C. would call a card. She'd be right to say it, even if I never told her a thing about him and how I was once in the two different places.

So where are we? Eight months, give or take? But you know what I say? I say she knew how many. I say she knew and she was just waiting for me to ask her to tell me. Not that yours truly would give her the satisfaction. Let's just say I made an educated guess. In other words, when she came up to get me with a bag of clothes and some candy, I could tell by the leaves. Meaning, it was when the leaves were coming off and all different colors.

This is what I did all the way down to Gotham. I watched the leaves. I watched them until you couldn't see them because of the buildings and then the tunnel. The next thing was Pennsylvania Station! You know what I said to myself? I said, "It's a small world." Here's why. Because it made me think of the program! I mean, the one they called "Grand Central Station." But did this make sense or did this make sense? Because let's not forget who was on that one back in the days he was on radio! Sure, I was on lots of them, but that's the one it made me think of!

I know I don't have to tell you it's too late for the last train out to Long Beach. Or maybe she just said enough was enough for the time being. So we go check into a hotel which is called The Clarendon. Let's face it, this was not the kind of establishment a person in your circle frequents. It is more like the type of place which goes with her shoes and what she does when she says she is going to business.

Here's something. She only paid for one room! This is because we stay in the room together. In other words, she says she's going to say it to me in words of one syllable. She says, "They only let you out because I said I would keep an eye on you!"

Hey, don't think I don't know the words which go with this subject. How's this? *Custody* and *jurisdiction* to begin with! But ask yourself, does she take the time to tell me? Forget it! She is too busy sleeping, and in the morning she is too busy telling the waiter what she wants for breakfast!

But when all is said and done, I've got to hand it to her. I mean, you've got to say this for her. She went all out when she picked a place for breakfast. Granted, we had to stay near the station. This is because she says we'll get something in our stomach and then get on the train out to Long Beach. But all things being equal, I say she went all out when she picked the Statler, which in that day and age was a top hotel good enough for your best people!

She says, "Order something solid. Look at yourself. You look like they turned a rock over and you came out."

She says, "For your information, I had no choice, whereas in my personal opinion, they worked a miracle." She says, "Believe me, you should get down on your hands and knees and thank God for what they did for you— because don't kid yourself, they told me plenty."

She says, "I promise you, if you are waiting for me to apologize, then I say don't hold your breath." She says, "If you want my advice, you had a lesson coming and you got it, take it or leave it." She says, "Because let's not forget all the heartache you put me through with this, that, and the other, not to mention vanishing into thin air, end of discussion, period."

She says, "Believe me, I'm here to tell you, I've got nothing to be ashamed of." She says, "So did you run me a merry chase or did you run me a merry chase?" She says, "Forget it, a call out to Jersey is next to nothing when you look at what you cost me in heartache over the years from the word go."

She says, "You're all wet if you're looking at you-know-who and pointing a finger." She says, "Just between you, me, and the lamppost, I did you a favor."

She says, "Finish your egg. It's paid for."

I said, "After I come back from the bathroom. I think I have to go to the bathroom."

She sits there looking at me. She says, "Granted, it was the first number which comes into my head, seeing as how the man used to be your father's district manager. So I think to myself two of a kind, they should live and be well and that's the end of it."

I said, "It's okay. I'll only be a minute."

She says, "Here. Take this. You should always have a dollar in your pocket."

So a dollar is what yours truly had for the subway. Whereas I don't have to tell you, they didn't get no big money for a token back in that day and age! Not to mention another thing of the subway of today. Meaning, you pay your fare, it's like buying a ticket where they're running a raffle for bodily harm! Don't kid yourself, T.C.'s scared to ride on them. To tell you the truth, here is one subject where yours truly has to go along with T.C.'s thinking!

I had to wait all day for her to come out. But it was okay. I liked seeing the leaves everywhere and also the look of the building. Believe me, it made me proud to see the caliber of school Janet Rose went to! On the other hand, I can't say it looked like its name. But then again, what does? Am I right or am I right? Does a camisole? And that's just for openers! How about Janet Rose herself? I mean, she looked more like her name was what they called her. Which I don't have to tell you was Binny. Let's face it, there's Barbara Luddy! But who can say what she looks like?

I just ran when I saw her! I just ran and grabbed her hand.

I said, "My beloved, my beloved!"

She said, "You." Then she said some things which don't amount to much as quotes. But here are some of them anyway.

"Did they do something to change your face?"

"How come you don't have the same face?"

"Your face, didn't anybody tell you?"

I said, "I don't know. Maybe it's because it's getting dark."

Hey, here are some firsts for you! I got to carry her books! Also, I got to see her walking in leaves! I saw her going up the subway stairs when we got to Eighty-sixth!

She got to the top of them and she said, "Actually, it might have been the bottle that damaged a nerve or something. The face is full of nerves. Did they tell you it was because of the bottle?"

Yours truly didn't have an answer for that one. So far as I could see, my face was still my face. In other words, it felt the same in all departments. Listen, I was still a picture-book boy back in that day and age. To be honest with you, nothing's changed!

"Red Dog, Red Dog, this is Blue Dog calling—do you read me, do you read me? Answer pronto, please!"

She said, "You better leave me alone."

She said, "I don't think you better hang around."

She says, "Look, you may as well know, I have a boy-friend now and his name is Neil."

She says, "That's the first thing. The second thing is, if I say we can do something, then it's only for this last time for old times' sake." She says, "I wouldn't want to have to tell him or my uncle about you. So if we do something, you have to promise me you won't bother me anymore. Is it a deal?" She says, "Because I went up to that place, you know, and it was really weird. But you're very sweet, the way you're carrying the torch for me. Except I can't have you around, is that clear? I have school and my homework and I really wouldn't want to have to get Neil or my uncle after you." She says, "So if I say we can do something just for old times' sake, then you have to swear you'll leave me alone."

She says, "Look, you didn't run away from there, did you?"

She says, "Turn a little that way so the light is better on your face."

She says, "Didn't anybody tell you what it looks like?"

She says, "You see this?"

She says, "It's a key to my friend Sylvia's." She says, "Her name is Sylvia Berman, and it's for me and Neil when her folks go away." She says, "You know what? They're away right now because Arnie's in dutch up at Hobart."

She says, "It's only over to Central Park West and Eighty-fourth. But do you swear to me that you'll never bother me again?"

She says, "If we went right now, we'd have about an hour before I have to be home."

She says, "So it's nothing or an hour, okay?"

She says, "Do you swear? Do you swear on your mother's grave?"

Oh, Mr. Capote, don't you see? I swore.

1 isten, I have to ask you something. What if we cut it off right here? I mean, with just the twenty-three. So *you* tell *me*, was the one with the bike the limit or was the one with the bike the limit? On the other hand, I can see where it's a touchy subject, yours truly making a recommendation like this. In other words, you're the expert, right?

It's just where to my way of thinking, there's this. Granted, forty-seven is what yours truly said, but maybe I bit off more than I can chew. Let's face it, sometimes your eyes (joke) are bigger than your stomach, *ha ha.*

But seriously, you think we could work out a deal on the basis of what we already have? I mean, I am not actually talking turkey yet, but does it hurt to throw out a few ideas before you and yours truly get down to brass tacks? For instance, what would you say to this, which is twenty-four instead of twenty-three? You see what I am saying? In other words, we make the next one *capstone*, which is the one I have been saving from when I first came across it and read what it means. So let's say *capstone* comes in right here. Which puts us where? In words of one syllable, it puts us past the halfway point, right? So then at that stage of the game we can say to ourselves that's it and that's it and that's it, and more or less just call it a day. Because I'll be honest with you. I'm tired.

Whereas here's another thing. In other words, it's time I told you, it's this thing which has come up with the refrigerator again. Listen, it goes without saying, you probably know all about it, okay?

"Red Dog, Red Dog, please call in!"

Believe me, no offense. You know what I say? I say I've really got to hand it to you. I say business is business, so what did I expect? So let's be honest with each other as regards this situation. Meaning, yours truly is sitting here and he's thinking to himself about what is stuck to the refrigerator. Hey, you think I mean that refrigerator? Listen, I mean this one! I mean this refrigerator in this kitchen!

But be this as it may, I don't have to tell you how forty-seven is definitely out of the question now, all things considered. So are we talking turkey or are we talking turkey? Because God is my judge, the thing which just dawned on me is one for the books! But okay, credit where credit is due. Didn't I say you were a top man? So what do I expect from a top man? Believe me, yours truly knows a top man doesn't get to be one just from sitting around and twiddling his thumbs! In other words, a top man has to look out for himself. Am I right or am I right? I mean, give me a break, okay? I promise you, yours truly was definitely not born yesterday.

You want to hear something crazy? Trees! I mean, saying Peartree's all the time just reminded me. Which is of how there were trees outside the window of Sylvia Berman's! Across the street outside of her brother Arnie's window. Hey, that's part of the mental picture. And the mirror!

So what's your opinion about all these things she stood there saying to me? Myself, I say who knows? It's how many years ago? Whereas just look at all the years yours truly keeps his word. Let's face it, I should go get my head examined! A person is fourteen years old, right? So do you go ahead and give your solemn word to such a person? I mean, for life? Is that ridick or is that ridick?

Hey, I was so dumb in that day and age! You know what? I was so dumb, you couldn't tell the difference between yours truly and his moron brother. Except for he was always going out and getting mud on him, whereas I was inside with the radio. But take you. Or take Norman. I mean, you take any of your top men and what's the answer? The answer is they weren't listening to any radio! The answer is your top men were listening to the teacher! Come on, be honest with yourself. In other words, this is how you get to be a top man, true or false? I mean, let's face it, you don't sit around listening to any vacuum cleaner or people going nibble, nibble, nibble! So am I saying something or am I saying something?

This is why I tell T.C. when it comes to the question of education and training she is all wet from the word go! This is why I tell T.C. she better leave the driving to yours truly! Granted, she says, "Lord, Lord." But I say I am the father of the boy, and the father of the boy is where? I'll tell you where he is! The father of the boy is at the door when the buzzer rings! And for your information, I'll tell you something else. The father of the boy doesn't tell you to sit on a curb and not be there when you can't do it anymore! That's who the father of the boy is!

You think there wasn't somebody there for when Buddy Brown came to the door? You think Buddy Brown ever had to wait a minute, but a minute wasn't anywhere close! Don't kid yourself. When it comes to hearing people throw paper, your Buddy Brown never had to do it nohow! Not to mention opening a closet and seeing them tell you they were dancing. And no Ben Bernie had to talk to him neither, in case you just happened to be wondering! Let's face it, Buddy Brown could sleep! Believe me, he didn't need any radio saying *A bit of a tweet-tweet, a fond cheerio, pleasant dree yums* and so on and so forth.

I mean, hey, don't make me laugh, okay? Like my hat is off to you for being a top man and looking out for yourself, but how about a little credit where credit is due?

Wait a minute! Wait a minute! Did I tell you *yowsah, yowsah, yowsah* was part of it? I can't remember if I told you. In other words, in the Old Maestro's sign-off, he said *yowsah, yowsah, yowsah* instead of saying yes sir.

I don't know. I mean, I'm remembering things and I'm forgetting things. But the thing of it is, which is which? Like you take *Hold the phone*, for instance. That's T.C. or Janet Rose? Oh, Mr. Capote, she was so wonderful. I saw her walking in leaves! I saw her go up the subway stairs! *Did you ever see a lassie go this way and that way and this way and that way?* Oh, Mr. Capote, I did!

Did I tell you about the potato chips? Hey, stop me if I told you, but when she comes out of school, she's got this little bag of potato chips. So when we get on the subway, I'm carrying her books. So here is the mental picture. Yours truly has his hands full. Whereas Janet Rose starts eating them. Like one for her and one for me! In other words, she's taking them out and putting them in my mouth! So you see what I'm saying? It's like the time we squished it back and forth until all of it was all gone! Naturally, it's just in a manner of speaking where it was. But in my analysis, this is what we were both thinking!

You see what I mean when I say Janet R. was in a class by herself?

So *you* tell *me* if you're so smart. Since when does your average individual think of a thing like that? Like just for argument's sake, let's say I said to T.C. where she should put a potato chip in my mouth. Strictly for the sake of argument, suppose yours truly said that. So if you're so smart, ask yourself the answer I'd get. Because I am here to tell you, this is what it is. "Let's not and say we did."

"Red Dog, Red Dog! Answer, please!"

She said, "Come over here and stand with me naked in the mirror."

She said, "Did you think about me while you were there in that place? Did you do it to yourself while you were thinking about me? God, it was a creepy place."

She said, "When you did it to yourself, did you have to use spit? Tell me. What did you think about when you did it? You have to tell me."

She said, "Do people say crazy things where you were? Tell me some of the things they said."

She says, "Do you want to get on the bed or do you want to stand here like this? Which do you like better?"

She says, "I know, let's dance. Did you ever dance with someone naked?"

She says, "I'm sexy, aren't I?"

She says, "Syl! Is that you?"

She says, "Syl, it's Binny! I'm in Arnie's room, surprise!"

She says, "You ought to hear the things Syl tells me. Brother, do you have a lot to learn about girls."

She says, "Turn a little so you can watch me do it. You have to keep watching the whole time. Can you see your thing in my hand in the mirror?"

She says, "Syl! Are you there? You don't know what you're missing, Syl!"

She says, "Keep looking. Look in the mirror. It's looking that makes it fun."

Here is something. The apartment was very nice. It was even nicer than Mrs. Hirsch's was. You know what? Sylvia Berman looked like Sue Cott looks. In other words, Channel 2, check it out. Black hair. Turn on your television and look at Sue Cott. The hair mainly. Not that I am saying I and mine have a color one. I'm just saying on my set it looks as black as it comes. Whereas you probably have color and know. Let's face it, I figure you and Norman both have color. Believe me, all your top people have it.

Listen, did yours truly make mention of where he used to call color at the top concession? Okay, it was just Long Beach and not Rockaway or Coney. But don't kid yourself, so far as the facts go, it was the top one!

Hey, I was just thinking something. What if they came in and asked Davie the three questions? I mean, can you just see that? The moron, he'd answer every one!

Here's something else I didn't tell you. Janet Rose has lipstick on, lipstick and all these things they do when they do their eyes.

She says, "This is Arnie's room." Then she takes off all her clothes.

She says, "Was that the door?"

She says, "Syl! Is that you, Syl?"

She wasn't the way she was the time I saw her come

into the living room. I mean, there was more of her. Like if you will pardon the expression, I will tell you what T.C. says, unless you think it's too off-color. Juglettes to jugs. I'm sorry, but that's a quote. Also, jism and jisette. That's another one. Granted, she maybe gets these things from "Charlie's Angels." But *you* tell *me*, is that any excuse?

On the other hand, you take *pulmotor*. Or somebody saying, "Drink it." Or, hey, "What is the tallest building in New York City?" You know what I say? I say you can't blame any of those on the wrong channels! Whereas the same deal goes for the pizza maker jumping. Tinkle, tinkle, tinkle, woof, woof, woof—they don't do that to you on any "Charlie's Angels." I guarantee you! They don't yank your hand so you go through the ice when you thought the puddle was frozen!

She gets all her clothes off. She says, "Jesus Harold Christ, will you hurry?" Then she goes over and stands in front of the mirror. Did I tell you we're in Sylvia Berman's brother Arnie's room and there is a mirror on the door of his closet? Hey, I don't mean your stick-on type which people get on with glue or something. Believe me, I don't mean this crap you can buy at your McCrory's or your Woolworth's or wherever! I mean, like this is a top mirror! You probably have mirrors like this on all your closets. You and Norman probably have them on all of them!

So I look at her looking at herself in the mirror. She says, "Will you come on, for God's sake! We've only got an hour!" She says, "Get your things off and come over here. Maybe you should see your face in a mirror."

It's like when I put Paki into the eye today. In other words, what comes out is different than what you expected. You put Paki in, right? But what comes out after Paki does? Is it your routine runny stuff? Twenty-two times it's routine, okay? But do they ever leave anything the same? Listen, do me a favor and don't make me laugh!

She says, "I am really actually developing, don't you think?"

She says, "Come on and get over here and I'll show you something up close."

She says, "Syl! I'm calling you, Syl!"

She says, "I'm sick and tired of you in here watching every move I make. Go outside and play!"

Hey, false alarm. That's not Janet Rose. That was you-know-who. Here's another one from her in case you want another quote. "So what's the matter with him? Two adults which are husband and wife having a little dance in the privacy of their own home! So *you* tell *me*, is this a crime?"

Listen, I'll be honest with you. I've got lots of quotes from her.

h ey, time out! I was just thinking about who says it, T.C. or Janet Rose. I mean, that thing about holding the phone. So what's your personal opinion?

Let's face it, I am too tired to think. Listen, it's this writing business. No kidding, I've got to hand it to you, sitting down and typing it up. On the other hand, I get the paper gratis. In other words, I'll be honest with you, they've got paper to burn in Payroll. Listen, the thing is, seventeen years. So am I entitled or am I entitled? Besides, one lousy letter, how much could I use up?

It's T.C. when she turns over! In other words, she is getting her Wednesday regular and she's already had the front, so then she's getting set to turn over! Meaning, now she's ready for the back. But she's not ready for you to start until she's got her finger where it goes! So what does she say? As God is my judge, she says, "Hold the phone."

I have to laugh. I really have to.

Bubble, bubble, bubble.

I mean, just think of it. This gick going plop on the bicycle seat.

Plop plop plop.

Or Buddy Brown, for instance. Splat splat splat.

There you go again, okay? You get down to the bottom of it, and it's all what? Don't kid yourself. It's splat splat splat! But that's only if you're the one down there on the bottom. Whereas if you're still up there where he was before he started falling, don't kid yourself, it's tinkle tinkle tinkle, woof woof woof.

You want to hear the payoff? The messenger who was on her way over to your place today? No gears! Take it or leave it, no gears. Not even three speeds! But what's the diff? She's walking anyway. A flat tire! Hey, my (joke) eye!

Ha ha.

Listen, I'll tell you who had speeds. You want to know who had speeds? The answer is Buddy Brown!

But the only thing of it was, he didn't have a bicycle, right? Let's face it, what the son of a bitch needed was wings!

S he says, "Syl, are you coming in here or do I have to come out and get you!" She says, "Come on, Syl, don't be shy!"

Her eyes are so brown.

Brown?

Wait a minute.

Yes, her eyes were so brown.

She says, "Come on, Syl! You don't have to do anything! Just come in and watch!"

She says, "Quit playing so damn hard to get, Syl! It's okay! He's crazy!"

I say her eyes were definitely brown. It was Buddy Brown which had blue ones. Except when he hit the concrete, what's the diff?

Splat splat splat.

She says, "Syl? Are you listening? Go get one of your dad's scumbags and come in here with your hairbrush!"

Did I tell you Sylvia Berman had the whitest skin I ever saw? Black hair and white skin. Oh, Mr. Capote, I think I'm getting another one. No kidding, I think I'm getting the world's biggest boner!

She says, "Look in the mirror and look at my cunny. Do you see my cunny in the mirror?" She says, "You think cunny sounds babyish? Because I think it sounds sexier." She says, "Tell me what your favorite word is. Look in the mirror and tell me. Cunt? Snatch? Nookie? Twat? How about ginch or gash? Neil says he likes slit the best. But I think cunny sounds sexier." She says, "Oh, look, he's all little and floppy. Little him needs Mama to suck him. Look in the mirror and ask Mama to suck him." She says, "Look in the mirror and tell me what it was like with my mother." She says, "It's okay. You can tell me. Look in the mirror and tell me." She says, "Did she make you do what I saw?" She says, "Look in the mirror and tell me if she made you." She says, "If we went to the bed, would you do it to me? Because Syl does. Look in the mirror and tell me if you want to see Syl do it to me." She says, "You can say if you want to." She says, "Sylvia, I am calling you!" She says, "Him and me are clearing the hell out!"

I was just kidding. No offense. Let's face it, that wasn't Janet Rose.

Hey, did I tell you what's up on the refrigerator? If I told you, you'd die laughing! I don't mean *that* refrigerator! I mean *this* one!

She says, "Do it. Do it to me. Do it the way I do it to you."

I'll be honest with you. There is nothing I would not do for Janet Rose! But the thing of it is, back in that day and age, nobody ever told you about the Devil's heel!

She says, "Oh, shit, do something." She says, "What's the matter with you? Don't you see I'm going crazy?" She says, "Oh, shit—Syl, will you do me a favor and come in here!"

I guess you know the next part, which is when she puts her finger there.

She says, "Watch me do it." She says, "Look in the mirror and watch." She says, "Talk to me. Tell me things." She says, "Tell me all the things you ever thought."

She starts getting sweaty. Her face gets red and different. The more her finger goes, the more her face gets different! She says, "Oh, fuck!" She's got her finger really going. Here's something. It sounds like this. It sounds like click. She says, "Oh, oh." I can hear it going click. She says, "Oh fuck, oh fuck." There's this sweaty thing all over her. It's on her face and everywhere! It's like it makes her change all over. Hairs! All her little hairs get big! She says, "Here it is, here it is!" But it's only what she's saying. She says, "Oh, you stupid asshole, please!"

I said, "Oh, my beloved, please."

But here's the thing. What did I mean? I said, "Oh, my beloved, please." And then it was like it was all light and everything afterwards changed.

So *you* tell *me*. You think yours truly missed something good? I mean, it's none of it so clear after that. It's like with the messenger, fair enough? In other words, I see the stuff go plop on the bicycle seat, I think after that I closed my eyes. To my way of thinking, I did. It's like you say to yourself you want the stuff on the bicycle seat to see a person who can't look at it! Hey, does this make sense or does this make sense?

Listen, I'm just going to let my hair down and tell you what's what. I mean, I hear myself saying, "Oh, my beloved, please." Then I hear this tapping on the door. And then there's the girl saying, "Binny? Are you all right? Because the question is if you really need me, I'll come in."

You know what? If you could hear the three questions, you'd die laughing! But I'll tell you the question they never asked me. Like this. "Were you up there in that house?" Hey, you want to hear the answer to that one? The answer is it wasn't even a house yet, end of discussion, period! Ask Namick. Ask Grady. Go ahead and ask the experts! And you want to hear the payoff? Which is that after it happened, they never even finished it!

So that's the answer to that question. Now go ahead and ask me another one! Like why don't you ask me what's up on the refrigerator?

Hey, as if you didn't know. I mean, let's not kid ourselves. Don't your top men always know everything?

"Were you up there in that house?"

Let's not be ridick!

A house has walls and that one didn't have any! It

didn't even have floors, for crying out loud. It had these boards like—and a shaft for where they were going to put in the chimney.

Hey, I'll tell you something else it had. Which was the concrete for the basement! But do they ever ask you about that one when they come in and ask you the questions?

The answer is I was in a real house and I was listening to the radio! Three guesses what the program was—because she said it was her favorite.

I don't know.

Ask Davie.

"What is the tallest building in New York City?"

I mean, give me a break, okay? You think I didn't know the answer?

I said, "How come they always call you Binny? Is that your real name really?"

She said, "You should get down on your hands and knees and thank God that he put on this block such a nice little boy to play with."

Hey, time out, time out! I need some deep ones. No kidding, I'll only be a minute.

Okay, I'm breathing, I'm breathing.

To tell you the truth, it's too fast. The thing of it here is this. It's going too fast. You go too fast and you get all balled up. It gets too fast and the next thing you know, you're meeting yourself coming and going!

Listen, I was just thinking of something. Those words I had to say so I could give you the quotes of Janet Rose. So in regards to those words, you think I don't know as well as the next one? Which is how it lowers me in your eyes because I had to use them? Whereas if we could just slow down for a minute, everything would get back on the straight and narrow.

228

"Red Dog! Come in, Red Dog, come in!"

That's better. That's good. Big deep breaths, enough said?

You think it is easy to open your eyes and be in Simon's? You think it is easy to drink it when they put it in a little cup and say do it? You think it is easy to stick it in when a certain brain has this crap which comes out of it?

You see what I am saying? Plop plop plop.

For your information, I took some time out for some deep breaths. So is that a crime?

"Red Dog, come in, Red Dog! This is Blue Dog calling— come in!"

I said, "Oh, my beloved, please."

So *you* tell *me*, does it make any sense? The Empire State Building?

"Red Dog! Red Dog! This is an emergency! Answer, please!"

Ask Namick. Ask Grady. Ask Davie.

"Answer me, Red Dog, answer me, please!"

She says, "Quit it with that shit now, my show is coming on!"

Janet Rose says, "Well, if you're coming in, then come in!" But I have to be honest with you, maybe it was blue eyes and yellowy hair. Listen, so long as it is Janet Rose!

I remember click click click.

I remember blue eyes. I remember blue eyes and yellowy hair. Go look at Bo Derek on "Charlie's Angels" except you have to have a color set! Or maybe it's Bo D. on another thing.

It's something on Channel 7! Bo Derek or Sarah Fawcett on Channel 7! That's the one, Sarah Fawcett, eyes are blue and yellowy hair! Or Angie something. Maybe Angie. Angie with a C.? Angie Campion? So *you* tell *me*!

She says, "Syl, show him how big Neil's thing is."

She says, "It's gorgeous out. Go play!"

She says, "Hold the phone, goddamnit, can't you see I'm turning?"

Janet Rose was like somebody sewing and then Janet Rose changed. No kidding, her face got red. It's getting sweaty and red. God is my judge, the sweat is coming out of her all over! It's making the hairs go from little to big! The facts are the facts. So much hair!

I have a boner! I have a boner! I have the biggest boner! I guarantee you, it's the biggest boner there is!

Somebody says, "Three's company."

Somebody says, "Three's a lucky number."

Did I tell you about the number on Paki? Believe me, if I told you, you'd be sorry if I did.

She says, "Let's play Simon says."

I remember a room. I remember a mirror.

T.C. says, "Wouldn't you like it if Syl came in?"

Somebody says, "In here? With all our clothes off?"

Janet R. says, "She'll take hers off just the way we did."

Somebody says, "Two of everything girls have."

T.C. says, "Three of everything."

Janet Rose says, "Three of these and six of these."

She says, "Just look at this child! Couldn't you eat him up alive? God is my witness, a face like an angel!"

Somebody says, "I'm tired of counting. I'm sick and tired of always counting."

Janet Rose says, "Simon says Syl gives Binny the hairbrush." Janet Rose says, "Simon says everybody has to look in the mirror." Janet Rose says, "Close your eyes." Janet Rose says, "You crazy dummy, I didn't say Simon says!"

I will tell you what I remember. I remember everything. It was such a quiet place. You could hear everything in it if you tried to. Think of the boys on Fourteenth. Think of the paper whizzing.

Janet Rose says, "Pardon me for living. Pardon me for just breathing."

Janet Rose says, "Well, are you going to do it or not? Because if you won't, I will."

Sylvia Berman says, "Will you look at little him! Is he ridick or is he ridick?"

T.C. says, "Lord, Lord, no balls at all. The pissant is nothing but mouth. Just a chickenshit clerk and all mouth!"

Janet Rose says, "Look in the mirror. Watch the hairbrush."

Sylvia Berman says, "Me next."

Janet Rose says, "Me first."

T.C. says, "Give it here, goddamnit!"

Somebody says, "The sonofabitch can breathe through his ears, and that's the whole story right there."

T.C. says, "Hike your legs up, honey, I'm going to honk you all the way home."

Sylvia Berman says, "Here's Grady! Here's Namick!"

T.C. says, "Come on, Neil, let's see you lay some pipe."

Janet Rose says, "Will you look at the hammers on those dudes!"

Somebody says, "Oh God, oh God."

T.C. says, "Open wide, girls, here come the heavy-duty drills."

Somebody says, "Davie, Davie, Davie."

It is a little room and there is a little light and there is a mirror on the door over there.

The mirror says, "Davie Davie Davie."

She says, "I'm warning you, you better hold the phone. You better keep holding it until I tell you."

231

But who can hold on to anything that long? Can the light even hold the dust? Don't kid yourself. How can you hold the phone when you have to get out of the Plymouth?

I'll tell you the God's honest truth. We had a mirror like that. But it was just your stick-on type from where she went to business. It was just crap. But yours truly listened to it and yours truly heard them! So how can you hold it when you hear a thing like that? You think you can hold it when you hear the mirror talking? I couldn't hold it anymore. It made me feel funny, the mirror talking! So I opened the door and guess who's in there grinning! You hear me? Because I heard it! I mean, let's not kid each other! You see what I am saying? They're in there! They're in the closet. They're in there and they're grinning!

He says, "The rhumba! The mambo! You name it!" He says, "Stand back, kiddo—you ain't seen nothing yet!"

"Red Dog! Blue Dog calling! Come in! Come in!"

Click click click.

What number are we up to, true or false?

Okay, time out, deep breaths. Time to start counting all over again.

You should see the number they put on Paki. I'm telling you, it's a number which would give you the creeps!

Number one, it's always Davie, Davie, Davie whenever she plugs it in.

Number two, the ice.

Number three.

Number four.

Number five.

Number six, the shoes which are not even white once.

Number seven.

Number eight.

Number ten, this way and that way and this way and that way.

Number eleven.

Number eleven, they said they were just dancing. They said the cha-cha-cha. They said it was just coming in!

Number eleven.

She says, "I'll just be a minute." But how long is one, fair enough? Number one, you go to the door and there's the mirror. Number two, you open it. Number three, it's them which are in there. But why are they both grinning?

Did you ever see a lassie go this way and this way and this way and this way?

Time out! Time out! Time out!

Oh, my beloved, please.

You-know-who is stopping to catch his breath now. You-know-who is stopping to do it. A certain person has to stop!

Number one, Simon's.

Number one, Simon says.

Number one.

All right.

I really have to laugh, you know?

Buddy Brown or Ben Bernie, true or false?

Somebody says, "Simon says if your name is Davie, take one step back." Somebody says, "Simon says if your name is Buddy, take one step back." Somebody says, "If your name is Buddy, take another step."

Somebody says, "Ha ha!"

Somebody says, "Pulmotor."

Somebody says, "Oh, my aching back." Then she turns around and she says, "Piss off, okay?"

I said, "What?"

She says, "You heard me, piss off. Get out of my face.

You're following me and I don't like faggot jerks following me, you understand?"

I said, "What?"

She says, "Don't hand me that shit! I been watching you for three blocks right in the goddamn handlebar mirror! You been looking at me and you been following me and I don't fucking like it, goddamnit, so go look at somebody else!"

I said, "I work in a bank. This is the direction I am going in. For your information, it just so happens we are going in the same direction."

She says, "Oh yeah? Oh yeah? You think I'm fucking crazy? You think I don't have eyes in my head? Look, faggot, I've been watching you in the fucking mirror, okay? Now get the hell out of my face before I call a goddamn cop! I'm counting to three, man—one, two..."

I said, "It is called Peartree's. I am just on my way to lunch at Peartree's. Ask anyone. Ask Gary."

She says, "I'm telling you for the last time, pansy—fuck off!"

I said, "Superfluous."

Or I said, "Effectuate."

So what's the diff?

But here is what she said. I am giving you a quote and it is a quote which is one hundred percent!

She said, "What?"

Which is when she gets it in the one on the left! First picas. Then inches. Then bingo! And she just stands there having her finish.

Click.

Granted, first there was the runny stuff no different than the rest. Like it's like the white of your egg before it gets cooked. Only more watery like, not so stiff. But then

God should strike me dead, you wouldn't believe what starts coming out next! I mean, it's like this lump of stuff, only it's bubbly and it's slow and then it's all the way out and goes plop.

God is my judge, it's making me vomit. But yours truly just stands there to stop and think. I mean, like the thing of it is, I can't move until I see what the whole story is. In other words, a certain person is saying to himself, "You better not move until you see what this is." Meanwhile, she is still standing there and she is still holding the handlebars just like this! I mean, let's face it, is this one for the books or is this one for the books? So you say to yourself, "Remember when the three of you are in the bathroom screaming? And remember when you open the door and there they are grinning? And how about the time Buddy Brown's halfway down and he looks back up and he catches you watching him go?"

You see what I am saying? Let's not kid ourselves. So long as the glass is there, some things you have to see for yourself! Because it goes without saying, those in the know are never going to tell! Whereas if you asked them to tell you, they say, "Don't be ridick." I mean, who's kidding who, okay? You ask them, what do they tell you?

Number one, the Empire State Building.

Number two, they say, "Drink it."

Number two, she says, "So we're trying out a few steps in the privacy of our own home. So we hear someone coming. Listen, don't forget it's August and you could die from the heat."

Number three, I wasn't born yesterday. You look and you see it's got the same laces, the same sleeves!

Number one, she says, "Do I have to apologize it's August and you could die from it, it's so hot?"

Number one, she says, "So if you were outside playing where you should be, so it wouldn't be such a big deal!"

Listen, I'll be honest with you, you know how you put on a face for the water you wash it with? So here is the question. How do you know the one you put on isn't the real one?

Forget it.

I mean, you take an individual who goes and gets her camera. So the next thing is, she says, "Oh, look at that!" And then she goes and sticks it on the refrigerator!

"Red Dog! This is Blue Dog! Give me a C.T., please! Emergency!"

So *you* tell *me*. You think he's out of range or something? Seven fabulous watts?

"Red Dog! This is Blue Dog sitting here, don't keep me waiting, please!"

Big breaths.

That's the whole deal right there, big breaths for when you need them.

She says, "Go play. Because I am here to tell you, in all your life you will never find a nicer child to play with."

She says, "Simon says faster and tip it up."

I was just kidding. I was just making a little joke so as to more or less break the ice. Believe me, you're all wet if you think you don't have to break the ice.

She says, "Don't you tell me little pitchers have big ears, by God, or I'll take him where he can't hear shit for Shinola!"

She says, "Simon says faster and higher!"

I said, "Simon says stand over here on this board."

Like you take yourself, for example, you're where? I mean, right this minute. Peartree's with Gary? Your fabulous apartment with your pencil and paper? The Hamptons or Palm Springs or Palm Beach? Hey, I say you're probably over at Antolotti's with good old Angie Luddy!

Just kidding. Just breaking the ice some more. Believe me, yours truly is not as dumb as his brother. Let's face it. I know where you are and who you are with and where you eat when you really want to put on the dog.

Three guesses.

Hint: At a certain fabulous restaurant with a certain fabulous author. Not to mention also two individuals who just happen to be members of my particular household! Am I right or am I right?

She said, "Higher! Higher! Go all the way in!"

Somebody said, "Don't you know what paraldehyde is?"

Somebody said, "Pulmotor!" I heard them say pulmotor!

She said, "Oh, my aching back, a flat."

I said, "What?"

She said, "Who's talking to you?"

I said, "What?"

She said, "Piss off, faggot! Get out of my face, you fucking creep!"

She said, "Faster and a little higher!"

She says, "You heard me, pansy—fuck off!"

She said, "Don't hand me any more of that shit-for-brains bullshit! You never offed nobody! And you weren't on no goddamn radio neither!"

She said, "Then give it to Syl if your arm's so tired. Jesus Harold Christ!"

I said, "Oh, my beloved, please."

She said, "I want the truth, were you up in that house or were you up in that house, true or false?"

She said, "I'm going to count to three, and if you don't have your ass out of here by the time I count to three, I am going to pick up this goddamn bike and bash you with it! You hear me, faggot? One!"

She said, "Then do it if you say you're going to do it! Oh, Jesus Eddie Christ! Show him how, Syl! Hold the little baby's hand."

She says, "Two!"

They said, "We are going to ask you three questions. Are you ready?"

I said, "How come they always call you Binny?"

She said, "Oh, nice, nice. Only move it up a little."

She said, "Come over here and just look at this picture. So *you* tell *me*, did you ever see such a gorgeous creature in all your born days?"

She said, "You bet your ass he ain't yours! Where'd you ever get it that he was? Mother of God, talk about shit-for-brains!"

They said, "Number one, what is the tallest building in New York City?"

She said, "Oh. Oh. Oh. Oh. Oh. Oh, Jesus Harold Christ!"

She said, "Come in here in this kitchen. I want you to see this. Take a look at the face on that up on the refrigerator! Is that a lovely creature or is that a lovely creature? You know what I call that? I call that a picture-book boy!"

They said, "It is just a question we ask people. There is no reason why it should distress you. Please answer the question. What is the tallest building in New York City?"

She said, "Dumbbell! Dumb cluck! Who *told* you to stay away from there! Did I tell you to stay away from there! Did I *tell* you? Answer me, imbecile, answer me!"

She says, "All right, three! Now scat, you little faggot!"

She said, "You never offed no goddamn anybody, you

crazy sonofabitch. You with your goddamn Ben Bernie every goddamn minute morning, noon, and night!"

She said, "Oh. Oh. Oh. Jesus, Jesus, Jesus."

I said, "Oh, my beloved, please."

She said, "Oh, Jesus Eddie Christ. Oh, Jesus Eddie Christ. It's coming, it's coming, it's coming! Oh, Syl, don't stop, don't stop!"

They said, "It is really very simple. What is your name, how old are you, and what is the tallest building in New York City? Now you have answered the first two questions with no trouble at all. So if you know the answer to the third question, just tell us. Please, don't be stubborn. You don't want to be stubborn, do you? Are you confused? Is that it? You mustn't be confused or frightened or stubborn. Do you understand? We are simply trying to find out something we have to find out. Everyone who comes here is asked the same three questions. You understand, don't you? But if you choose not to answer, then how will we know what we need to know? And if we don't know what we need to know, then how can we help you get better? So please, just answer the question and we can all be done with this and you can go to sleep. Will you answer the question, please? What is the tallest building in New York City? Just name a building, any building. You can do that for us, can't you? Won't you do that for us, please? It doesn't matter if it's the right answer or not. It can be the wrong one, but it will still be right. Please. You mustn't keep us waiting. You see what Everett has there? So let's not have any unpleasantness. Just answer. Just name a building, any building—it can be any one you want. But, really, you must try. Or a city. Would you rather name a city? Pick a city. Just name a city. It doesn't matter which one. But you must make an effort. You really must. Will you do that for us? Just try. And then you can drink this and we'll leave you alone and you can have a nice, long sleep. Try now. Please. Name a city. You don't want Everett to put that on you. But if you won't answer, what choice do we have?"

Forget it.

In this day and age, you can't hide nothing nohow.

I know where you are.

"Red Dog! Red Dog!"

here's the thing about the major rules. Which is that you think them through enough and you come out with the opposite of what you started with! Tonight, for instance. Am I sitting here with a dollar in my pocket? Don't kid yourself—it's just Paki and the seven-watter and the thing which went plop on the bicycle.

"Red Dog! This is an urgent! Answer!"

Number one, I come home.

Number two, I come home.

Number one, I look around.

Number one, I wash my hands.

Number

Number two, I sit down on the toilet.

Number

Number one, it's this thing I see on the refrigerator.

Number two, I go and wash my hands.

"Red Dog! Red Dog!"

She said, "Just look at this shoe and this sock! Imbecile! Dumb cluck! Now we have to go all the way home because God in heaven gave me a moron for a child!"

Hey, I really have to hand it to you, all of you sitting there and breaking bread together. But that's okay. You have to expect it. Take it or leave it, your top men always stick together. I wasn't born yesterday, believe me. And here's the other thing. I mean, so far as the members of my household go, it's like Everett says. Hey, I give you my word—no hard feelings. Enough said?

Like she puts this picture up on the refrigerator. So guess who has to come home from school and see it. She said, "Just look at that face! Is that a face or is that a face?"

It was a room. There was light. There was a mirror and I was looking in it.

Listen, who's kidding who? The face they're seeing is not the real one you have!

She said, "Go look in the mirror and look at your face."

I said, "Face?"

Hey, she never had her finish. She was just making it up! But listen, you think when she said I was just a messenger, she was just making that up too? In other words, is this a question for the experts or is this a question for the experts? Granted, you could ask Norman for his analysis, but do me a favor and don't do it in front of T.C. and you-know-who.

On the other hand, to my way of thinking, it's on the refrigerator. Am I right or am I right? It says *Him and me*.

So what's your best guess? I mean, the four of you get together, does you-know-who still get a decent split? In other words, there is the question of the future. So how does it work, as one professional to another? In other words, you or Norman, which one does the typing up?

Whereas so far as T.C. goes, forget it! She says Exrox. She says, "Him and me is clearing out." She wrote down, "Your Swansons in the uvin." Hey, let's face it. T.C.'s got a head on her shoulders. But can you and Norman count on her when it comes to spelling even oven?

She said, "It's coming! It's coming! Don't stop!"

She said, "As God is my witness, I want the truth! Were you up there with that child in that house?"

They said, "Everett?"

She said, "Oh, Syl! Oh, Syl! Everybody look in the mirror! Oh, it's coming! Oh, look, look, everybody look!"

She said, "As I live and breathe, did you go near that child up there? Answer me! Do you hear me? This instant! Did you even say boo to that child? Imbecile! Do you hear me? Answer the question!"

They said, "Everett, if you please?"

Listen, if you're looking for a dummy, then you know where to look.

Hint: In Davie Jones's locker, okay?

Who's kidding who? Nobody's face is ever their real one! I mean, he steps back into the coat rack, right? In other words, now is when they have him where they want him. But did he give them the face he really had? Or take when Janet Rose had the hairbrush hanging out of her. Like she says she had her finish. But you know what I say? I say it's only her face which had it!

Hey, do me a favor and don't make me laugh.

What a boner I get when I think about it! Ask Sylvia Berman. She saw me thinking about it and getting one! Let's face it, what I couldn't do with a big boner like this. Ask Janet Rose! Listen, if you-know-who gets up to go to the bathroom, do me a favor and ask T.C. But only if a certain person put his head down and went to sleep—let's face it, little pitchers have big ears.

On the other hand, don't do it if you think it will make things worse with Norman. I mean, just between you, me, and the lamppost, I don't want to get any lower in that individual's eyes.

Hey, I've got a good one for you. Not a stitch on either one of them, except she's got on her shoes! I mean, go know, okay? Can you just see a person with her veins popping out and all she's wearing is these shoes? Be honest with me, the cha-cha-cha in shoes like those?

It's like I told you, you have to look, seeing as how whatever it is, they don't want you to see it. Did Buddy Brown? You think he thought he'd see me looking back? I'll be honest with you. It's like I'm not one hundred percent the pizza maker is climbing or jumping. In other words, it's one or the other, but I am not one hundred percent which. But go ahead and ask yourself why! Because the answer is it looked like both! And yours truly looked!

Listen, just between you, me, and the lamppost, it's three rooms. Myself, I'm in here, as I don't have to tell you. Whereas the refrigerator is over there.

She said, "Will you just look at the face on that! Couldn't you just eat it up alive?"

"Red Dog!"

It says *Him and me is clearing out.*

Tell the truth, doesn't it give you a boner when I talk about Janet Rose? I promise you, you can tell me. Go ahead and let your hair down. You think this was the thing of it with Norman? You think it was on account of how he was always getting these boners whenever yours truly made mention of Janet Rose? Listen, when Andre comes over to the table, you ask him what's his opinion. Except only if you-know-who already put his head down and went to sleep. Or you could do what my policy is in a PG. In other words, you handle his ears and he'll take care of the eyes himself. Believe me, he's had his education and training in this particular department. No thanks to T.C., of course. But am I the one who's pointing a finger?

Hey, or ask Norman who told him about Ann Shepherd and who she really is! In other words, you deal with yours truly, even if the deal falls through, it's never a total loss. Ask Namick! Ask Grady!

Okay, so she was on her way to your place and she doesn't get there! Let's face it, is she the first which didn't? Listen, number one, no telling what you could have caught from her! Number two, whatever you figure it cost you in so many dollars and cents, we'll work it this way. Go ahead and double the figure and cut it out of Norman's end of the movie rights. You see the direction of my thinking? In other words, the way I see it is this. If the man would have played ball with me in the first place, you never would have come into the picture! The other thing is, he's a family man. So he knows the situation you get in.

Tell the truth, is the boy there? Because the way I see it, it's way past his bedtime. No kidding, T.C. in this department, you can't depend on!

You and Norman, does he go for those pink peppered vodkas too? Whereas T.C., it's a sidecar! Am I right or am I right? Look, on this one I'm entitled to a straight answer—did you order a Roy Rogers for you-know-who? Because I wouldn't want him getting no Shirley Temple! One Roy Rogers and then a full glass of milk! Enough said? Who knows, tomorrow he'll maybe feel strong enough to give the colored a run for her money!

Did I make mention of the fact that your coloreds have ten-speeds in this day and age? Whereas look at some of your professionals! I'm telling you, I checked. Balloon tires and not a single gear, as God is my witness! You see what I am saying? Or is it your personal opinion yours truly is making another mountain out of a molehill?

Hey, it just this minute dawns on me, we're all at private tables! Except I don't have no Andre to go get me my Swanson's. But big deal. Listen, all I got to do is reach over to the "uvin."

Ha ha.

Okay, I take it back, I take it back! It's just I keep on trying to think up a couple of my own icebreakers. But let's be honest with each other. There's more to it than yours truly being no sleeper and no eater. Face facts! Yours truly is also no talker!

You know what I like? I like to look in the mirror and listen to Janet Rose talking. I like it even better when there is no mirror to look in. I like it when she says, "Baby, baby, baby." I like it when she takes the sheet and wraps it all around it. I like it when she says, "This will make him better. Oh, baby hurts all over." I like it when she says, "There, there. Hush, hush. Now go right to sleep right this minute."

Oh, Mr. Capote, I thought the hairbrush would only take a minute. But who ever stopped to tell me how long a minute is?

No kidding, can I really level with you? I mean, speaking as one professional to another? Because I am here to tell you, my arm can't take much more of this! Believe me, I've really got to take my hat off to you and Norman, writing down all those best-sellers and then turning around and getting them all typed up! Hey, you fellows must have some real arms on you! No offense, but T.C. is a married woman. Ask Namick. Ask Grady.

I said, "Oh, my beloved, please!"

Let's face it, nothing is a minute. Just between you, me, and the lamppost, it's all too long to hold the phone.

She goes, "Oh, oh, Jesus Harold Eddie Christ!"

She goes, "Binny, my arm is killing me!"

She goes, "Will you get a load of the face on that!"

Oh, Mr. Capote, I am so tired!

I liked it when she said, "Hush, hush."

Here's something.

Number one, the optic chiasm!

Number two, the hypothalamus center!

Number three, the anterior artery!

Hey, it's in the book. The title is *Your Body and What Is in It.*

"Red Dog! It's Blue Dog calling! Please, my beloved, please!"

Did you ever see a lassie go this way and that way and this way and that way?

We are talking about enough picas to go through all three! But do they ever tell you that? Do they ever do it on any of the channels? Do they say, "He is right-handed and he is large"?

The answer is I am. The answer is I do not have to push. The answer is, check it out. The answer is, go ask Buddy Brown.

Forget it. I was just kidding. I promise you, I was the

one which stayed inside. Whereas guess who always went out to play and always comes back with mud on!

You know what I told the boy? This is what I said. I said, "A three can take a tenner if the three thinks it through enough." You see what I am saying? You see what they make you say? Let your hair down and be honest with me! It's like the Empire State Building, right? I mean, they make you say these things! But say you don't! They go, "Everett?"

Listen, do me a favor, okay?

You go in there. *You* look at him. *You* watch him catch his breath and get the last of the winks he's got coming by way of getting his fair and honest share! Then you come back out here and *you* tell *me*, enough said?

On the other hand, who's kidding who? Number one, I don't have to tell you, he's not there in the first place! Number two, you've got a lot to learn!

Believe me, I am not pointing any finger. Not yet!

Granted, to her way of thinking, she thinks she has her reasons. In other words, it's a free country. She wants to deal direct, then she wants to deal direct. End of discussion, period! You know what I say? I say more power to her!

Except you got a couple of sidecars in her, she'll start talking Grady and Namick and forget about turkey! You see what I am saying? In other words, speaking strictly as the father of the boy, it's a hot story one way or the other. But ask yourself, "Is this an individual which knows her onions?"

Answer me this. So who picks up the tab for this, you or Norman? Because if it's a three-way split, I say forget it. The boy's got a dollar in his pocket, whereas T.C.'s got carfare! On the other hand, I don't have to tell you what you could get for the seven-watter. In other words, if you're going dutch, maybe you fellows could see your way clear. Meaning, the boy will be good for it, and meanwhile you and Norman could hold on to the walkie-talkie for more or less collateral. Unless you boys are thinking about doing the decent thing and divvying the check up between you.

You know what I liked? I liked to hear her talk. I liked it when she walked and talked! I saw her walk in leaves.

You know what they told Davie his split would be? The answer is a third!

I promise you, you don't have to tell me. You ask for a Roy Rogers in the C.B., what you are going to get is a Roy Rogers in a class by itself! True or false? Believe me, I wasn't born yesterday! To make a long story short, I won't kid around with you. Which is when all is said and done, it is the best thing which could have happened! I mean, you and Norman and T.C. all breaking bread together. Listen, the three of you can really sit down and talk turkey. Because I want to be honest with you. Where yours truly is concerned, let's face it, I've got no head for business. But you take T.C. Granted, she's no Gothamite, but does she have a head on her shoulders or does she have a head on her shoulders? The thing of it is, so what if her favorite is "Charlie's Angels"! You think "Young Doctor Malone" didn't go out to millions and millions of decent American families?

Hey, yours truly's regards to Andre. And this goes ditto for Norman, okay? Let's face it, bygones is bygones. It's all water under the bridge. End of discussion, period. God is my judge, no hard feelings.

"Red Dog! Red Dog! Can you hear me?"

Tell the truth. Is that a boy or is that a boy? Could they eat him up alive or could they eat him up alive? I mean, go ahead and talk about a face! Listen, just between you, me, and the lamppost, you are looking at what the father of the boy looked like back when it was my day and age. Ask anyone! Ask Namick! Ask Grady!

Whereas to her way of thinking, who gets his picture so it goes up on the refrigerator?

Talk about a certain person who didn't know the first thing about what a face really is!

I have to laugh. God is my judge, I really have to.

No kidding, no hard feelings. The way it worked out, it's better for all parties concerned. I mean, as regards talking turkey, yours truly can see where he made the wrong start in the first place. In other words, I'd be the first to admit, I should have stuck with a different one! With No. 4 maybe. I don't know. Maybe No. 8. Look, at this stage of the game, what's the diff? It is just where I am sitting here thinking this. A different start would have come out different.

Be honest with me. Is Johnny there into the bargain?

Face facts, it's high time you should be honest with me. Is it a table for five because Johnny himself barged in at the last minute?

Hey, I don't believe what I am sitting here with in my pocket! In other words, it just dawned on me how I almost forgot it. On the other hand, Paki's in the other one, so it comes out even steven.

You know what? I was just thinking. Like if I put my hand in which one, you think I would find a dollar in it?

I liked it when it was in her mouth. It was the sky

with its arms down and holding me. I liked it when she made believe she liked it. I liked it before everything stopped making believe.

Are you ready for the payoff?

Can you believe it, the three questions they ask you? In other words, you wake up and they see you do it, so they come in and they ask you the questions.

Number one, what is your name?

Number two, when were you born?

Number three, what is the tallest building in New York City?

Listen, let's face it, it could be worse, enough said? I mean, for argument's sake, suppose they ask you these three instead?

Number one, is there steel in Pakistan?

Number two, what's it like in the C.B.?

Number three, who pushed Buddy Brown?

Hey, so how come they skipped the biggest one of all? Which is how long is a minute! So *you* tell *me*. Could yours truly give them what to hear on that one or could yours truly give them?

Ask the hairbrush. Ask Namick. Ask Grady.

I said, "It makes me afraid for you to be asking me questions like that." I said, "Please do not ask me those questions." I said, "I know the answers. But please don't ask me to say them."

They said, "Everett?"

I said, "They are dumb questions. Ask my dumb brother."

They said, "Everett?"

I'll bet it's getting light out. I'll bet it really is. You can't tell from the kitchen here because in this kitchen there is no window. But I bet it definitely is!

I said, "Why are there mats on the walls?"

I said, "Why does everybody call her Binny?"

I said, "She said her name was Janet Rose."

I'm tired. It's fast. Woof, woof, woof.

"Red Dog!"

They said, "Drink it."

They said, "Here. Like this. Just drink it down fast."

In Simon's, when I saw them, this is what I thought. I thought they are here where she is! I thought she is in a place where knives are!

I said, "Why are those on the walls?"

They said, "Like this. Just hold your breath and do it fast."

When the boy backed up into the coat rack, this is what I thought. I thought Davie was the one which did it. I thought Davie was the one which made him back up.

Ha ha, Buddy Brown.

They said, "Drink it. Don't make us have to make you."

I said, "Just give me a minute to catch my breath."

I thought it's me which is climbing and jumping. I thought it's me which is letting me do it. I thought if you are everything, they won't see where you are. I thought the sky could see. I thought nothing couldn't. I wanted to be blind!

The sun came through the blinds.

I was on the hassock watching.

Wasn't I on the hassock watching?

I said, "It has the same laces. It has the same sleeves."

They said, "Yes, of course. But it's not what you think it is."

I never looked it up. I never looked up *pulmotor*. I said, "Simon says come stand over here on this board."

They look soft when you see them in the movies. I saw

one in a movie once. But they are not soft when they put you in one. It is only the laces which are soft.

Lanuginous. I saw the hair of Janet Rose's you-know-what.

I was a picture-book boy. This is what she said. She said I was a picture-book boy. And then she did not say it anymore.

I thought the sky had eyes. I thought the sky had arms.

I never had a Roy Rogers. And did I ever touch a drop? But then they come and say it's paraldehyde, ha ha.

We moved and everything was always mud. There were houses going up.

I said, "Just let me catch my breath."

They said, "Count to three. Then take a deep breath."

I was seven, going on eight. Wasn't I always on the hassock? Wasn't the hassock the safest place?

The sun was coming through the blinds. It was like this. It was the light. Little things that came and went. She moved her arms and made a wave.

They said, "One."

This was the major rule which Davie broke. Davie broke the major one. They said don't play around the houses. They said stay away from the ones going up. But then there was only one that was.

They said, "Two."

She said just look at that child. She said as God is my judge. She said I could take a bite out of him, that's what an angel he is. She said look at this when you want to see what gorgeous looks like. She said come over here and look at this picture.

She said, "Your face, it's changed." She said, "Did they change your face up there?"

She said, "Do yourself a favor and go outside and play."

They said, "That's it. That's three."

When we moved, we took the hassock with us, didn't we?

I said, *"Hold the phone!"*

I said oh my beloved, please.

I said. No, I said, "God is my judge, I was here on the hassock!" I said, "The room saw me sitting here!"

They said, "Take the pulmotor down to the basement."

They said, "Let's play Simon Says."

"Oh, Red Dog, oh my beloved, please."

h ey, time out.

No kidding, it's definitely time for a big time-out.

No kidding, it's too fast.

Let's face it, it's what? It's light outside? So it's already getting to be light?

Look, the big bucks start rolling in, here's hoping a certain somebody sets off enough to the side for one of your top makes of a watch! Somebody says to him eight o'clock, he'll know what eight o'clock is!

Hey, no kidding, it's fast. It's really getting fast.

She says to me, "Keep pumping, keep pumping, it'll only take a minute." She says to me, "I'm going into the hardware and I'll only be a minute." She says to me, "His little arm is tired? He said his little arm is tired? Harold Jesus Christ, Syl—show him what an arm is!" She said to me, "Shit-for-brains, if you had any arm on you, it wouldn't take me but a minute!"

You know what I say? I say fuck them with their

minutes! I say you want somebody dumb enough to wait one, go get a dumbfuck like Davie! Hey, ask him! Ask him your dumbfuck questions, all fucking dumbfuck three of them!

On the other hand, you don't know shit enough to ask a moron to name a city. Even after you already told him the name of the biggest one of all! Listen, you think I don't know what your analysis is as regards who did the pushing? You think just because an individual is honest and aboveboard, he has to sit here and listen to your shit? You think yours truly was born yesterday just because he has been sitting here and being nothing but one hundred percent? Let's not be ridick!

"Mayday, Red Dog, mayday!"

Hey, do me a favor and don't make me laugh, okay?

You think I don't know this paper has been looking at me? The whole time I've been doing this, you think I didn't know? Forget it, bigshot! Don't flatter yourself! You-know-who is no Davie!

So what if this paper looks at me! Why shouldn't it? For your personal information, so does the whole goddamn kitchen! The light's looking! And I don't mind telling you, I don't fucking blame it! Hey, hotshot! You want to know the big-ass secret? Stick to mirrors and leave the rest of the shit to the morons who don't even know better!

Like I could look at the glass over there! Like it's just the little window in the oven. But you think everything isn't a mirror? You see what I am saying or do you see what I am saying? In other words, a certain someone gets up from here and goes over there and gets down on his hands and knees. Hey, you hear me, bullshit artist? You! Bigshot! Top man! You think I can't look in my face like the best of them? Sure, sure, the window's got this crap all over it from the goddamn Swanson's! Because like God forbid she should clean it off when the dumbfuck cunt might miss her "Charlie's Angels"! Whereas don't kid yourself, hotshot! You think glass is what they say it is? You go into Simon's and the knives are inside a glass counter and the glass you look down at is a goddamn mirror!

So like I could do that, enough said? So where's your paper then? Not to mention your whole motherfucking kitchen! Bingo, buddy boy! Because where does the motherfucking dust go if I motherfucking do it!

So strictly for argument's sake, let's just say I get good and fed up with all this bullshit and the caliber of individual you sit down and break bread with. Stop and think a minute! You think I can't quit looking at your paper! You think I can't get down on my knees and go look in the glass like the best of them! Ben Bernie said *besta*! So like what do you say, you hotshot sons of bitches, when a certain someone has to sleep? Because maybe it just so happens whereas this is what's on the agenda! Fair enough? I mean, enough said? You think I don't have eyes in my head!

Number two, let's not forget who is the one with the voices! Like do me a favor and wise up! Like let's just us look at this eyeball-to-eyeball. There is no Young Fucking Doctor Anything unless you-know-who steps in to do it! Or how about any fucking voice you name! You yourself, for instance, or Janet fucking Rose!

Hey, who the fuck are you, any of you, anyway? You think I don't know you made up the name you sign your fucking books with? Hey, just the way you-know-who made up all of the ones in this letter! I mean, who's kidding who?

You know what all of you are? You are just me talking to me and myself in the glass of a fucking oven!

You hear me, T.C.? You took him away! But you're just me and he's just me—and when I sign off, you're all just fucking nothing!

You hear me, all you sons of bitches in your fancy fucking famous places? You're fucking nobody because I am who you are! You're not even somebody in a closet dancing!

Hey, T.C., you listening? I motherfucking dare you! Go on! Go ahead! Tell them I'm the one which did it and did it and did it. Tell them I said Buddy fucking Brown! Tell them who was the picture-book boy and who went splat as flat as his picture. Hey, T.C.! Hey, Norman! Turn on the seven-watter! No shit, I want you to hear this. Who do you think Janet Rose is? And how about Norman Mailer? No shit, no shit, listen, please listen. I am begging you just to listen.

Tinkle tinkle tinkle.

Nibble nibble nibble.

Woof.

Click.

Plop.

No shit, were you all ears?

"Red Dog, I beg you, my beloved. Please, answer!"

Forget it! You're all anybody! You're just one thing which leads to another!

"Red Dog! Please. My beloved."

Oh, you sons and sons and sons of bitches!

You know what? You know fucking what I am going to fucking tell you? Even blind, I can see what any of them can! *One* eye! Hey, I can see Pakistan, and I say one eye is just for openers!

Look at this. It's 13010.

Did you hear it? Click. It was Paki coming open.

Dope! I told you, live and learn!

Oh, you silly sonofabitches, you don't know nothing nohow! But, hey, be a sport and do a guy a favor. Tell you-know-who where *capstone* went when he gets to the day that's not there.

"Binny! I beg you! Please answer your father, please!"

Here's looking at you, Mr. Ben Bernie. You went away just like the rest of them did—but God is my judge, I never stopped loving you ever.

Hey, Davie, here's mud in your eye! Here's plenty of mud for both, you dumb cunt of a moron brother.

Bottoms up, shit-for-brains! It's time to call it a night, okay? Meaning, chapter and verse, enough said? Now open wide for Blue Dog.

Oh, Davie, sweet Davie, my Davie, this one's for you and for real and for keeps.

My darling. My beloved. There's no world, no window. There is just a mirror.

End of discussion. Yours truly. Period.

P.S. *And now the time has come to lend an ear to—au revoir, pleasant dree yums, think of us when requesting your thee yums—until the next time when possibly you may tune in again, keep the Old Maestro always in your schee yums, yowsah, yowsah, yowsah—au revoir—may*

good luck and happiness, success, good health, attend
your schee yums, and don't forget we'll try to do our besta,
yowsah, yowsah, yowsah—au revoir, a fond cheerio, a bit
of a tweet-tweet,
     and good night and God bless you
            and pleasant
                dree yums